KILLER YEAR

•

Stories to Die For...

•

EDITED BY LEE CHILD

St. Martin's Paperbacks

This is a work of fiction. All of the characters, organizations, and events portrayed in this anthology are either products of the authors' imaginations or are used fictitiously.

KILLER YEAR

For information address St. Martin's Press, 175 Fifth Avenue, New York, NY 10010.

Library of Congress Catalog Card Number: 2007046344

ISBN: 978-1-250-06732-6

Printed in the United States of America

St. Martin's Press hardcover edition / January 2008
Minotaur Books Paperback Edition / January 2009
St. Martin's Paperbacks edition / July 2015

St. Martin's Paperbacks are published by St. Martin's Press, 175 Fifth Avenue, New York, NY 10010.

10 9 8 7 6 5 4 3 2 1

Copyright Acknowledgments

•

For the ones who lit the flame—
and those who will keep it burning

Contents

•

Acknowledgments

•

The members of Killer Year, the Class of 2007 would like to thank their International Thriller Writers (ITW) mentors (James Rollins, Allison Brennan, Gayle Lynds, Ken Bruen, Anne Frasier, Harley Jane Kozak, Lee Child, Tess Gerritsen, Joe R. Lansdale, Douglas Clegg, Jeffery Deaver, David Morrell, and Duane Swierczynski) for their kind support throughout this debut year. Having a chance to work with all of you has been our honor.

Our deepest thanks to Ken Bruen, Allison Brennan, and Duane Swierczynski for contributing high-caliber stories of their own as well as providing guidance and friendship.

Many warm thanks go to our editor, Michael Homler, and the wonderful team at St. Martin's: Sally Richardson, Andrew Martin, George Witte, Matthew Baldacci, and Hector DeJean.

Special thanks to our fabulous agent Scott Miller, who had a vision; M. J. Rose, for taking a chance on a group of unknowns; Laura Lippman, for her everlasting grace; and our esteemed editor, Lee Child, for agreeing to take us on. We appreciate each and every one of you.

Introduction
by Lee Child

•

I won't tell you how old I am, but I'll give you a clue: the first record I bought was "She Loves You" by the Beatles. Back then I lived in England, and 45 rpm singles cost six shillings and eight pence, exactly one-third of a British pound, which was a substantial but feasible sum for a boy in my position. LP records were a different story. There was something called retail price maintenance—essential government support, or evil price-fixing, depending on your political persuasion—that made an LP's price exactly thirty-two shillings and fivepence ha'penny. Way, way more than I could afford. I could have mowed my whole neighborhood—if it had had any grass—and still come up short. LP records were strictly for birthdays and Christmas, two a year. But I loved them. The smell, the feel, the sleeves, the shiny vinyl, the tiny shimmering grooves. And the music.

Then, late in the sixties, a couple of record companies came out with samplers, both loosely from the world of progressive rock. Full-size LPs, proper sleeves, the smell, the feel, the grooves . . . twelve tracks, maybe two from bands I had heard of, plus ten others I had never heard of. All at the amazing price of seven shillings and sixpence! Just ten pence more than a single! I was all over them, naturally. And they were wonderful. I was introduced to many, many bands that I love to this day.

That's what you've got in your hands right now.

A sampler.

We've included three writers you might already know, and thirteen more you'll soon come to know. A total of sixteen stories, with introductions to the new writers from veterans with about a thousand years in the business between them. How's that for value?

The three familiar names are Allison Brennan, Ken Bruen, and Duane Swierczynski. Allison is the new poster girl for success, proving yet again that talent is always enough. Ken is a cult fixture, and has been for years—and will be for years more: to look at him, you might think he'll keel over any minute, but when you know him, you realize he'll outlast everybody . . . well, maybe not Keith Richards, but it'll be close. Duane is in the early stages of what will be a stellar career. Some people just have what it takes, and Duane has more than his share.

The new guys—in order of appearance—are Brett Battles, Robert Gregory Browne, Bill Cameron, Toni McGee Causey, Sean Chercover, J. T. Ellison, Patry Francis, Marc Lecard, Derek Nikitas, Gregg Olsen, Jason Pinter, Marcus Sakey, and Dave White. I've gotten to know most of them quite well. They're quality people, and quality writers. But they're more than just thirteen nice guys and thirteen new names. They're a . . . what? A cooperative, a group, a band of ruffians, smart enough to join forces in an organization they called Killer Year. The idea was to make some noise and generate some buzz. And it worked. (Why else would all those veteran bestsellers write their introductions? Not because they were getting paid, I assure you.) My friend M. J. Rose has contributed an essay to this book that explains the context better than I can. And my friend Laura Lippman has written a coda to sum the whole thing up.

Which leaves me to say just once more: this is a sampler. I think you'll enjoy these stories—they're all excellent, and some of them are just plain great. If you agree, bear this in mind: short stories are far, far harder to write than novels. So if you like these guys' stories, check out their novels—I promise you, they'll be to die for.

The Class of Co-opetition
by M. J. Rose

•

The point of this collection of stories is to thrill you, the reader. And no one expects you to care that the publishing biz is in dire straits. But to appreciate the spirit in which this collection of stories came together, it helps to understand something about the publishing industry at this point in time.

With margins low, distribution costs rocketing, limited or no marketing budgets for all but the top 15 percent of titles, and little major media interest in all but the biggest authors, book sales drop a little more every year and fewer and fewer authors can live off their fiction efforts.

Ours has become a risk-averse industry that more and more puts all its eggs in the same baskets year in, year out: a few brand-name authors, yet there are more than one thousand novels traditionally published every month.

These days even some of the biggest and the best authors will attest that their job is as much about selling as it is writing, because the support they get from their publishers is no longer enough to spread the word among booksellers, let alone readers. Authors hiring outside publicists and webmasters, buying additional advertising, subsidizing book tours, not just talking about marketing but doing something about it . . . all these things are no longer the exception but the rule.

You might think, because of all this, that there's an every-man-for-himself attitude among writers, each one trying to outfox the other for limited ad dollars, blog reviews, special events or promotions. Yet one group of writers who routinely practice backstabbing, larceny, and murder is doing the opposite: working together to promote each other's books.

In the fall of 2004, International Thriller Writers—ITW for short—was created at a mystery and suspense book conference called Bouchercon. Our goal was to celebrate the thriller, enhance the prestige and raise the profile of thrillers, create a community that together could do more, much more, than any one author—or even any one publisher—could for the genre.

Now ITW, with more than five hundred members who have more than two billion books in print, is changing the rules for how books are sold and marketed, and how writers work together.

Superstars have rolled up their sleeves to work alongside mid-list and debut novelists to apply some fresh thinking to a stale industry.

And nowhere is that spirit of co-opetition more evident than in this book. The authors of this collection are in essence in competition with each other; if you look at the statistics, the average "avid" reader only buys 2.5 books a year.

And yet this smart, savvy group of debut authors came up with a plan to give fresh verve and energy to the clichéd phrase "strength in numbers." They've turned it into "creativity in numbers."

To support these debut authors, ITW offered to mentor the Class of '07 because we recognized our same spirit in them: a group of writers willing to band together and help each other rather than view each other as competition. To do something different. And to do it right.

We wanted to help, not just because we were so damned impressed with the creativity of the idea but because once upon a time—be it twenty-five years ago or last year—each and every one of ITW's members was a debut novelist.

And most of us remember every single difficult step of that process.

For some of us that means remembering the people who helped us.

Or that there was no one to help us.

And how isolating that was.

Wouldn't it be great if ITW as an organization could help the debut authors who are going to be the future of our genre?

So over the summer of 2006, the full ITW board of directors approved the idea to adopt Killer Year 2007 and take some of the tough work out of being a debut novelist by helping each author through their baptism by fire into the publishing world.

Lee Child, Jeff Deaver, Tess Gerritsen, Gayle Lynds, David Morrell, Jim Rollins, Anne Frasier, Douglas Clegg, Duane Swierczynski, Cornelia Read, Harley Jane Kozak, Allison Brennan, Ken Bruen, and Joe R. Lansdale all signed on to be mentors.

This idea of cooperation among potential rivals is a

variation on a theme we're beginning to see in other places on the Web, from group blogs to social networking sites like MySpace or cultural hotspots like YouTube.

For an industry losing readers to video games, movies, digital cable, blogs, and a creeping apathy about books, it seems a no-brainer.

But, as ITW member and author Tim Maleeny said about the program, "It's no small irony that it took a bunch of writers who probe the darkest side of humanity to see the light."

Perfect Gentleman
by Brett Battles

•

I first encountered Brett Battles's work in his debut thriller *The Cleaner*. The book landed on my doorstep one early afternoon. I glanced at the opening page, figuring I'd read a few pages, then go about with my day. Instead, hours flew by, and the entire book was devoured in one sitting. The best word I can use to describe his writing is *addictive*. Razor-sharp prose bites deep, cuts to a raw nerve, and leaves you wanting more . . . and more again. Here's a taste of his work, a short story titled "Perfect Gentleman," a small glimpse into a major new talent. So enjoy the story—a tale of murder and revenge in a remote corner of the world—and you'll soon be lost . . . lost and forever craving more. Just don't say I didn't warn you.

—James Rollins,
New York Times bestseller of *Map of Bones*
and *Black Order*

You won't like me.

Whatever. I've stopped caring.

I'm not a bad guy, but you're not going to believe that. People like you never do. You hear about what I do. You see how I live. You think, sleaze or deviant or something like that. Maybe you're right. Maybe I'm all those things. I certainly don't think God's waiting for me to show up at his front gate.

Again, it doesn't matter. This isn't really about me, is it? It's about Joseph Perdue.

Now there was a guy you really hate. A real asshole. But you people only chose to see one side of him. You made him out the hero. Someday you'll probably call him a martyr for the cause. For the American way. That's what happens to the dead, isn't it? No one cares about the truth.

I remember the first time he came into the bar.

That's not really surprising. I remember every time someone new comes in. It's part of my job. First I need to make sure the guy (they're always guys) doesn't look like an obvious problem. If he's too drunk or too belligerent or has got a bad rep, I point them to another bar and say they got a special show that night and he shouldn't miss it. Works every time. If he doesn't seem like he'll be a problem then I size him up, figure out how much we can expect to get out of him, and what he might be looking for.

On the evening Perdue came in, the usual pop crap was blaring out of our far too expensive sound system. Occasionally I've been known to sneak in an old Skynyrd album or *Dark Side of the Moon* by Pink Floyd. God, I love that album. But the girls always protest, and I seldom make it through "Speak to Me" before I have to flip back to Christina Aguilera or Gwen Stefani or Gorillaz. When Perdue walked in, I'm pretty sure the song playing was "Perfect Gentleman" by Wyclef Jean.

Perhaps I should have taken that as a sign.

It was a slow night, a Tuesday. Our big nights are Thursdays, Fridays, and Mondays—the first two because around here everyone is ready to start the weekend a little early, and Mondays because that's when we hold our weekly body-painting contest. Nothing like some fluorescent paint, some beautiful young women, and a few fluorescent black-light tubes to fill up the place and bring in the cash.

Event evening or not, we still had a full complement of girls, somewhere between twenty and thirty at the beginning of the shift. That number would depend on how many girls were sick, how many had found someone for an extended absence, and how many just didn't show up.

No idea what our exact total was that night. I do know that Ellie was there. She was up on the stage with five or six others grinding away. But I've gotta say, whenever Ellie was onstage, it was as if she were dancing alone. That was her power. She was a superstar. The killer bod and the killer personality and that killer something that wouldn't allow you to take your eyes off her.

You don't get a lot of superstars. Maybe one or two per bar. Ellie was our one.

In strip bars in the States, the girls had routines, elaborate moves choreographed to the latest hip-hop favorite. But not here.

Of course, my place isn't really a strip bar. And it's nowhere near the States. It's in Angeles City in the Philippines. Perhaps you remember Clark Air Base? Used to be the biggest U.S. base outside of the States. The old main gate is only a couple miles from the door of my bar. But then there was Mt. Pinatubo erupting ash over everything, and the Filipino people threatening to erupt in anger if the U.S. didn't finally withdraw.

We withdrew.

Well, the government did. Us ex-pats, we stayed. And over the years we've been joined by more.

This is the part where you realize you hate me. Yeah, my bar is one of those kind of bars. A go-go bar. At my place, you can watch them dance, buy them a drink, talk to them, and then take a girl out for the night or for a week if you want. You just gotta pay the bar fine, and it would be nice if you tipped the girl after.

And this is the part where I tell you I take care of my girls. I try not to let them go out with jerks—it happens, but not as much as it does at other bars. I do what I can to protect them. I try to keep them out of too much trouble. I know it won't matter, but there are a hell of a lot worse *Papasans* around than me.

So go ahead and hate me, but the business will still be here. The guys will still come. And so will the girls. Because for them the money's better here, and there's always a chance they might get taken out of the life to live in Australia or the UK or America.

Perdue, if I remember correctly, glanced at the narrow stage—more like a runway down the center of the room back then before I remodeled—then took a seat in an empty booth on the far side.

He wasn't alone for long. That's not why people come to the bars in Angeles City. They come for the laughs, for the cold bottles of San Miguel beer, but most of all they come for the brown skin girls so willing and available.

A couple of my waitresses in their uniforms of tight,

pink hot pants and white bikini tops approached him together. Only half interested, I watched the encounter,
still unsure if the guy was one of those who was only
gauging the talent and would soon be leaving, or was
someone we could milk a few pesos out of, maybe even
hook him up for the night.

One of the waitresses, Anna, giggled while the other
one, Margaret I think, looked over in my direction and
said something to our new guest. Perdue looked at me,
then removed a wad of bills from his pocket and handed
a couple of notes to each of the girls.

Now I was intrigued. Guys usually didn't pay for anything the moment they arrived. What happened next
surprised me even more. Perdue got up from his booth
and walked around the stage to where I sat at the bar.

He nodded at the stool next to the one I was sitting
on. "May I?"

"Please," I said.

"Thanks. I think the view's better from over here."

Indeed it was. Superstar Ellie with the do-me-now
looks was swaying back and forth less than ten feet
away.

"Joseph Perdue." He held out a thin, rough hand.

"Wade Norris," I said.

His grip was stronger than I expected. Whoever Perdue was, he was more powerful than he let on.

"You American, too?" he asked.

I nodded. "Ohio. Columbus."

"Never been there. I'm from Wyoming, myself."

"Yellowstone?" I asked. It was the only place I knew
in Wyoming.

He smiled at me. "Nah. Laramie. Cowboy country."

Anna walked over and handed Perdue a San Miguel, then set a cup on the bar behind him with a slip of paper inside noting the beer.

He held his bottle out toward me. "Cheers, Wade."

I obliged by clinking the bottom of my bottle against the bottom of his. We both took drinks, his deeper than mine.

"I hear you're the *Papasan*. You run things."

Run would be a good word for it, I thought. I wasn't the owner. He was thousands of miles away in the Netherlands. But I was the decision-maker, and gatekeeper.

I shrugged, then said, "You enjoying Angeles?"

"Seems pretty nice. But, you know, all these bars around here seem pretty much the same. You all got the neon, the mirrors with all the names painted on them, the big bells. The only difference I can see is the girls. Some places have a better group than others."

I couldn't argue with his assessment. There are over a hundred go-go bars in Angeles City, all offering pretty much the same thing: prerecorded music and liquor and women.

"So how does ours rank?"

"About average." He nodded toward Ellie. "Except for her. She brings your score way up."

I couldn't help but smile. The fish was circling the bait. Now all I had to do was hook him.

While Perdue took another drink, I caught the attention of Kat, the bartender. With a quick, almost undetectable motion, I indicated our new customer's interest in our superstar. Less than a minute later, Ellie had made her way off the stage and walked across the room to where we were sitting.

"Hey, Ellie," I said. "How you doing?"

"I was getting hot," she said. She pulled at her bikini top, like she needed to get air between the flimsy fabric and her C-cup breasts. She looked at Perdue and smiled. "Who's this?"

"Another Yank," I said. "Joseph Perdue."

She held out her hand and gave him a look even the most disinterested man would be hard-pressed to resist. "Nice to meet you. I'm Ellie."

"Hi, Ellie," Perdue said. Instead of shaking her hand, he kissed it, the whole time his eyes never leaving her face.

I knew the deal was done then, and twenty minutes later I was proved correct.

"He wants to pay bar fine, Papa. What do you think?" Ellie asked me. She and Perdue had moved to the booth he'd occupied when he'd first arrived. Now she had walked back over to me alone while her potential boyfriend for the night waited.

"He seems all right," I said. "What do you think?"

"I think he has money," she said.

"Then, by all means, have a great night."

It didn't surprise me when Perdue came in the next night and bar fined her again. And I wasn't particularly shocked that he'd decided to bar fine her not just for that evening, but for the rest of the week. The fish had not just swallowed the hook, but the hook and the line and the rod. Ellie was a hard one to resist.

Of course, the deal was good for everyone. I was happy to collect the cash. Ellie was happy to be out of the bar for more than just a few hours, and was definitely happy about her cut of the bar fine. And Perdue, presumably, was happy to be spending time with a beautiful girl at least twenty years younger than he was.

Honestly, after that night, I thought I wouldn't see the guy again. I figured he'd probably bar fine her for the remainder of his trip and when she came back to work, it would mean he was on the long flight home to the U.S. But two days later, he showed up in the middle of the afternoon.

It was Friday, but we wouldn't really get busy until after dark. At the time, we only had two customers, so the day shift girls—about half as many as I'd have on that night—were huddled together in cliques talking or sitting alone texting their boyfriends, both foreign and Filipino, on their mobiles.

I had only been there about thirty minutes, but as usual, my ass was glued to my favorite stool at the bar. If anyone else ever tried to sit there, Kat or one of the other bartenders made them move. "Papa Wade's chair," they'd say.

When Perdue came in, he took a few seconds for his eyes to adjust from the bright sunshine outside to the dim interior, then spotted me and walked over.

"Alone?" I asked.

"Ellie said she had to run home to take care of something. I'm meeting her at Mac's in an hour."

Mac's was the main restaurant in the district everyone ended up in. But Perdue didn't sound happy about it. In fact I'd say he was pretty annoyed. But I didn't push. My job was to make the customer feel as good as possible about his time in Angeles. Getting into the middle of a relationship between one of my girls and her *honey ko* was never a good idea. Unless, of course, it was because he was treating her badly.

Whether you believe it or not, we're a family. And a hell of a lot better one than those most of my girls had grown up in back in the provinces. We watch out for each other. We're there when times are good or times are bad. We know enough to give each other room when we need it, when to let hope simmer and not discourage it, and when to snap each other back into reality—albeit our reality—when we had to.

But what we really have to do is be careful not to crush the dream. In this make-believe world of faux love and real sex, it's the dream that keeps a lot of the girls going. It's the chance that maybe, just maybe, the guy they've got temporarily wrapped around their finger might fall for them hard. Maybe they can get him to spend his entire vacation with them. Maybe they can get him to call them, and email them, and send them money after he's returned home. Maybe—and this is the big one—maybe he'll even marry them and take them away from the islands.

It happens all the time. Only with thousands of girls working the business, a few a month leaving for better lives is a small percentage. Still, the dream is there. And I have always been careful not to get in the way of even that narrow chance.

"So you been having a good time?" I asked.

I figured the only answer could be yes. He would have sent Ellie back by now if he wasn't.

"Took her down to Manila yesterday. Had a little business to deal with. Thought she might like to do some shopping." Finally Perdue cracked a smile. "I guess I was right."

I laughed. Take one of the girls shopping, and she'd stay with you for free. It was their religion, but one they seldom indulged in unless it was on someone else's dime. "So I'll take that as a yes."

The smile slipped again. "For the most part."

We drank in relative silence as the perpetual sound track of Justin Timberlake and Robbie Williams and even vintage Spice Girls played on, only at slightly reduced afternoon levels.

"Can I trust you?" Perdue asked.

I looked over at him, a knowing grin on my face. "Of course," I said.

It was my standard answer. Truth was, I already knew what he was going to tell me. It was going to be some variation on "Ellie's not like the other girls," or "I haven't slept more than an hour at a time since I took her home," or "Do you think you can meet someone special at a place like this?" They were all a prelude, a setup to talking himself into believing he'd fallen in love. Perhaps Ellie had actually found her ticket out of town.

But even as the thought came to me, I questioned whether it would really pan out. After you've worked here as many years as I have, you get a sense of the guys. And my sense of Perdue was that he wasn't looking for a wife.

"I'm serious," he said. "Can I trust you?"

I lifted up my beer. "You can tell me whatever you want. It'll just be between us."

For a few seconds, I thought he wasn't going to say anything. He leaned toward me. "I'm Homeland Security," he finally said, his voice barely audible above the music. In fact it was so low, I wasn't sure I'd even heard him right.

"What?" I asked.

"Homeland Security. You know what that is, right?"

I'd been living in the Philippines since the late nineties, and hadn't actually set foot Stateside since before 9/11. But with CNN International and the large American ex-pat community—most of whom were former military—you couldn't help knowing a little bit about what was happening back home.

"That's, like, antiterrorism, right?"

"That's just part of it. But, yeah, that's our main focus."

I wasn't sure what to say. I mean, we get all types in the bar. Maybe he was trying to impress me. Homeland Security, it did sound important. Maybe I should have been impressed. But I wasn't.

"I'm here looking into a few potential rumors. We want to neutralize any problems before they develop."

" 'Neutralize'?" I repeated. I think it might have been the first time I'd ever heard it used like that in conversation. "That's why you're in Angeles? Or why you're at my bar?"

"The Philippines," he said. "Mainly in the south. Two months now. I came up here for a little relaxation."

Now we were back on familiar territory. "Glad we could help you with that."

The corners of his mouth went up and down in what I could only guess was a quick smile. "When I was in Manila yesterday . . ." He let the words hang as he took a sip of his San Miguel.

"On your business," I offered.

He nodded. "On my business. I heard something disturbing. It came to us through a very dependable source. But you know how these things are."

No, actually, I didn't. And I had no idea why he was even telling me any of this. But he was the customer, so I wasn't about to stop him. Besides, it wasn't just the girls who fell into a routine. Someday I could tell this story to my other *Papasan* friends. They'd love it. *The secret agent confesses all to Papa Wade.*

"Seems there might be trouble here in Angeles," Perdue finally said.

I almost laughed out loud. Terrorism? Here in Angeles? Gangs, yes. But terrorists? Something that would concern the government of the United States of America? Not possible.

"I think maybe your source is screwing with you," I said.

"That's what I thought, too," Perdue said. "But I did a little checking this morning, and now I'm not so sure."

"We've never had any of that kind of trouble. And I'm sure we're not about to, either." I suddenly had no desire to continue talking about this. I didn't want to know. I was happy with my beer and my girls and my life. Terrorism was a problem for somewhere else.

"Yeah, well, they didn't have that kind of trouble in Bali before, but we all know what happened there."

That stopped me.

Bali was the thing someone always threw out on those rare occasions when conversation turned to terrorism. And Bali scared the shit out of me. That had been in 2002. Two bombs at nightclubs in the tourist district. A couple hundred people died. All of us in Angeles knew at the time it could have just as easily happened in front of one of our places. And then, over weeks and months, we forgot about it, pushing it out of our minds, and returning to the belief that it could never happen here.

"I'm not sure you should be telling me this," I finally said.

Perdue leaned in. "I'm telling you this for a very good reason. I need your help."

"My help?"

"I got a name and a picture from my source in Manila. He's been involved in kidnappings and executions in the south, but it appears his *comrades* have ordered him to set up shop here in your part of the country. The funny thing is, when I saw the picture, I knew I'd seen him recently. Here."

"In Angeles? It's a big city."

He shook his head. "On Fields Avenue." Fields is the main street that runs through the bar district. "I want you to look at the picture. Tell me if you recognize him."

I could feel a bead of sweat growing on my brow, not unusual for hot and humid Angeles City, but definitely unusual in my bar where I kept the AC on all the time so it was always comfortable.

Perdue reached into his pocket, and pulled out a photograph. He handed it to me.

"Well?" he asked.

I looked at the picture. It was fuzzy, out of focus. To me, and I'm not an expert at this, it looked like the picture had been taken from a distance using a zoom lens.

The subject was a man. A Filipino. I guessed anywhere from twenty-five to thirty. He was sitting on a motorcycle facing the camera. His brown skin looked extra dark, probably from spending too many daylight hours in the sun. Other than that, there was nothing to distinguish him from a couple hundred other guys who drove motorcycles in the city.

"I don't know," I said, honestly. "Could be familiar, but it's not a great photo."

"His name's Ernesto de la Cruz, does that help?"

Acting is a big part of being a *Papasan*. You've got to always be happy, always on. You've got to act like the jokes your patrons are telling you are really funny. You've got to pretend that there's never a bad day on Fields Avenue.

So when I heard the name and looked at the picture again, I didn't flinch.

"Never heard of him," I lied.

Perdue looked at me, a stupid little smile on his face, his eyes on my eyes. It was like he knew I was lying, like he was waiting for me to take it back and tell him the truth.

"Sorry," I said. "I don't know him."

He hesitated for a half second more, then broke off his stare. "You keep that picture. Maybe you can show it around. See if any of the girls know who he is. But don't tell anyone I'm looking for him."

"And if someone does know who he is?"

Perdue picked up his beer. "See if you can find out where he lives."

"I don't know if I want to get in the middle of anything here."

"You're a good American, right?"

I didn't respond right away. I didn't like the direction

this was going, but when he cocked his head and narrowed his eyes, I said, "Sure."

"Then finding out where he lives isn't going to be a problem, is it?"

"I didn't say I could find out."

"I have faith in you."

After he left, I asked Kat for a match, then burned the photo. I wasn't able to relax until the last of the image blackened, then turned to ash.

I knew who Ernesto de la Cruz was. He was a local. Helped me out sometimes at the bar—washing glasses, stocking beer, that kind of thing—when one of my regular guys needed a day off. He was a good kid. Smiled a lot. Always respectful. As far as I knew, he'd never been south of Manila.

A terrorist? Not even remotely possible. Of course, the moment Perdue mentioned Ernesto's name, I knew this wasn't about terrorism.

Ernesto de la Cruz was Ellie's boyfriend. And I would bet everything I own that Perdue knew that, too.

That evening, I asked Marguerite—she was one of my girls and Ellie's best friend—to text Ellie and tell her I wanted to talk to her. I'd trained the girls to know if they received a text like that, they were to stop by the bar at their next opportunity and see me.

I didn't expect to see her until the next day, and I was right.

It was just before noon. The bar wasn't open yet, but I was already there. Ellie knocked at the front door, and I let her in.

"You want me, Papa?" she asked, once we were alone inside.

"How is everything?" I said.

She hesitated only long enough for me to notice. "Okay. Fine."

"Mr. Perdue's treating you all right?"

"Joe took me to Manila. He buy me lot of things."

"So he hasn't hurt you?"

There was that pause again. "No. Why?"

"When was the last time you saw Ernesto?"

"What?" My question obviously surprised her.

"Have you seen him this week?"

"No. Of course not."

It was a pat answer. If the girls were on an extended bar fine, the house rule was no contact with any boyfriends. The reason was to avoid exactly the problem that seemed to be developing here.

"Ellie. Tell me the last time you saw him."

"Last weekend," she said quickly. "Sunday, I think."

The girls were as good at lying as I was. But unlike their temporary boyfriends, I'd long ago developed the ability to know if one of the girls was telling me the truth or not.

"When, Ellie?"

The sparkle in her eyes disappeared as she realized she'd been caught. "Yesterday," she said. "Joe went out for a while in the afternoon. I meet Ernesto at his place. But only for an hour. I don't lie."

That had probably been around the same time Perdue had stopped by the bar. "And before that, when?"

"The day before Joe take me to Manila."

"Jesus, Ellie. You know the rules."

"What? What's wrong?"

"Perdue must have seen you. He was asking about him."

"Joe wants his money back, doesn't he?" She looked horrified. "I'm sorry, Papa. I shouldn't have seen him. I'll pay you back, I promise."

I shook my head. "It's not the money."

"Then what?"

I contemplated stopping right there. I should have, but I didn't. "He wanted to know if I could find out where Ernesto lived."

"Why?"

"I don't think Perdue is a good man."

The true meaning of my words took a moment to sink in. When they finally did, she stepped away from me and turned for the door. "I have to tell Ernesto!"

I grabbed her arm, stopping her. "You can't go anywhere near Ernesto."

"But Joe will try to hurt him."

"Tell me how to find Ernesto. I'll tell him to get lost for a few days. Maybe he can go down to Manila."

"You'll do that?"

"Yes," I said. "Do you know when Joe's leaving town?"

"Monday, I think."

She told me where Ernesto lived, then, almost as if she didn't want to say it, added, "He pushed me."

"Who?"

"Joe," she said. "It was late, but I wanted to go out dancing. He said he was tired. I teased him and he pushed me into the wall."

I held my tongue as a surge of anger grew inside me.

"He said it was an accident. That he was just teasing back, but he wasn't. He pushed me. He'll hurt Ernesto."

"Go to your place," I said. "Stay there until Perdue leaves town. I'll tell him you got sick. I'll give him back his money if he asks."

"What about Ernesto?"

"I'll find him. It'll be okay."

Only it wasn't okay.

Ernesto shared a room in a dingy building about a mile from Fields Avenue. When I got there, the normal chaos of a typical Angeles street had been replaced by something much more sinister.

White vans blocked off each end of the street, but it didn't stop the curious from walking around them to see what was going on. The real action was toward the middle of the block, in front of Ernesto's building.

Whatever had happened seemed to have just ended. A dozen soldiers stood near the entrance. They were wearing full battle gear and held machine guns at the ready. At first I thought they were all Filipino, but the closer I got, I realized that though they were wearing identical dark uniforms, most of the men appeared to be either Caucasian or African-American.

My immediate thought was *Americans*.

I moved with the crowd, reaching a spot almost directly across the street from the building's entrance. I knew enough not to put myself out front, and I held back, allowing others to stand in front of me.

After about ten minutes, two men appeared in the doorway. They were carrying a stretcher, complete with a sheet-draped body on top. By the way everyone was acting, I knew the dead man wasn't one of theirs. And when Joseph Perdue emerged from the building a few moments later to the backslaps of his colleagues, it was pretty evident who was on the stretcher.

Homeland Security had gotten their man.

It was nearly 10:00 P.M. when Perdue showed up back in my bar. For the first time in a long time I wasn't sitting on my usual stool. Instead I'd taken over the back booth, and left instructions not to bother me unless it was really important.

Perdue spotted me right after he came in. He got a beer from Kat, then walked slowly back to my table, not even glancing at the girls on the stage. That was probably a good thing. While I hadn't told any of them what had happened, most had found out Ernesto was dead through other means, and had a pretty good idea Perdue had something to do with it. The looks they gave him were nothing short of venomous.

"How ya doing, Wade?" he asked.

"Fine. You?"

"Doing just great."

He slid into the other side of the booth without waiting to be asked.

"Haven't been able to get anything about the guy in your picture." I figured ignorance was the best route to take.

"Don't worry about it," he said. "Problem's taken care of."

I said nothing.

"Look. I'm going to be leaving town a little early. Heading out in the morning. Don't know when I'll be back."

"Have a good trip."

"Actually I came by to thank you. I had a great time. Lots of fun."

"That's what we're here for," I said, less than enthusiastically.

He took a deep swig of his beer, then set the bottle on the table. "Good-bye, Wade." He stood up. "You take it easy, all right?"

I shook his hand. Didn't want to, but there was no sense in causing a scene. He was leaving town, so I wouldn't have to worry about him anymore.

"Have a safe trip wherever you're going," I said.

"I'm heading home," he said. "Well, D.C., actually. I'm getting promoted."

"Good for you."

"Yeah, it is."

I'd been so wrapped up in wishing he'd just get out of the bar, that it wasn't until after he left that I realized he hadn't said anything about Ellie. Not one word.

Kat was the one who found her. We actually shut the bar down, and I sent the girls out in every direction. But leave it to Kat to hunt her down.

Ellie was only a few blocks from the dormlike room she shared with over a dozen other girls. She was in an alley—Angeles is rife with them—on the ground, her knees pulled up to her chest and her head lolled back with her mouth open. There was a long gash running from her left temple nearly all the way to her mouth. Blood was running from the wound, so I knew she was still alive.

The story I got later was that when she heard Ernesto was dead, she went crazy. All she could think about was killing Perdue. She got a knife and went to Perdue's hotel. The rest is pretty easy to imagine. She was no match for him. The only reason he didn't kill her—and I'm guessing here—is because he thought damaging her would be a worse fate.

As it was, what he had done to her in less than fifteen minutes took three operations and several months to repair. Even then it wasn't perfect. The scar that ran down the side of Ellie's face would always be with her. A reminder not only of Perdue, but of Ernesto.

"Can I ask you a few questions?" the man said.

It was a Monday evening, and in less than an hour the place would be packed for the weekly body-painting contest. But at that moment we were only half full.

"Of course," I said.

"Something to drink?" Ellie asked the man. Since returning to work a couple weeks earlier, she had asked if she could work behind the bar with Kat. Who was I to say no?

"Just some water, please," the man said.

He was the nervous type, who probably felt a lot more comfortable in a suit than in the casual wear he had on at that moment.

Ellie set a cold plastic bottle of water in front of him.

"Thanks," he said.

"I'm Wade Norris," I said.

"Curtis Knowles." He held out his hand and we shook.

"What can I do for you, Curtis?" I said, already knowing what he was going to ask.

"I'm with the FBI," he said.

"A little out of your territory, aren't you?"

He smiled. "I'm just part of an investigation, that's all."

"And your investigation brought you here?"

Knowles looked around. "It is one of the more unusual settings I've been in. I'll tell you that much." He unscrewed the top of his water, but didn't take a drink. "I'm looking into the disappearance of a federal employee."

"Don't tell me," I said. "Joseph Perdue, right?"

"I realize someone's already talked to you about this."

"You're the third person in two months. One of the others told me Perdue'd been kidnapped."

"We don't know anything for sure."

"He said it was in retaliation for that kid he killed, if I remember right."

"Terrorist."

"What?"

"The terrorist he killed. Perdue had uncovered information that linked the man to potential attacks that would have happened right here on your street, Mr. Norris."

"Really?" I said. "Hadn't heard that part."

"It was in the paper."

"I stopped reading the paper years ago. Too depressing."

Knowles removed a small notebook from his breast pocket, and opened it to one of the pages. "According to my notes, you said you remember Perdue coming into the bar twice, is that correct?"

"I haven't thought about this since the last time one of you guys came by. But that sounds about right."

"People have reported seeing him with . . . a woman."

I smiled. "So he was getting in a little fun while he was here."

"The woman was not someone he was *seeing*," Knowles said. "Perdue was a good family man."

"Was?"

Knowles paused, caught by his own words. "At this point, we believe he is most likely dead."

"I'm sorry to hear that."

"We also believe he was in contact with this woman as a potential information source. One of the people we talked to thought she might work here."

"Get you another beer, Papa?" Ellie said.

"Yes. Thanks." I looked at Knowles. "She wasn't one of ours. I remember everyone who takes one of the girls out."

"Everyone?"

"It's my job."

Ellie replaced my old bottle with a new one.

"He probably just met her on the outside."

"I would have found out," I said, then took a drink of my beer. "Mr. Knowles, there are a couple thousand girls who work in the bars here. Who knows where she came from."

Knowles nodded. "You're right."

"Why do you think she's so important?"

"We don't know for sure, but we think maybe she set him up."

"Sounds like you're reaching," I said, trying to appear sympathetic.

Another nod from Knowles. "I won't take up any

more of your time." As he pushed himself off the stool, he said, "If we have any more questions, we'll get back to you."

"I'll be here," I said, then saluted him with my bottle.

Knowles smiled, then walked around our new stage and out the front door.

I knew Perdue was trouble when he'd stared at me after I told him I didn't recognize the picture of Ernesto. There was no bluff in his gaze, no false toughness. What I had seen was the look of a man who didn't like to be crossed. I'd seen it before, back in my service days in the corps. Other marines who were more like machines than real men—in their minds, they felt like all they had to do was look at the enemy, and their adversary would crumple to the ground.

They were hard. They were single-minded. They were dangerous as all hell.

And I'd been one of them.

After Kat found Ellie and we'd gotten her to the hospital, I'd gone alone in search of Perdue. I found him easily enough. He was in his room at the Paradise Hotel. I knocked on his door, told him I was looking for Ellie and wondered if he knew where she was. Of course he let me in.

I eased the door closed behind me, then I buried the pointed metal rod I'd been holding against my leg under his rib cage and into one of his lungs. I watched his face for a moment as he realized too late the danger I represented. I was just a lazy old *Papasan,* after all. Drunk half the time, and mellowed by the women that surrounded me.

He tried to grab for me, but he was already too weak.

I should have probably said something damning, something to sum up his failures as a human being. Instead I pulled the rod out and shoved it up again. This time into his heart.

See, I was Homeland Security, too. It was just that my homeland extended only a couple miles beyond the door of my bar.

By morning, the old stage in the bar had been ripped out, and a hole dug deep into the ground beneath. Perdue went into the hole, along with some dirt and rocks and concrete. Then we got to work on the new stage. I made this one a little wider.

The girls love it.

"Thanks, Papa," Ellie said after Knowles had left.

"Nothing to thank me for. How about a dance?"

"Not today," she said. But this time, unlike all the previous times I'd asked her to try out the new stage, she actually smiled.

I was breaking her down. One day, she'd get up there and she'd dance again.

On that day, drinks will be on the house.

Killing Justice
by Allison Brennan

•

I.

Senate Pro Tem Simon Black sat in his high-back leather chair signing letters, the tall, narrow window behind him framing the Tower Bridge at the far end of Sacramento's Capitol Mall, the morning sun making the elevator bridge appear golden. His secretary, Janice, escorted Matt Elliott into the office, offered him coffee—which he refused—then quietly retreated.

Simon had been expecting the confrontation since Elliott called him before six that morning, and said nothing, allowing the tension to build.

It didn't take long. Elliott slammed his fists on the antique desk and leaned forward, his knuckles white. "You bastard. You stacked the committee!"

Simon placed the pen precisely on the blotter, sat up straight, and clasped his hands in front of him.

"Sit down, Senator Elliott."

The pulse in Elliott's neck throbbed. He pushed away from the desk and paced, running both hands through his dark hair. "You promised you wouldn't fuck with my bill package."

That was true. Simon had always planned to quash the so-called children's safety legislation on the Senate floor at the end of session, when it would be too late for Elliott to raise the money and qualify an initiative. Simon hated the fact that in California, when the legislature—which had been given the power to pass or defeat legislation—didn't cater to the cause of the year, the rich and powerful would raise a few million dollars to put their pet project on the ballot.

He hated it except when it benefited his interests.

The truth was, if Senator Matt Elliott had the time, he could have qualified an initiative for the November ballot even though it would force his party to take a position on "tough on crime" legislation. Didn't Elliott see that? Wasn't the future strength of their party more important than one bill?

"Kill the bill now, Simon."

Jamie Tan's words came back to him. The head of the Juvenile Justice Alliance, which operated nearly two hundred group homes for juveniles in the criminal justice system, had made it perfectly clear that if Elliott's bill passed, they'd pull all support. It was an election year and they wanted to take no chances on a vote by the full Senate. The bill had to die in committee.

Worse, Tan had brought the head of a prison reform group and one of the two major trial lawyer organizations into the meeting. The warning was clear: screw them, his election well would run dry.

That was the biggest problem with term limits, Simon realized. Before, the leader had the power. Now, special interests had power. James Tan would be around longer than Simon Black, and Tan knew it.

Simon had no choice but to back down. If he lost even one seat this election cycle, he'd be unceremoniously dumped as leader.

"Put Paula back on the committee," Elliott demanded, stopping in front of his desk.

"Forget it, Elliott. My decision is final."

"I'll bury you, Black."

"You? You're the outcast of our party. No one trusts you. You're just as likely to vote with the Republicans as vote with us. So you won Paula over to *this* issue, but you know damn well she'll never agree with you on your other pet projects."

"This isn't a pet project. My bill will save lives."

Black waved his hand in the air. "Don't start believing your own press releases," he said.

"Damn you, we can make a difference!"

"Do you realize what's at stake? Do you know how many people will lose their jobs if your bill passes? Do you understand that the state is under court order to decrease the prison population? All your bill would do is make the crisis worse."

"Tell that to Timothy Stewart! Wait, you can't. He's *dead.*"

"That's what this has all been about. You want to destroy an entire industry because of one mistake."

"*One?* The Stewart case is only one *example* of the problems with the current system."

Simon's phone beeped. On cue. He'd told his secretary to never leave him alone with Matt Elliott in his office for more than five minutes.

"Yes, Janice? Right, I'll take it."

He covered the mouthpiece. "Get out."

II.

Senator Matt Elliott hung up with the fiery Paula Ramirez, who was as livid as he was that Black had replaced her on the Public Safety Committee. Matt had spent the entire three years of his legislative term working on Paula, earning her trust and respect. It all came to a head when he asked for her support of this bill, against their party line. Matt was the maverick, the others expected him to vote however he damn well pleased, but Paula was one of theirs: a dyed-in-the-wool, intellectual, steadfast liberal.

And he'd won her over on this issue. He'd also grown to like her, though they still didn't see eye-to-eye on most criminal justice issues.

It was Hannah Stewart, the slain boy's mother—for whom "Timothy's Law" had been named—who'd swayed Paula. Her raw, honest testimony that Matt, a former prosecutor, could only attest to, not recreate. She'd been to hell and back in the five years since her son had been murdered, and had been with him from the very beginning.

And now he had to tell her that not only was the bill dead as the result of political posturing and corruption, but he didn't have the time to qualify an initiative for this year's ballot. It would be put on the back burner until the next election.

His chief of staff, Greg Harper, knocked on the door. "Mrs. Stewart and her sister are here."

"Send them in."

He stood, walked to the door to greet them. Matt felt

like a prosecutor again, giving bad news to surviving family. He'd always hated that part of the job, and this was worse because he knew Hannah.

"What's wrong?" she asked as soon as they sat down on the couch facing his desk.

She'd always been perceptive. Even when she was on the emotional ringer during Rickie Coleman's trial, she'd picked up on the subtleties of the court testimony.

"Paula was removed from the Public Safety Committee," Matt said. "She was replaced by someone who opposes Timothy's Law."

"Why?"

"I told you this was going to be a tough sell."

"But after Senator Ramirez agreed to support Timothy's Law. We had the votes, correct?"

He nodded.

"And she was removed why? Because someone didn't want the bill to pass?"

"Essentially."

"You mean the Senate leader."

"I'm not going to lie to you. Politics reigns supreme in this building. We knew what we were up against— the group-home industry is worth tens of millions of dollars and growing. All they are doing is slowing down the tide against them."

"It's happened since Timmy," Hannah said. "It'll happen again. Is that a justifiable cost for human lives?"

Matt had nothing to say. He agreed with Hannah. "I'm sorry."

Hannah turned away from Senator Elliott and looked at her niece in the stroller. Rachel was a beautiful child, perfect in every way, round and plump with chubby hands and deep dimples. The dimples ran in their family—both Hannah and her sister, Meg, had them.

Unlike Rachel's twin indentions, Timmy had had a solitary dimple on his left cheek.

She squeezed her eyes shut as the wave of pain hit her, palatable. Unconsciously, her hand fiercely rubbed her forehead.

"Hannah, you okay?"

It was the senator speaking. She lied. "I'm fine."

"I know you're disappointed. I'm furious about this, and I promise you I'll take it to the voters. I'm not going to sit back and let this power play go unnoticed. My chief of staff is crafting a press release, and I'm having a press conference—with Paula—immediately after the committee hearing."

Hannah nodded, though she only heard part of what he said. She'd known this could happen. And, really, why had she come to testify in the first place? It wouldn't bring Timothy back. It wouldn't piece together her destroyed marriage.

You did it to save other children.

And now other children were still at risk because of politics. Politics that allowed juvenile sex offenders to move quietly into neighborhoods without anyone knowing. Politics that allowed those perverts to live across the street from an elementary school, to watch the little boys and little girls walking to and from school every day.

They could slip out because people who had no idea how to care for these criminals were put in positions of authority. Did they even understand that their young charges hurt other children? That it was only a matter of time before they escalated from sex crimes to murder?

What was the difference between a seventeen-year-old paroled rapist and an eighteen-year-old paroled rapist? The public was allowed to know when the older predator moved into their neighborhood, but not the other.

"Hannah?"

It was her sister Meg's motherly tone. The sign that she was worried.

Rachel started fussing in her stroller and Meg reached for her. Hannah interrupted.

"Let me take care of her," she said.

"All right," Meg agreed, her eyes following Hannah as she left with the baby.

Matt had known Hannah for more than five years, ever since he was the prosecutor in her son's murder case. She'd always been a quietly strong woman, even though he'd never forget the pain in her eyes. How could he? Five years later it was still there, a permanent reminder of the uncaring bureaucrats and a callous system that made it more profitable to house sex offenders in middle-class neighborhoods than in prison.

Of course, the group homes were officially "non-profit," but the people that ran the facilities also owned the food supply, laundry services, van companies. Investors quietly bought up houses in middle-class neighborhoods and leased them out to the nonprofits at inflated rates. Then there was court-ordered counseling, attorney fees, private security companies—Matt had only touched upon the money trail of those connected with these facilities.

"How's she holding up?" Matt asked when the door closed.

"Hannah's strong. She's gotten through the worst of it, and now that the divorce is final I think she'll be okay. It's just—"

"What?"

"Every time Hannah speaks, she relives Timmy's murder."

Matt hated thinking he was partly to blame for Hannah's pain. He'd sympathized with her, he took care of her needs, but he'd never failed to use Timmy's murder to advance his goals. While his goals were for the protection of all children, he'd lost sight of his own humanity in the process. And the idea that maybe everything he'd asked Hannah to do had kept the wounds festering, instead of healing.

He wished he could help Hannah move forward, reclaim her lost life. Five years was a long time to grieve.

But he'd never lost a child to violence.

III.

HANNAH PUSHED her index fingers into her temples, pushing back the agony.

She'd lost her only child. Then she'd lost her husband. Eric wasn't dead, but he was dead to her.

"Why weren't you watching him? How could you let this happen?"

He'd apologized, but the damage was done. Eric

thought she was responsible. That her actions and inactions had resulted in Timmy being stabbed six times after enduring a rape.

Rickie Coleman said he didn't mean to kill Timmy, that he was scared of going to jail if he was caught. And the judge only gave him nine years. For *manslaughter,* not murder.

The sixteen-year-old Coleman lived right down the street from Timmy's school in a group home for juvenile sex offenders. Timmy had passed by that house every day, unaware of the depravity that hid behind the door.

If she'd only known, she'd never have let Timmy walk home alone. Or even with friends. She would have picked him up. Or arranged a neighborhood carpool.

Dammit! His school was only three blocks from home! He should have been safe.

She worked only ten minutes away and had adjusted her work schedule in order to meet Timmy when he came home from school every day.

But he never came home that day. She called every friend and ran from her house to the school, calling his name, her panic growing.

She ran right past the house where Timmy lay dead in the backyard, to be discovered three hours later when the owner came home from work.

The house next door to the group home.

Rachel let out a yelp and Hannah cleared her head. Remembered where she was . . . in a restroom in the California state capitol.

"Sorry, sweetheart," she said and changed the wet infant's diaper. Rachel reached up and pulled Hannah's long brown hair. Hannah was in the handicap stall, which she'd often used when Timmy had been in a stroller. Now, she needed it for privacy more than safety.

"Sorry, Rachel," she murmured as she reached under the stroller. Her hand touched the cold metal.

Are you sure?

Of course she was sure. Her son was dead, her marriage was over, and she had nothing left but distant memories of happiness and current memories of pain.

Rachel gurgled in her stroller, reached again for Hannah's hair. She allowed the baby to grab a handful, a tear falling onto Rachel's little pink dress.

"I love you, Rachel," she whispered. "I hope your mommy forgives me."

Hannah loosened the gun which she had strapped down with duct tape under the stroller that morning when she'd volunteered to load Rachel's stroller into the car.

She had watched people coming and going through security during her numerous trips to the capitol. The guards passed the strollers around the metal detector and only took a cursory glance at the contents. Diaper bags and backpacks were run through the X-ray, but not the strollers themselves.

After more than a year of delays, bill amendments, and testimony that made her heart bleed, Hannah had suspected that Timothy's Law would never pass. She'd hoped she was wrong, that the bill would get out of committee, but she'd brought the gun anyway. Just in case. And her instincts had been right.

She and Meg had grown up on a farm in the Central Valley and their father taught them to shoot at a young age. Hannah never expected to use a gun on a human being.

Senator Black was anything but human.

"Let's tell your mommy you want a walk," she told Rachel, securing the gun in the small of her back, under her loose-fitting blouse. "Auntie Hannah has a meeting."

IV.

"I'M NOT GOING to sit here and pretend none of us knows exactly what happened today. Senator Ramirez was unceremoniously removed from the Public Safety Committee after faithfully serving for seven years. Why? Because she supported Timothy's Law."

He stared at his fellow committee members one by one. They in turn looked disgusted, bored, and angry. Angry at *him,* perhaps, because he was shining a high-wattage light on the dark dealings of the capitol.

Good bills were killed because of special interests every day of the week. Matt's bill was simply another casualty.

"We've heard enough," the chair, Senator Thomas, said. "You're getting very close to being censured."

"Censured? You think I care about being *censured* when you sit there and abstain on a bill that would protect children?"

"Senator Elliott, that is enough."

Out of the corner of his eye, Matt noticed Hannah Stewart enter the committee hearing room. She came in through the rear entrance and sat in the back row.

He couldn't drag her through another hearing, not

like this. Her face was ashen, and she was as skinny as he'd seen her during the trial when her sister told him she'd lost weight, going from 140 pounds to less than 110.

"It may be enough for this room, but I will continue to fight for child safety legislation even if some of the members of this committee believe in politics over innocent lives."

He retook his seat, Thomas staring at him icily. He stared back. He wasn't going to let them get away with it. He knew what he would tell the press.

Without fanfare, the committee voted. Three ayes, four abstentions.

Failed.

The next time he looked up, Hannah was gone.

V.

THOUGH HANNAH had grown up listening to her father's tirades about the corruption of government, she'd always believed in the system. That good people ran for office—people like Matt Elliott, the man who'd prosecuted Timmy's murderer. The man whose eyes teared when he told her the judge was going to give Coleman a lenient sentence. That Rickie Coleman would be a free man at the same time Timmy should have been graduating from high school.

Senator Elliott was not to blame. He'd done what he could.

It was Black's fault. Simon Black, the man who'd stacked the committee for the sole purpose of killing Timothy's Law. A man who cared more about politics than a little boy who'd bled to death, alone, crying for his mommy. . . .

Hannah screamed, but no sound escaped her tight throat. She heard Timmy's silent pleas every time she closed her eyes, every time she tried to sleep. But never in daylight, never like this.

She pretended to look through her purse as she watched the traffic in the corridor. It didn't take long before she saw the group she needed. Six women of different ages, walking with briefcases and purpose. She quickly trailed after them, standing only a foot from the rear as they opened the door and piled into the waiting area.

The short woman of the group announced them. "Betsy Franklin with the Nurses Coalition. We have a meeting with Senator Black."

The secretary checked the schedule, nodded, and told them to have a seat and she would let the senator know that they'd arrived.

If any of the women noticed her, they must have assumed she also had an appointment with the senate leader. They didn't comment. She didn't offer an explanation.

She sat in a chair while Nurse Betsy Franklin spoke to Black's secretary. Hannah hadn't been in this office before, but she was a good observer. She watched as the secretary vaguely nodded toward a door behind her and to the left. Was Black's office right on the other side of the door? Or down a hall?

Now that she'd made her decision, an eerie calm descended around her.

Killing Senator Black wouldn't bring Timmy back

from the dead, but it would punish him for what he'd done to stop justice. It would make a statement: that people who had the lives of others in their hands could not callously disregard the dead, or the living.

"Janice, I'll just be a sec." A tall, lanky man with a boyish face and graying hair walked past the secretary with a half smile at the nurses. He opened the door, closed it. But Hannah saw what she needed to see. A short hall, then double doors.

Where that bastard worked.

Rickie Coleman was to blame for killing Timmy. But what about the system that put him there in the first place? Even though Coleman was now in prison and the staff fired, that house was still open and operational in her old neighborhood. Nearly every day she drove by, watched as the so-called counselors, who looked barely old enough to vote, escorted the six teenage boys from the house to an unmarked van. Followed as they drove across the county to "school." Their school was housed in a recreation center that also held a preschool and several after-school programs. They put those sexual predators in the same building with innocent children.

When she'd gone to the Recreation Board, she was told that, "There have been no reported problems. And they pay their rent on time."

She'd been in the building enough over the last six months to know that she couldn't simply walk into the pro tem's office. The secretary would ask if she had an appointment. And she doubted that Senator Black would talk to her, even if she did tell him she wanted to see him.

Hannah, are you sure you want to do this?

She wasn't sure of anything. She couldn't sleep, she

could barely eat. She'd never wanted to move, but she couldn't live in the same house where Timmy had lived. She was in limbo, going through the motions of life.

Her soul had died the same day as Timmy.

The man left Black's office ten minutes later and Hannah jumped up.

"Ma'am, you can't—"

Hannah closed the door and ran to the double doors, opening them at the same time as the secretary opened the outer door.

"Sergeants!" the woman called.

Hannah closed the door.

She'd noticed Matt Elliott had locks on his doors, and was pleased to find that so did Senator Black. She turned it.

"Ms. Franklin?" Senator Black asked, confused, as he rose from his desk.

Recognition crossed his tanned face as he stared at her.

"Hannah Stewart," she said, though it was unnecessary. "You killed Timothy's Law."

Fists pounded on the door behind Hannah. She drew the gun.

"Senator? Senator?" a muffled voice called through the door. "Get the sergeants!"

"Mrs. Stewart—" Black put his hands up, slowly. He stared at the gun, not at her.

Her enemy cowered in front of her. Sweat formed along his receding hairline. She should kill him now. But her hand trembled, so she held the gun with both hands; her purse fell to the floor with a *thud*. She jumped, heart pounding.

She'd never shot a person before.

"You sacrificed innocent children for politics," she said, surprised that her voice sounded normal.

"Mrs. Stewart, put the gun down."

He tried to sound tough, but his voice cracked at the end. He was scared. He feared for *his* life when the lives of the innocent meant nothing to him.

"That group home, the same one that Rickie Coleman slipped out of to kill my son, is still in operation. And because of *you,* it will not be shut down."

"That's not the role of state government—"

"Bullshit!" Swearing surprised her as much as her volume. "You stacked the committee! You killed my bill!"

"Mrs. Stewart, it's only legislation—it can't bring back your son."

"Timmy! His name is Timmy! Do you know how many juvenile sex offenders escaped and hurt children? Do you?"

"Mrs. Stewart—"

"We don't know because they're minors and their records are confidential! And because the people who run those homes make millions of dollars they'll never be shut down. The group home in my own neighborhood? The owner makes three times the market value every month on an inflated lease. Is that the price of a child? Seven thousand dollars a month?"

Black took a step toward her and Hannah fired the gun.

VI.

"SENATOR, they're evacuating the building," Greg exclaimed as he ran into Matt's office, his lips in a tight, white line.

"What's going on? Bomb threat?"

"There's a gunman in the building."

"They'd lock down if there was a gunman loose, not evacuate," Matt said. His instincts hummed.

"I'm just relaying what the sergeants told me. He's in the historic building; the annex has been locked down and is being evacuated. It's mandatory."

Matt waved his hand dismissively at Greg and turned on the television by remote.

". . . capitol building is being evacuated. Nothing more is known at this time."

The picture switched from a reporter outside the east entrance of the capitol to the bureau chief. "Sources in the building tell NBC news that every office has been ordered to evacuate immediately. A gunman is in the building. Wait—"

The reporter listened to his earpiece. "A shot has been confirmed fired. Three separate sources report that a shot has been fired on the second floor of the historic building. Sources indicate the shot may have come from Senate Pro Tem Black's office, a Democrat from Los Angeles."

"Simon," Matt whispered.

He pictured the look on Hannah's face when he told her about the committee.

Suddenly, the last five years took on a different face. For the first time Matt clearly saw what he'd done. The last major case he tried before filing for office was the Timothy Stewart murder. It was the judge's idiocy that had propelled him to seek the senate seat. He'd wanted to fix the system in a way that a prosecutor couldn't—by changing the laws.

And then he brought Hannah Stewart in to help his cause. She'd seemed the perfect spokeswoman for reform; an eloquent, attractive mother, a person the press and the people could relate to. She joined his bandwagon to change the laws, to ensure that children were protected and violent predators—whatever their age— were locked up where they couldn't hurt others.

It had been his cause because he'd lost in court when he hated to lose—and rarely did. Sure, Rickie Coleman had been convicted, but the judge threw out the first-degree murder charge—believing Coleman when he said he didn't intend to kill the boy—and Coleman ended up with manslaughter and a nine-year sentence.

Matt had wanted to change the system, fix what was broken, and he'd used every means possible.

Including a woman so devastated by grief that she hadn't truly lived in five years.

He suddenly knew who the "gunman" was.

He had unwittingly created her.

VII.

THE SERGEANT-AT-ARMS, Bob Bush, ran a hand over his mustache, a nervous habit he'd thought he'd broken. In charge of capitol security for the past twenty years, he'd had his share of situations. But never had a shot been fired in the capitol under his watch.

"CHP is on alert," Jefferson said.

They stood outside Black's office, which had been immediately evacuated after the gunshot. He'd just debriefed the secretary, who didn't know anything.

"Where's the damn security tape?"

A security camera outside the senator's office would have recorded who'd passed through the door.

"They're viewing it downstairs right now," Jefferson said, listening to his earpiece. "They have an I.D. Hannah Stewart, Caucasian female, forty-two."

"Who the hell is she?"

A commotion outside the door had Bob turning. He saw Senator Elliott trying to bypass the shield they'd set up around the office.

"Senator, you need to evacuate," Bob said, turning around to talk to Jefferson before he'd finished his sentence.

"I know Hannah."

Bob stopped, turned to him. "She won't pick up the phone. We've been trying to call in to the office for the last ten minutes."

"She'll talk to me. Please, let me go in."

"I can't do that, we don't even know if Senator Black is alive. SWAT is getting into position, a guy is climbing a tree outside on the West Lawn."

"Don't shoot her."

"He's been ordered to assess the situation and report."

"Please, Bob. I can defuse this."

"What's her story?"

"She testified on one of my bills in Public Safety. It was defeated today."

"She's holding Black hostage because a bill got killed?"

"No. She's holding Black hostage because her son got killed and she doesn't think anyone cares."

VIII.

THE SERGEANTS would not let him go in, but that didn't faze Matt. He had an idea.

He ran upstairs to the third floor to the Republican leader's office. The floor was oddly deserted. The windows in the gallery were sealed shut, but those in the member offices could be opened. Matt walked in through the leader's "escape" door—an unmarked entrance directly into his office from the side hallway. Few legislators kept their private door locked.

Matt crossed to the window behind the desk, directly above Black's office. He opened the window. A portico traversed the west steps of the capitol building, but stopped before reaching the offices.

Matt looked down, swallowed heavily. A three-foot ledge ran under the windows, but if he slipped . . . the drop was already precarious because of the seventeen-foot-high ceilings. But broken ankles were the least of his concern now. To his left was a spindly palm tree, to his right the top of a tree with long, narrow leaves. It didn't look sturdy enough to climb down, but if he fell from the ledge, the tree would prevent him from hitting ground.

He knew Black's little secret—after hours, he often opened that window and leaned out to smoke cigars. Not once had Matt seen him lock it.

Without hesitating, Matt flung open the far window and climbed out, holding on to the ledge, his legs dangling over, and assessing the drop. He hung there only a moment before falling. . . .

Slam. Right on the ledge. His knees protested, but no broken bones. He teetered a moment, grabbed a thin branch to steady himself. He shook off the pain, shimmied along the ledge to Black's unlocked window, and pushed it open.

Hannah stood over Black's desk, a gun aimed at his chest. Black's face was ashen and he lay awkwardly across his chair.

He was too late.

IX.

"WHAT THE HELL was that?" Bob Bush exclaimed at the faint *thump* that came from outside the building.

Jefferson listened, then said, "SWAT reports that a man jumped from the third floor onto the balcony and has entered Black's office."

Bob bit back expletives. "Who?"

"No confirmation yet. He was wearing gray slacks and a white button-down, rolled up at the sleeves. Dark hair, approximately six foot one inch—"

"Matt Elliott. Ring the office." Dammit, did the senator want to get both himself and Black killed?

Bob held the phone to his ear as it rang and rang.

X.

"LET ME ANSWER the phone," Matt told Hannah.

"Why are you here?"

"Hannah, please."

She didn't respond, and Matt slowly reached over to Black's desk, watching Hannah's eyes the entire time. He pressed line one, picked up the phone. "It's Matt Elliott."

"Senator, what are you doing?" Bob Bush exclaimed.

"Black is alive. Give me ten minutes."

He hung up as Bush protested. "Hannah," he said, "you don't want to do this."

He glanced at the Senate leader. There was no blood; she hadn't shot him. Something was still wrong. Black's mouth moved rapidly, but no words came out. He was pale and his left eye seemed to look in a different direction than his right. Heart attack? Didn't matter, Black needed medical attention immediately.

"You don't want to kill him."

Hannah looked at him with blue eyes filled with pain so tangible Matt's own heart broke.

"No one cares about Timmy," she whispered.

"You care, Hannah. You've done everything you can. I'm not going to let anyone forget about your son."

Tears welled in her eyes. "Today—today he would have been fifteen."

Matt had forgotten. He'd breathed nothing but the Timothy Stewart homicide for five and a half years, but he hadn't remembered the child's birthday.

His mother would never forget.

"I'm so sorry, Hannah. I've done everything I could to make sure no other mother suffers like you have."

She shook her head. "He—" she waved the gun at Black, swallowed. "People like him don't care. All they see are numbers and statistics. And money. Always the money. Like the life of a child has a price on it! All they had to do was give parents information. Give us a chance to protect our children. I'd have walked Timmy home myself every day if I knew those sex offenders lived in that house. But no one can protect the children if we don't even know what we're up against!"

Matt was concerned about Black. His breathing was shallow, his face clammy, and an odd sound emanated from his throat. Maybe it was a stroke, not a heart attack. Hannah seemed not to notice.

If Black died, she'd be charged with murder. Matt didn't know if he could live with that on his conscience.

"What about Rachel?"

Hannah blinked, really looked at him for the first time. "Rachel?"

"How can you protect your niece if you go to prison? What is Meg going to tell Timmy's cousin? Rachel needs you. Meg needs you. She's stood by you from the very beginning. She sat next to you during Coleman's trial *every single day*. Think of how she will feel if you go to prison. Or if SWAT shoots you?"

Matt had spied the SWAT team member in the tree across the path, and blocked his direct line of fire. He couldn't let Hannah die.

He couldn't let Black die.

"I'm nothing," she whispered.

"Hannah, you're living in hell. Let me help bring you back. Please."

She stared at him. "Promise me one thing."

"What?"

"You won't stop until Timothy's Law passes."

"That I can promise you." Arms outstretched, he took a step toward her. "Please hand me the gun."

She nodded.

His momentary relief that she was giving up the fight dissipated as Hannah brought the gun to her head.

"No!"

He leaped toward her.

The gun went off.

XI.

Three months later

"Matt, Sandra Cullen is here to see you."

"Thanks, Bonnie."

Bonnie was the last of his staff. When he announced last month that he wasn't seeking reelection, his entire staff found other jobs. He didn't blame them, though there were still six months left in his term. He didn't care that he was staffless. He had nothing he wanted to accomplish—at least in this building.

He'd already done all the damage he could.

Sandy closed the door behind her. She was a petite woman, skinny through excess energy. She'd been the district attorney of Sacramento County for coming on twelve years, and his former boss. He had complete respect for her. It was Sandy who had tried to stop him from running for state senate. He'd accused her of playing politics—he was taking out a member of her party. But in hindsight, she'd wanted to spare him the pain of failure.

An idealist in government simply tilted at windmills, she'd said.

"I'm not going to try to change your mind," she said, "because you're going to make a damn fine DA."

When Sandy had announced her retirement, Matt had tossed his hat into the ring. She'd endorsed him immediately.

Already, he felt like the world that had crashed down three months ago was rising just enough to allow him to breathe.

"Thought you might like to know that my office just accepted a plea on Hannah Stewart's case. She'll continue to stay at Napa State Hospital for twelve months."

"No jail time?"

Sandy frowned. "I know you think I'm callous, but I couldn't fight for jail time on this one. I would have got it. But in a trial, I think I would have ended with a hung jury. She wanted—and needed—to go to the mental hospital."

"Thank you."

"I read in the paper that Black was released from the hospital yesterday. Is he coming back? It was unclear."

"He's still incapacitated from the stroke. He doesn't have mobility on his left side at all, though he's regaining his speech."

"Have you seen him since?"

"No."

"And Hannah?"

He paused. "Once." It had been awkward for both of them. He thought originally she'd been too embarrassed and grateful that he'd knocked her hand away before she killed herself. Instead, she'd blamed him for her failed suicide attempt.

"I just don't want to live anymore."

"Matt, I always said you were too good for this building."

He shook his head. "Wouldn't it be better for more people like us to be here? Then maybe we *could* make a difference."

"When Hell freezes over," she said.

Bottom Deal
by Robert Gregory Browne

•

The author of the exceptional novel *Kiss Her Goodbye,* Robert Gregory Browne has an artist's gift for creating other worlds so believable one would swear they exist. And they do—just begin reading "Bottom Deal," and you'll be gripped by the gritty, colorful world of Jennings, ex-cop, ex-husband. He's one of those archetypal figures for whom all of us root while admiring their bold insouciance, feeling the depths of their pain, and waiting breathlessly to see how they're going to get themselves—and those they're trying to save—out of the current mess. A short story, when as beautifully executed as this one, is an abbreviated, luminous moment of life. Settle into your favorite chair and enjoy.

—Gayle Lynds,
New York Times bestselling author of
The Last Spymaster

Three months after he was kicked out of the Tally-Ho Casino for copping cards, Jennings called in a marker and snagged a matinee gig in their second-floor lounge. The contract, such as it was, had a special stipulation that he never set foot on the casino floor.

That included the private rooms.

Cockney Carl Baldwin, the casino owner, whom Jennings had once helped out of a pretty large jam, warned him that he'd better not go back on his promise.

"As it is," Carl told him, "you're lucky to be alive."

The Tally-Ho was a dump several blocks west of Fremont, populated by locals and a healthy dose of low-income tourists. The gig didn't pay much, but then the show Jennings gave them in return wasn't worth a whole helluva lot either. Mostly card tricks, a few coin gags, and a mentalism routine he'd ripped off, patter and all, from Max Maven. He'd go table to table as a couple of cheap ceiling-mounted video cams followed him, projecting his "amazing feats of sleight-of-hand" onto a large-screen TV for all the tourists to see.

They seemed to like it, the tourists, giving him rousing rounds of applause between sips of watery piña coladas. He made cards disappear, dealt perfect hands of poker, and changed a blue deck into red right before their startled Midwestern eyes.

Jennings didn't really hear the applause. It wasn't much more than a buzz in his head, a cue for the next bit of canned patter, while his mind retreated into that dark cave it seemed to find so comforting these days. Either that, or he was strapped into his Time Machine, reminiscing about those long-ago days before God, or whoever, decided—as Cockney Carl would say—to take a giant two-bob bit on his head.

It was all pretty pathetic, when you thought about it. But that's the way it was for Jennings. He was on autopilot, headed nowhere fast.

Until Holly Addison's murder changed everything.

*   *   *

"I say we go for all three," Scully said. "Bing-bang-boom, all in one night."

It was about 7:00 P.M. on a warm Thursday. They were sitting in the snack shop of the Golden Sands Bowling Center, the thunder of league night protecting them from prying ears.

Scully had a printout in front of him, three of the entries highlighted in yellow. The header read, "Stateline Security Systems."

"Bing-bang-boom, huh?"

Scully nodded. "One right after the other."

"You realize," Jennings said, "we take down one, it seems like a random act that maybe nobody but the homeowner cares about. We go for all three, we'll make Stateline Security and the boys at Metro Patrol Division look pretty bad."

Scully shrugged. "Boo-friggin'-hoo."

"Come on, Scully, think. When cops look bad, they work harder. That's more heat than we can afford."

"Isn't that an oxymoron?" Scully asked.

"What?"

"Hardworking cops."

Jennings looked at him. There was a time when he might have thought this was funny, might even have made the joke himself. There was also a time he would've smacked Scully upside the head and told him to watch his mouth.

Instead, he said, "Don't let greed get in the way of your common sense."

"You're one to talk."

Jennings ignored the comment. "Just pick one and give me the particulars."

Scully did, choosing the house that he thought offered them the highest return for their labor. They dis-
cussed strategy for a moment, then Jennings said, "That's
the one we hit, then. Tomorrow night."

Scully raised his eyebrows. "What's your rush?"

"I'm starting to get the itch again."

The itch.

Everybody knows it—has felt it at one time or another. Whether it's booze, smack, sex, smokes, coffee, or
a late-night snack when you're already tipping the scale
past buffalo butt.

For some, it's a crawling sensation that starts in the
gut and travels up toward the brain. And if it isn't stopped
somewhere along the way, all rational thought is abandoned. The only thing that matters is scratching that itch
before it pulls you under.

For Jennings it wasn't booze or drugs or sex or cigarettes or even steak and eggs at midnight.

It was the game. Texas Hold 'Em, Omaha High,
Seven-Card Stud. He'd played them all and played them
well.

"Tomorrow night," he said again.

Scully shrugged. "I got nothin' better to do."

Jennings decided to drive awhile before heading back
to his apartment. The Vegas air was hot and dry and he
enjoyed the feel of the warm wind streaming in through
his open window. He considered looking for a game,
then decided against it. The more you scratch, the more
it itches, right? Start now, and he was likely to be at it
all night.

He was just turning on Carson when his cell phone rang. Probably Scully, concerned about some overlooked detail. Flipping the phone open, he said, "Yeah?"

"Nick?"

Not Scully. The voice was female. Familiar.

"Nick, it's me. Holly."

Talk about your blast from the past.

Jennings hadn't seen or spoken to Holly Addison in three long years. All at once the Time Machine kicked into high gear and a boatload of memories flooded his brain.

"Nick, you there?"

"I'm here," he said. "How you been, Holly?"

"Not so good." Her voice was shaky. She was quiet a moment, except for her breathing, which sounded labored, upset.

Then she said, "I think someone's trying to kill me."

Her real name wasn't Holly.

She was born Rebecca Jane Addison, a corn-fed kid from Nebraska who one day filled a ratty suitcase with clothes, kissed her drunken mother good-bye, and hitched a ride to the nearest Greyhound station.

Ever since Rebecca had watched *Showgirls*—one of Mom's DVD rentals—she'd dreamed of going to Vegas to seek her fame and fortune. Her face and body, she had decided, were a heckuva lot easier on the eyes than that Nomi chick from the movie, and there were very few men who were likely to disagree. Especially the ones who paid for the privilege of her company.

It was a familiar story with all the usual props and scenery, and Rebecca, now Holly—short for Hollywood, because she was always blathering on about movie stars—would be the first to admit that she was a walking cliché.

But she had no regrets. Making a living as a professional escort wasn't all that bad.

"It's just a different kind of show," she'd once told Jennings. "And I'm very good at it."

Jennings had always believed that people should play to their strengths, but the words sounded hollow. He sensed a kind of sadness in Holly. Twenty-three years old and she already carried that battle-worn resignation that hits all of us when we finally realize the future isn't as bright as we once thought it would be.

He'd known her for a couple years by then, back before the world caved in on him. He'd met her while working a homicide downtown.

Sergeant Nick Jennings, Detective First Grade.

You wouldn't know it by looking at him now, but he'd spent seven years on the homicide squad, and six prior to that in uniform. And in those years he'd managed to cultivate quite a list of informants.

Holly was at the top of that list.

But just as his life started its nosedive, Holly's was on the rise. She met and married a real estate developer from California who pretended not to know what she did for a living. Jennings figured it gave the guy a secret thrill, thinking he'd tamed a wildcat.

"Who woulda believed it," she said to Jennings. "Just like Richard Gere and Julia Roberts."

He was happy for Holly. Her future was bright after all. The night she left Vegas, he bought her a cup of coffee and gave her a good-bye peck on the cheek. Told her if she ever needed him for anything, just call.

That seemed like an eternity ago. To say he'd never thought he'd hear from her again was a bit of an understatement. Yet here she was, all these years later, taking him up on his offer.

"Nick?"

There was a flash of static on his cell line. Vegas was full of dead zones. Pulling to the side of the road, he said, "Where you calling from, kid? You in town?"

"At the Diamond."

A little upscale for the Holly he knew. Then again, maybe not. "What about Mr. Real Estate?"

"Chuck and I split up."

That was a surprise. "Then what's going on? What do you mean you think somebody's trying to kill you?"

She let out a long, shaky breath. "I don't want to do this on the phone," she said. "Buy me a cup of coffee. One hour, the usual place."

Then she hung up.

Jennings popped a U, his eight-year-old Crown Vic groaning in protest, and caught a red light at the intersection. Red lights in Vegas are notoriously long, and he found himself half-wishing he had a good book or a magazine to pass the time.

I think someone's trying to kill me.

This wasn't the first time he'd heard something like that come out of Holly's mouth. She'd always had a flair for the dramatic. She wasn't exactly the Girl Who Cried Wolf, but it would be just like her to follow up three years of silence with a proclamation that her life was in danger.

He stared out at the red light, willing it to change. Three or four days seemed to pass before it turned green again. Then, just as he took his foot off the brake, he heard a screech of tires behind him and—

—*wham!* Someone hit him.

The impact sent a jolt through his spine as the Vic lurched forward toward the intersection. Jennings hit the brakes, brought the car to an abrupt halt, then checked his rearview mirror.

All he could see were two blazing headlights that sat above the bumper of what looked like a big black Humvee.

He leaned out the window and craned his neck. The Humvee, of course, didn't have a scratch on it, and he could just imagine what the rear end of the Vic looked like.

Before he could let loose the string of profanities waiting at the tip of his tongue, the Humvee's driver and passenger doors flew open and two fullbacks in Hawaiian shirts climbed out.

This couldn't be good.

He shifted his foot to the gas pedal, ready to bag out, but the driver pulled a Smith & Wesson nine millimeter from the small of his back and leveled it at him. "Stay right there, Houdini. Hands on the wheel."

Jennings watched the driver approach his window and cursed himself for leaving his piece back at his apartment.

"Let me guess," he said, putting his hands at ten and two o'clock. "You don't have insurance."

No reaction. The driver was all business and Jennings wondered what that business was. The face was impassive, eyes as black as a shark's. Hired muscle, no doubt. Had called him Houdini, which meant he knew who Jennings was.

Hawaiian Shirt Number Two came around the passenger side and folded his arms across a chest that, to Jennings, looked like a wall of nicely tanned cement. The driver reached in through the window, popped the door open, then swung it wide and stepped back. "Get out."

Jennings did what he was told, faint strains of a funeral dirge streaming through his brain.

"Get in the Hummer," the driver said.

A few steps later, Jennings was climbing into the back of the Humvee wondering when or if he should make a move. Another time and place, he would've been all over these guys. Uh-huh. Sure.

Being a cop gave you a kind of arrogant self-confidence that tended to make you feel invincible. Being an ex-cop didn't do diddly-squat.

Hawaiian Shirt Number Two brought out his own Smith and shoved in next to Jennings as the driver got behind the wheel. Doors slammed shut.

"FYI," the driver said, turning in his seat to look at Jennings. "We work for Garlin Enterprises. You heard of it?"

There weren't too many people in Vegas who hadn't. Emile Garlin was the biggest adult entertainment mogul in the city, responsible for a chain of gentleman's clubs and cathouses throughout the state. His most popular enterprise was an upscale exotic dance outfit just off the Strip called Garlin's Girls. All the stars went there. So did a few ex-cops.

"Sounds familiar," Jennings said, staring out at the rear of his car, which was crumpled in a way that almost looked painful.

"Last Saturday," the driver said, "you played a private game in Whitehead Springs. That sound familiar, too?"

It did. He'd taken about twenty large off some punk who thought he was the next Bob Tyner—Tyner being one of the greatest card mechanics on the planet. Two days later, Jennings lost that twenty and ten more to a guy who really *was* the next Tyner.

"What's your point?" he said.

"The kid you played was Emile Garlin's stepson. Says you screwed him out of eighty grand."

"Eighty grand?" Jennings said. "Do I look like I've got that kind of cash? The kid's lying."

"Be that as it may, it wasn't his money to lose. Mr. Garlin comes back from a business trip, finds out he's eighty light, and the kid points the finger at you. Given a choice, who do you think Mr. Garlin's gonna believe— his poor misguided stepson or a brain-fried cardsharp like you?"

"I take it that's a rhetorical question?"

The shark eyes just stared at him. "He wants his money back. With interest."

Jennings took another look at his wounded car, managing to muster up some of the old cop swagger, then told the driver exactly what Garlin could do to himself and how.

The driver stared at him a moment longer, then faced front and backed the Humvee up. Shifting into gear, he hit the gas and slammed into the rear of the Crown Vic, the impact swerving his car to the right, knocking it into a utility pole.

Ouch.

"Mr. Garlin anticipated you might put up a protest." He reversed the Hummer again, then rammed the Vic a third time. The bumper fell off.

"Hey!" Jennings said. "I'm still making payments on that thing."

The driver backed up several yards now, then stomped the gas and angled the nose of the Humvee into the side of the Vic. It crumpled with a horrific groan.

Jennings started to rise out of his seat, but Hawaiian Shirt Number Two planted a hand on his chest and shoved him back. It felt like he'd been hit with a brick.

The driver set the brake, climbed out, then went around to Jennings's side and pulled the door open, pointing the Smith at him. "Get out."

Get in, get out. Make up your mind.

Jennings glanced at his mangled vehicle, thinking the only way it would ever move again was chained to a tow bed. Making a mental note to *always* carry his piece, he stepped back onto the street.

"A hundred large," the driver told him. "Two days. And next time it won't be the car."

He had the Vic towed to the nearest junkyard, then caught a cab to Abe's Diner, a dingy café off Charleston that catered to the lost and lonely. Back in his days on the force, he'd spent a lot of time there loading up on coffee and pie. It was also the place where he and Holly would regularly rendezvous to discuss business.

He was a good forty minutes late by the time he got there and Holly was nowhere to be found. Figuring he may have gone through a couple more dead zones on the ride over, he checked his phone and, sure enough, there was a voice message waiting for him. He dialed his number, punched in the code.

After a beep, Holly's voice came on the line, shakier than ever. "Nick, where are you?" She paused, her breathing uneven, sounding as if she was on the edge of panic. "Okay, I'm gonna go to your apartment. I just hope you haven't moved."

He hadn't. And this was no cry of wolf, he was sure of that now. The fear in her voice was all too real. He immediately punched a button, dialing her back.

A moment later, a pay phone at the far end of the diner started to ring.

She wasn't carrying a phone.

Feeling a sudden sense of urgency, Jennings did a 180, went outside and flagged the cab, which hadn't yet left the parking lot.

In all the years he'd known Holly, he'd never heard her sounding so desperate. And as the cab took him back across town, he thought about how happy she'd been when Mr. Real Estate proposed. Almost giddy.

He wondered what had happened between them. And who had she hooked up with that made her so scared?

Twenty long minutes later, the cab dropped him off in front of his building. It was decades old and looked it, a fifteen-unit, U-shaped pile of stucco overlooking a small courtyard and an even smaller pool. Jennings quickly pushed through the front gate and climbed the stairs toward the second floor, hoping that Holly still had a key and had let herself in.

In the past, it wasn't unusual to come home and find her parked on his couch, watching TV. This was at the beginning of his infamous fall from grace and he had to admit that he'd found her presence comforting. In those days, she was the only one he could talk to. And the only one who would talk to *him*.

He was nearing the top of the steps when a teenage girl in a Megadeth T-shirt came flying out of the darkness and nearly collided with him as she ran down the stairs, her long blond hair trailing behind her. A split-second later, Jennings heard a splash from below and wondered if she'd fallen into the pool.

As he reached the second-floor landing he glanced down at it, a bright rectangle of blue, and his gut immediately clinched up. Silhouetted against the light was a body. Not the kid—but a woman's body. Floating.

Scrambling back down the stairs, Jennings took a flying leap into the water and swam toward the deep end, where the body undulated on the surface. Grabbing hold of her, he turned her over, but one touch and he knew he was too late. There was no sign of life there. No pulse. Nothing. A neat round bullet hole adorned the dimple of her throat.

And while the face was older, there was no mistaking who it was. He recognized her immediately, his sudden dread morphing into an almost overwhelming sense of guilt.

Holly Addison had had every right to be frightened.

Holly Addison was dead.

* * *

He wasn't surprised when Cassandra walked in the door.

Detective First Grade Cassandra Jennings was a ranking shield on the homicide squad. The minute his name came over the wire, she had undoubtedly requested to take the lead.

Her reasons wouldn't be complicated. Jennings had made another mess and, as usual, Cassandra felt obligated to clean it up. He supposed somebody could have cried conflict of interest, considering their history, but without interest, there *is* no conflict, and Cassandra hadn't shown any in him in quite some time.

The moment he realized Holly was dead, he had shouted for a neighbor to call the cops. They converged on his apartment complex like a swarm of blue bees, roping off the crime scene, dragging her body out of the water, waking up everyone in the complex for questioning.

He'd known it was only a matter of time before another part of his past showed up, and here it was, in a neatly tailored suit and dark, short-cropped hair. As lovely as ever.

This was turning out to be one helluva night.

"You okay, Nick?" Cassandra's expression was somber. A look he'd seen at dozens of crime scenes. Professional, yet sympathetic. Jennings couldn't help feeling that familiar stirring of the soul when she spoke, or the sudden stab of pain that went with it.

"I've been worse," he said.

It was a pointed remark, not lost on her, but she recovered quickly and gestured to the guy in the doorway behind her. "This is Jerry Kravitz. He came on board after you left."

Left. That was a nice way of putting it.

Kravitz was tall, broad-shouldered, and hostile-looking. Jennings imagined the guy had heard quite a bit about Nick the burnout. They exchanged curt nods, then Jennings returned his gaze to Cassandra. "Any luck with the canvass?"

"Why don't *we* ask the questions," she said, leaving no doubt that the chasm between them was as deep as it was wide. "Mind if we sit down?"

He gestured to a sofa whose seat cushions held stacks of newspaper and an open cardboard box full of pilfered casino decks. "Just throw that stuff on the floor."

They made room for themselves and sat, Cassandra throwing a disapproving glance at the box, probably making a mental note to confiscate it.

Jennings stayed in the faded armchair he'd been warming for the past half hour, after he'd changed into a dry T-shirt and jeans. "Fire away," he said.

Cassandra brought out a small spiral notepad. "How long had Holly been in town?"

Jennings shrugged. "Tonight was the first time she'd called me in years. Said she was staying at the Diamond."

"On somebody else's dime, no doubt." This from Kravitz.

Jennings looked at him. "What makes you say that?"

"She was a pro, right?"

"Ex," Jennings said. He hadn't known this guy two minutes and already he didn't like him.

"I thought tonight was the first time she contacted you."

"That's right."

"Then how do you know she wasn't working?"

Truth was, Jennings didn't, but he said, "She quit that life when she got married." He looked at Cassandra. "You know all this."

Cassandra nodded, but Kravitz said, "Once a party girl, always a party girl."

Jennings knew the guy was baiting him, but said nothing.

"Did she tell you why she was back in town?" Cassandra asked.

"I talked to her for a total of about twenty seconds." He gave them a quick rehash of the phone call and Kravitz's eyebrows raised.

"She actually said that? Somebody wants to kill me?"

Jennings nodded.

"So why call you?"

"Maybe she trusted me."

Kravitz snorted. "Lotta good it did her. She say who this alleged killer was?"

"She wouldn't talk on the phone."

"Of course not." Kravitz was clearly skeptical.

"Where did she want to meet?" Cassandra asked. "Here at the apartment?"

"Over at Abe's. But I was late, and she was gone before I got there. Used the pay phone to leave me a message."

Cassandra jotted some notes on her pad. "Why were you late?"

"Getting my car towed. I had an accident."

Another eyebrow raise from Kravitz. "What kind of accident?"

"A *car* accident," Jennings said. Who was this dope? "I ran into a utility pole."

"Oh? You been drinking?"

"No. I'm not big on booze."

"What *are* you big on?"

"Minding my own business," Jennings told him.

"Uh-huh," Kravitz said. "What about firearms? You own any?"

Jennings stared at him. "Nine mil. Drawer in the kitchen, next to the can opener—in case somebody sneaks up on me while I'm heating up the chili." He paused, then said, "If you're thinking I'm good for this, forget it. The weapon's clean and I've got cell phone records, a tow-truck driver, and a cabbie to corroborate my story."

"Oh, don't you worry," Kravitz said. "We'll be checking into all of that. And once the ME's report comes back, we'll be taking a very close look at the timeline."

Jennings wouldn't expect anything less, but this guy was really starting to irritate. He glanced at Cassandra but she was still jotting notes. Then she said, "I don't suppose you'll have any objection to an ISID?"

An Instant Shooter Identification was an updated version of the old dermal nitrate or paraffin test. A tech brushes diphenylamine on your hand and if it turns blue, kiss your butt good-bye. Jennings couldn't believe she was even asking. "You're kidding, right?"

"I wish I was, Nick, but you know I don't have a choice, considering your history with Holly."

Jennings tried to keep his voice calm. "We were friends. That's not how I treat my friends."

"Friends with benefits," Kravitz said. "Depending on how much cash you had on hand."

All right, enough was enough. Jennings got out of his chair and Kravitz immediately rose to meet him.

Cassandra shot up between them. "Easy, boys, easy."

Kravitz relaxed his posture and smiled. "Sorry, Cassie, but you get something stuck to the bottom of your shoe, you just want to scrape it off. Know what I mean?" He held Jennings's gaze. "If I'd been on the force three years ago, I would've grieved for you and Cassie just like everybody else. But I didn't know you then. Don't know if you were a decent cop or a good husband or a loving father."

Cassandra frowned. "Cut it out, Jerry."

"Let me finish." Kravitz kept his gaze on Jennings. "But instead of taking a cue from Cassie here and handling your grief like an adult, you took all the goodwill the department offered you and turned it into mud."

"Jerry—"

"And that tells me all I need to know about what kind of man you are, Jennings. *That's* how you treat your friends. You hurt people. So why should we give you the benefit of the doubt now?"

Jennings felt as if the top of his head was about to explode. He glared at Kravitz, barely able to contain the urge to strangle him right then and there.

Thing is, Kravitz was right. Every word he'd said.

But Jennings didn't need this dredged up along with everything else tonight. And he could see from Cassandra's expression that she wasn't particularly happy about it, either. "Jerry, go outside."

"You telling me I'm wrong about this guy?"

"I'm telling you to go outside. We're in the middle of

a murder investigation and I don't need you two stand-ing here trying to prove who's got the most testosterone."

Kravitz smiled again. "Is it even a contest?" He shot a glance at Jennings, then swept past him and headed out the door.

After he was gone, Jennings said, "So how long have you been sleeping with that idiot?"

Cassandra's face went cold. "Are you gonna agree to the ISID or not?"

"I've got nothing to hide," Jennings said. "Get the tech in here, we can do it right now."

She turned and headed for the door. As she reached the threshold, she looked back at him, quiet contempt in her voice. "For the record, Nick, I know you'd never hurt anyone intentionally." Then she added, "You just can't help yourself."

His hand didn't turn blue.

The only one surprised by this was Kravitz, who, for whatever reason, seemed to have an emotional invest-ment in Jennings's culpability.

Jennings told them about the girl who tore past him on the staircase right before Holly went into the pool. They noted it dutifully, asking if Jennings had recog-nized her.

"Just some kid," he said. "Looking scared."

"You happen to notice if she had a weapon?"

Jennings shook his head. "I don't make her for the shooter. I never heard a shot, and somehow I don't see a teenage girl packing a suppressor. But the speed she was moving, I'd lay odds she saw something. Or someone."

"We'll put it out there," Cassandra said. "But I'm not expecting much."

They left the apartment complex after the crime scene unit had done its damage and most of his neighbors were questioned. Jennings wasn't privy to the answers. Cassandra made it clear that his involvement in the investigation was not wanted, needed, or in any way condoned.

He was a witness. Nothing more. Which was fine with him.

But Cassandra wasn't convinced. "I know you were fond of her, Nick, but leave this to Jerry and me. There's nothing worse than an ex-cop on a mission."

"All I want is a nice hot shower," he said. "You two have fun."

He watched from the window as the caravan drove away, Cassandra at the wheel of her gray Infiniti, Kravitz riding shotgun. Beyond them, he could see the lights of the Strip bleeding into the darkness, a world that seemed to exist in an alternate universe.

He thought about Cassandra and what they'd once had and wondered how he'd let himself sink so low. He was a man who defined his life by putting "ex" in front of everything. Ex-cop, ex-husband . . .

Ex-father.

Foregoing the shower, he doused the lights and climbed into bed, jeans and all, letting the night drain away from him as he rolled onto his back and stared up at the moonlight that played across his ceiling.

Images of Holly crowded his head. The sweet smile. The perfect body. The sad eyes.

The bullet hole adorning her throat.

Why had she come back to Vegas? Had she come alone? Who was she afraid of? Was her assailant friend or foe?

It wasn't up to him to answer these questions, but there they were, accompanied by that unmistakable feeling of guilt he knew so well. True to form, Nick Jennings had once again failed someone he cared about.

Three and a half years ago, his daughter, Michelle, had been the object of that failure. Snatched out of her own bedroom while he and Cassandra slept just six feet and a wall of plaster away. They never heard a thing. And two weeks later, her body was found in a drainage ditch.

While Cassandra somehow managed to find the internal fortitude to continue on with her life, Jennings fell hard and still hadn't landed.

Now, he felt an itch rising inside him and for the first time in years it wasn't the thought of a game that got it going. It was a different kind of itch, the one he'd always felt at the beginning of a new case.

A sudden sense of resolve washed over him and, despite his ex-wife's admonitions and his own protests, he knew he wouldn't rest until he'd scratched that itch.

Cassandra was right. There's nothing worse than an ex-cop on a mission.

"I'm sorry, what was your name again?"

"Kravitz," Jennings said. "Detective Jerry Kravitz."

"And did you wish to speak to Mr. Hartley or Mr. Fine?"

"Mr. Hartley."

"I'm afraid he's out of the office. Can I have him call you back?"

After discovering that cell phones don't react well to pool water and cursing himself for never getting a land-line, Jennings had found a battered pay phone about a block down from his apartment building. This was a long-distance call using an old phone card he'd managed to scrounge up, and there weren't too many minutes left.

"It can't really wait," he said. "Is there another number I can call? A cell phone maybe?"

"Actually, Mr. Hartley's on vacation and doesn't want to be disturbed. He does check in a couple times a day, but—"

"It's about his wife."

Up until now, the voice on the phone had been generic. A typically efficient female receptionist in tenor and tone, which, to Jennings, was practically a miracle at eight o'clock in the morning.

Now the voice faltered. "Is Mrs. Hartley in trouble?"

"Why would you ask that?"

"I just assumed that since you're with the police . . ."

"Do you know Mrs. Hartley?"

"Just in passing. They split up several months ago."

"That's right," Jennings said. "Any idea what caused the breakup?"

"I'm afraid I wouldn't know."

"Come on, now, you're right in the middle of rumor central."

"Sorry, Detective, I don't believe in speculating about people's private lives."

"Sure you do," Jennings said. "Otherwise why would you ask if Mrs. Hartley's in trouble when most people would've asked if she's okay?"

"Is there a difference?"

"You know there is."

Another pause. This one longer. "Las Vegas," she said, finally. "He's spending the week in Vegas."

"Isn't that a coincidence."

"I beg your pardon?"

"Never mind," Jennings said. "Where's he staying? The Diamond?"

"He usually stays at the corporate condo. His secretary should be here in a few minutes. Shall I have her call you?"

"Just give me the address," he said.

She hesitated again. After a few moments he heard the clacking of computer keys, then, "Do you have a pencil?"

"I'll manage."

He memorized the address and was in the middle of thanking her when the line suddenly went dead.

His minutes were up.

He managed to scrounge up enough change to call Scully for a ride and a new cell phone. An hour later, they pulled up in front of a cluster of town houses located about a half mile from the Strip.

Scully killed the engine. "You ready to tell me what's going on?"

"Surprise visit to an old friend," Jennings said. "You wait out here."

"You kidding me? It's already ninety degrees."

"I need you to keep an eye out. If my ex-wife and her new boyfriend show up, give me a jingle, then get your butt out of here."

Before Scully could protest, Jennings threw his door

open and crossed the sidewalk to unit nineteen, the corporate getaway for Hartley-Fine Real Estate, of which Chuck Hartley, Holly's ex-husband, was CEO.

He leaned on the buzzer. No answer. He tried again. Still nothing. Moving to the window, he took a peek inside but saw only the usual trappings of corporate wealth: expensive but generic furniture, reproductions of famous paintings, a well-stocked wet bar. Everything looked neat and tidy.

Jennings stepped away from the window and pulled his wad of bump keys from his pocket. He had several makes, each with its key cuts trimmed down to maximum depth. When he found one that fit the door lock, he shoved it in, then took his pocket knife, held it by the blade and used it like a hammer, knocking the key deeper into the lock. He hit it several times until the cylinders finally fell into place. When he turned the key, the lock clicked open.

He'd been smart enough to bring his piece this time. Taking the nine mil from the small of his back, he carefully started inside. He was halfway through the door when he realized he wouldn't need it.

Things had just gotten complicated.

"Let me guess," Scully said. "*He* lost the argument."

Jennings turned. "I thought I told you to wait in the car?"

"I'm fryin' out there. I figured this place would be air-conditioned." He sniffed, made a face. "Not that it's doing this guy any good."

Beyond a small dining area was a doorway that led

into the kitchen. A man of about forty-two lay faceup on the linoleum, staring lifelessly at the light fixture overhead. He was wearing only boxer shorts.

"Is this the old friend you were talking about?"

"Never seen him before," Jennings said. When he'd first spotted the body, he'd thought it was Chuck Hartley, Mr. Real Estate. But he remembered Hartley being much bigger and blonder than this guy.

He crossed to the kitchen for a closer look. There was a bullet hole, another neck shot. Stepping around the pool of blood, he crouched down and grabbed hold of one of victim's hands. Rigor had already set in. He'd been dead for a while.

"If you're finished spreading your DNA," Scully said, "we'd better get outta here."

"Go work on your tan," Jennings told him.

"Suit yourself. But you got five minutes before I bag out."

When Scully was gone, Jennings crossed through the living room to a short hallway that led to a bedroom and bathroom. Stepping into the bathroom, he flicked on the light, checked the sink. Two toothbrushes in the holder.

Jennings popped open the medicine cabinet and found the usual assortment of bath products: a couple wrapped bars of soap, some dandruff shampoo, shaving cream and a razor, and a couple sticks of deodorant—his and hers.

Had Holly been staying here? If so, why lie about the Diamond?

Maybe the toothbrush and deodorant belonged to someone else. Some young fluff the dead man had picked up off the Strip. Some young fluff who had vacated the premises shortly after drilling a hole in the guy's neck.

But if that was true, how did Holly fit in?

Jennings went into the bedroom and glanced around. The bed was unmade, clothing strewn on the floor: jeans wadded up in a corner, a pair of panties and a dark blue T-shirt at the foot of the bed.

Jennings picked up the shirt—size small—and stared at the words plastered across it: IRON MAIDEN. There were a couple long blond hairs stuck to the fabric.

The image of a scared kid in a Megadeth T-shirt and flowing blond hair tumbled through his brain. The girl on the staircase. She, not Holly, had been the houseguest here.

But who was she?

He moved to the corner, snatched up the jeans and patted the pockets. They were empty. Crossing to the dresser, he yanked open the drawers but found only boxer shorts and a few pairs of socks. He was about to turn away when he spotted something in the trash can next to the dresser. Reaching in, he pulled out a small, crumpled piece of pasteboard. It was an insert for a mini-DV video tape box.

He stared at it a moment, his mind clicking, then glanced at the bed and the clothing on the floor. Had someone been making a home video?

A home video with an underage kid?

He looked around for camera equipment, but found none. There was, however, a row of track lights facing the bed, and the bulb wattage was much too high for everyday use. This was a makeshift movie set, plain and simple.

Crossing to the nightstand now, he yanked the drawer open. Inside was a phone book, a clutch of keys and a wallet. Opening the wallet, he found a driver's license inside, the face of the dead man staring up at him.

Joseph Edward Fine. Chuck Hartley's partner.

"So who do you think did it? The kid?"

They were back in Scully's Jaguar and headed across town. After listening to Scully whine for ten minutes, Jennings had finally given him the details.

Jennings shook his head. "They were both professional hits. No question about that now. But I'm still trying to figure out how Holly fit in."

"Maybe she and this Fine guy were having an affair. Maybe that's why she and Mr. Real Estate broke up."

"So she and Fine start getting into underage porn? You don't know Holly. That's about as believable as the title on this car."

A few minutes later they pulled into Abe's, which had been owned and operated for the last thirty years by a guy named Carlo Pronzini. Scully was complaining of hunger pains, so they found a booth in back and ordered breakfast. A few minutes later, Carlo came out of the kitchen and greeted Jennings. "Heard you stopped by last night. You shoulda said hello."

"Who'd you hear this from?"

"Your ex and her partner. They came in asking questions about you and Holly. Real shame what happened to her."

"So what'd you tell them?"

"That she stopped by around ten. Which was a surprise. Figured I'd seen the last of her after she snagged the rich guy."

"You talk to her?" Jennings asked.

"Just to say hello, say it was good to see her. She didn't look all that thrilled to be here, though. Kept looking out the window like she was expecting the sky to fall."

"She happen to mention what the problem was?"

Carlo shook his head. "She didn't seem all that interested in conversation. Not with me, at least. She made a few phone calls, then a cab pulled in and she was gone."

"A *few* calls? How do you know that?"

"Saw the coins drop, heard her talking. Your name was mentioned more than once."

Jennings nodded. "She was leaving me a message."

"No, this wasn't *to* you. It was *about* you."

"Oh? In what way?"

"Something about you being someone they could trust. That you'd be able to help them."

Kravitz must've had a field day with that little tidbit of information. "Them?" Jennings said. "Any idea who she was talking to?"

"Not a clue. But, whoever it was, she was planning to meet up with him."

"Yeah?"

Carlo nodded. "She gave him your address."

Jennings considered heading to the Diamond to see if Holly had been shacked up with someone, but he was pretty sure that Cassie and Kravitz had already covered that ground. No point in giving hotel security a reason to start making phone calls.

As they pulled away from Abe's, Jennings thought about Holly's call. Not the one to him, but to whomever she'd given his address. It was obvious now that they'd done something to get them in nice and deep with a very nasty crowd—a professional crowd—and had expected Jennings to pull them out.

Could it have been Fine she was calling? Or what about Hartley? His receptionist said she thought he was staying at the corporate condo, but there'd been no sign of him. So where had he disappeared to?

Back in the old days Jennings would simply have gotten the pay phone records, but that wasn't possible now. There were no friends to call for favors, because the only friend he had was sitting next to him. Scully may have been a good R&D man when it came to home invasions and such, but his connections with the Metro Police Department were nonexistent. And the only decent informant Jennings had ever had was lying on a slab with a bullet in her neck.

He remembered how Holly had liked to play up the cloak and dagger when they worked together, offering to get him photos and other evidence, her flair for the dramatic often superseding her good sense. Everything was a movie to Holly. Always had been.

So what role had she been playing last night?

Scully, ever the deep thinker, said, "What does Carlo put in those eggs? They're starting to back up on me."

Jennings ignored him. A sudden thought had surfaced, an image straight from the Time Machine: Holly letting herself into his apartment to leave cryptic messages on his bathroom mirror.

He'd found no such message this time, but Jennings had assumed that Holly was headed *toward* his apartment when she was shot. What if she had kept her key and had already let herself inside? What if she had left some kind of message behind that he'd simply overlooked?

"Take a left," Jennings said.

Scully belched. "Where we headed?"

"Back to my place."

When they got there, his door was splintered and hanging open. The place had been ransacked. Every stick of furniture overturned, cabinets ajar, newspapers and a couple dozen casino decks scattered across the floor.

"Add a little water," Scully said, "and you'd have Hurricane Katrina."

Apparently Jennings wasn't the only one who thought Holly had left something behind.

But what?

He found it in the shower, pressed deep into a new bar of soap that lay in the tray above the spigot. If he had bothered to bathe last night, had bothered to wash off the chlorine that had soaked through to his bones, he would have found it then: a locker key.

Holly had once told him that after she first arrived in Vegas she'd lived out of a locker for nearly a month. A locker at the Greyhound bus station.

He turned to Scully. "Let's go downtown."

Twenty minutes later, they waded through a crowd of

passengers heading for a departing bus, and worked their way to locker 223. Jennings slipped the key in, turned it.

There was a manila envelope inside. Dumping out its contents, he found a wallet-size photograph and a bright pink cell phone—which would explain why Holly had used the pay phone at Abe's.

Jennings stared at the photo. Two girls stared back at him with reticent smiles: a much younger Holly, about sixteen, and a smaller girl who couldn't have been more than six. There was something oddly familiar about the smaller girl's face.

His stomach clutched up when he realized what it was, and suddenly everything made sense. Holly wasn't the only member of her family to kiss her drunken mother good-bye.

The girl in the Megadeth T-shirt was Holly's sister.

Picking up the phone, he clicked it on, immediately noticing a symbol in the upper left corner that indicated there were photos waiting to be viewed.

He thumbed a button, flicking quickly through the photographs, feeling his heart pump faster with each new frame.

"Guess we know what they were after," Scully said, looking over Jennings's shoulder. "Is that who I think it is?"

Jennings nodded. "That B&E we were planning for tonight? We just found a new target."

He waited for them in the upstairs hallway. The alarm system had been sophisticated, but relatively easy to breach. A window overlooked the front drive.

Despite the size of the house, a fifteen-room Tudor in

the heart of Red Rock, the support staff—according to Scully's contact at the security company—was minimal. The maid left at five every night, the gardeners were contracted, and the hired muscle, whom Jennings had no desire to tangle with, lived off premises. Wife and stepson were away for the weekend, so that left only the owner and the lone security man who accompanied him at all times.

Despite his wealth, the owner apparently believed in keeping his life as uncomplicated as possible. His house was tastefully furnished, but offered no overt signs of the man's considerable fortune. Even the car he drove was modest: a black Ford Expedition.

As it pulled into the driveway, Jennings receded into the shadows and watched as the headlights went dark and two men emerged. To his surprise, however, there was a third person in the car.

Yanking open the rear passenger door, the security man barked an order. A moment later, Holly's sister climbed out, her movements slow and clumsy as if she'd been drugged. She was wearing the same black T-shirt she'd worn the night before.

Jennings saw not only a younger version of Holly, but something in her that reminded him of his own daughter. His Michelle. And with that reminder came an even stronger sense of resolve.

The security man turned to his boss, his voice muffled through the windowpane. "I still say we should get rid of her. Cut our losses."

"Not until she tells us where it is. Get Tank and Brian over here to do a little work on her. I'm gonna go upstairs and take a hot one."

The security man nodded and grabbed the girl by the arm, pushing her toward the house. All three of them disappeared from view and Jennings heard the front door slam.

Crossing the hallway, he disappeared into the darkness of a bedroom.

The owner was stepping out of the shower, pulling on a neatly monogrammed terry cloth robe, when he realized Jennings was standing just inside the bathroom doorway. Startled, he recovered quickly. "What is this? Who are you?"

"Just call me Houdini," Jennings said. "I owe you a hundred large, remember?"

Emile Garlin's eyes narrowed. He reached for a telephone on the wall.

"Don't bother. The line's been cut." With a quick flourish, Jennings produced Holly's cell phone and set it on the counter. "Why don't you try this one instead. It's what you've been looking for, right?"

Garlin eyed the phone, then slowly shifted his gaze to Jennings. "I don't know what you're talking about."

"Come on, Emile. You've already killed two people to get it. Probably three."

"I think you're mistaking me for somebody else."

"Am I? You look remarkably like one of the guys in those photos."

"What photos?"

"Don't waste my time," Jennings said.

As if this was some kind of cue, Garlin suddenly moved toward him, but Jennings produced his nine mil. "Easy."

Garlin stopped in his tracks, his voice flat. "You're a dead man."

"I got the life sucked out of me a long time ago. Not much damage you can do now."

There was no sign of fear in Garlin's eyes. He just looked annoyed. "What do you want?"

"I'm curious," Jennings said. "Did you know that Holly and I were connected when you sent your goons after me?"

"Pure coincidence," Garlin said. "But those are the hazards of living in a small town." The guy wasn't even breaking a sweat.

"How do you sleep at night, Garlin?"

"Meaning?"

Jennings gestured to the cell phone. "Consenting adults is one thing, but fourteen-year-old girls?"

"I see you don't spend much time on the Internet," Garlin said. "Teens are all the rage. And I didn't create the market."

Jennings felt something tighten inside. Felt his finger against the trigger of the nine.

When he'd first played the photos back, he'd wondered what Garlin would have to say about them. Slimeballs can rationalize anything.

He and Scully had talked it through, and had a pretty good idea how the whole thing had played out. A lot of it was conjecture, sure, but he didn't think they were too far off the mark.

There had long been rumors of a Lolita Club in Vegas, an elite and very secretive group of businessmen who traded teenage girls like baseball cards and videotaped their adventures. Even as a cop, Jennings had assumed it was an urban myth, but the photos on that cell phone had dispelled any doubt that it really did exist.

Joseph Fine, of Hartley-Fine Real Estate, was a member of that club. Shortly after Chuck Hartley and Holly broke up, Fine had decided to let his old buddy in on his secret, showing him a few videotaped samples, hoping maybe to cheer his partner up.

But Hartley wasn't into jailbait. He was, in fact, appalled by what he saw. And one of the girls on the video looked remarkably like Holly. So much so that he went to his estranged wife and told her about it.

The rest played out like a bad spy movie, Holly and Hartley doing a whacked-out version of Nick and Nora Charles, using the Diamond hotel as their base of operations. Hartley had feigned interest in the club, had offered up a good deal of money to get a closer look, had even snagged a personal tour of Garlin's underage bunny ranch from the man himself.

And all the while, he'd had Holly's cell phone with him, snapping surreptitious, and very incriminating, photos.

Somewhere along the line he'd asked Fine to arrange a private rendezvous at the corporate condo. The choice of girls was obvious: Holly's sister.

Then something went wrong. Somehow Garlin had been tipped off about the photos—probably by Fine, or maybe even Hartley himself. Whatever the case, Holly had already stored the phone in the Greyhound locker. Then she'd gone to the condo, grabbed her sister, and called Jennings.

Fine had been a casualty of the cleanup crew. And

Hartley had been the man at the other end of Holly's phone call from Abe's.

Jennings could see her standing there at the pay phone, looking out at the parking lot where her sister was waiting, giving his address to Hartley, not realizing that Hartley was already in Garlin's custody.

Later, as Holly and her sister left Jennings's apartment, they were confronted by Garlin and his security man. And Jennings, true to form, was a day late and a dollar short.

That was about to change.

There was a muffled sound of a door slamming. Jennings had no doubt that the Hawaiian-shirt boys had just arrived.

"Reinforcements," Garlin said. "You're one shout away from history."

"Doesn't matter," Jennings told him. "The great thing about cell phone photos is that you can send them instantly to anyone on your network. You'd be surprised how many newspapers and law enforcement agencies share the same service. Not that it makes much difference at this point."

Garlin studied him as those last words sunk in. Then his expression changed almost imperceptibly. There was fear in his eyes now. He nodded to the nine. "What do you plan on doing with that?"

Jennings smiled. A smile that hid the rage he felt. A rage that had been building for three long years and had finally reached the boiling point.

The answer, he thought, was fairly obvious.

*   *   *

The papers were still talking about it three days later. "The Garlin Mansion Massacre," they called it. Four dead at the hands of an unknown assailant. A young runaway, one Teresa Jean Addison, was found cowering in a closet.

The photos of the Lolita Club bunny ranch, its inhabitants, its owner, and a few of its better known members had made international headlines. Teresa Jean got her fifteen minutes of fame on the nightly news, talking about her ordeal.

On the afternoon of that third day, after Jennings had just finished up his show at the Tally-Ho lounge, he found Cassandra waiting for him in the parking lot.

"I suppose it's too late for an ISID," she said.

Jennings stole a line from Garlin: "I don't know what you're talking about."

"My partner thinks you're good for that thing in Red Rock."

"When are you gonna stop sleeping with that idiot?"

"He's coming after you, Nick. Consider yourself warned." She started to turn away, but Jennings stopped her.

"Let's pretend for a moment that I did do it," he said. "What would be my motive?"

"We all know how you felt about Holly. Or maybe you just didn't want to see another little girl wind up in a drainage ditch."

They were silent a moment, thinking about that and what it meant, Cassie's eyes showing a trace of tears.

"You're forgetting who you're talking to," Jennings

said. "I'm just a screwup, remember? A guy who can't help himself."

She studied him sadly a moment. "That's the problem, Nick. It always has been."

Then she turned and walked away.

Jennings watched her cross toward her car, feeling the tug of emotion that always accompanied her visits, as infrequent as they were.

Someday, he thought. Someday he'd make it right with her. And as he watched her drive away, he took his cell phone from his pocket and dialed.

Maybe Scully could find him a game.

Time of the Green
by Ken Bruen

•

Fake city
Yeah, trot 'em out
        A phony
        A con man
        Grifter
        Flimflam guy
I know 'em all
Been 'em all
To
Varying degrees of success
Currently, I'm washed up in the West of Ireland
Time on my hands
But not on my wrist
That I'm gonna fix
Bring that sucker to the bank
Shooting craps
And
Dude, I can sure shoot the shit
You'll have noticed . . . my accent . . . see, I'm . . . talk-
    ing real slow so you can keep up
Accents
More changes than a Brixton hooker on one of them wet
    November evenings, I've been there, Brixton, too.

I flit from accent to accent like an alkie on down gear
And you're thinking,
"Why?"
'Cos I can.
Failed actor
Yeah, maybe that's it. Try it on for verification. I hadn't
    what it takes, for acting. That zombied sponge abil-
    ity to soak it up.
And odd to tell, I'm not real good at taking direction.
    But hang me out to dry, shoot me now, I 'fess up.
I wanted the kudos without the graft.
Is that so wrong? Seems to me to be the spirit of the zeit-
    geist.
I left London in a hurry, hung some paper and it was com-
    ing back to bite me in the ass and hard. Got me a cheapo
    flight outa there, in like, jig time. Just a carry-on.
If I'd a little more of a window, I'd have gone to Prague,
    they like me there
But Galway was first up and like I said, speed was of
    the essence.
I'd never been to Ireland, swear to God.
My periods Stateside, I knew lotsa micks.
Mad demented bastards
And like, I mean, do they ever—ever, shut the fuck up?
A woman asked me,
"Don't you love their lyricism?"
She was kidding, right? Wasn't she?
The harps, all the swearing
            Fook this, fook that
            By jaysus
            Yah bollix

What's with that?

You want a crash course in cussin', get you in the mick mode, watch *Deadwood*. The effing and blinding, set you right up.

Our plane circled over Galway airport, no sign of us landing. A middle-aged woman at the window seat, smelling of Chanel and stale gin, said

"Seagulls on the runway."

I asked,

"And that tells us what?"

She gave me a cursory glance, then,

"We might be diverted to Knock, now that'd be a hoor."

As in whore?

Then she let out a breath, said,

"Ah, there's Tommy, he's shooing them."

For a moment I thought he was shooting them. I asked,

"And Tommy, that's his job?"

She clucked her tongue, said,

"Don't be an eejit, he's the air traffic controller."

Right

With a final look at me she said,

"You must be English."

Welcome to Ireland.

I had two credit cards, good for tops, twenty days, then the flag went up. With about a hundred in sterling.

Man, I love a challenge.

I was wearing my Armani suit, the real job. Not one of those knockoff units. Most times, let the suit do the talking, gets you halfway there. In the lounge, I

changed my cash to euro and had to check the time
on the airport wall. My one aim, well, first one anyway, was a Rolex Oyster, the whole nine.

My old man, the original loser, wore a Timex, plastic
strap, to accessorise his soul, once, between beatings,
said to me,

"A man's arrived when he wears The Oyster."

Stuck with me.

I'd never quite got it together to attain one. And hey, I
didn't want it to fulfill his dream

Fuck him

It was solely to roar

"This is for you, Pops."

To stick it up his ass

We buried him two years ago, cheap box, cheap service.
My mom, glass-eyed on Valium, threw a dead rose
into the hole, said,

"He was a good man."

I looked right in her eyes, said,

"You stupid cunt."

Liar, too

Last I heard, she was down in Boca, working on her skin
cancer.

Coming out of Arrivals, I hailed a cab, took a moment
and decided to go American. The flag still flew for
the micks. The Brits, now they were always thin ice.
The driver, his face a riot of broken veins, purple
blotches, asked,

"How's it going?"

I never quite worked out the *it*. Was *it* life, the weather,
work?

Most times in Ireland, *it* was the weather. I was sorely
    tempted to answer,

"It's a hoor."

Went with,

"Going good, buddy, and you, how you doing?"

Lots of vim in there

Worked

He put the cab in gear, no automatic for this guy, and
    he asked,

"Yank, right?"

"Outa Boston."

Why not? The Kennedys owned it and they still had
    sainthood here. He asked,

"Where to?"

"A good hotel, in the city centre?"

"Ah, you'll be wanting the Great Southern."

It would be neither southern nor great but it certainly
    had notions. The driver lit a cigarette. I asked,

"Don't you guys, like, have a smoking ban?"

Blew a cloud of smoke at the Sacred Heart medallion
    on the dash, said,

"Ary, fuck that."

My kind of country.

I used my American Express at the hotel and it was hard
    to focus for a moment, my British birth always got
    me those moments, despite how I'd immersed my-
    self in America, damn near raised there, the home-
    land still sang in me, if anything British can be said
    to sing. The receptionist provided me with a spacious
    room, overlooking Eyre Square, the heartbeat of the
    city. I booked for a week and they seemed delighted.

The porter who showed me to the room reminded me
   of the first man I ever killed, he didn't even look remotely like him but something in his gestures, I
   dunno. A Mexican, named José, he'd tried to stiff me
   on a deal and it was the first time I got to use a knife.
   I wasn't very adept then and it was messy, stuck him
   in the throat first and of course, geyser of blood, been
   a time since then but they say, you never forget your
   first. He sometimes came in my dreams, a gouging
   spilling hole in his brown neck. I'd kinda liked old
   José, made me laugh.

The porter was showing me the amenities and I slipped
   him ten euro, got rid of him. I unpacked my holdall,
   one white shirt, black Levis, and my Converse. Picked
   up the phone, got room service, ordered a bottle of
   Jameson, club sandwich, ice and they said it would
   be along in jig time.

I was in the shower when it came and I shouted,

"Kick ten bucks on for your tip."

Heard warm appreciation.

Clean, change of clothes, and double Jameson over ice,
   I let my breath out, said,

"Good to go."

Had me a warm-up jacket from the Yankees and slipped
   that on, checked my reflection in the full-length mirror. Tousled blond hair, even features, bordering on
   bland and tallish. My beer gut holding, barely. Crin-
   kled my eyes, gave me that warm look, your regular
   affluent but not showy guy.

Next three days, I hit the shops, hit them hard. Galway's
   a walking town and suited me. Lots of quaint pubs,

some cobbled streets, and a definite carnival buzz. It was May, summer walking point.

Brown Thomas, a department store, with prices to rival Fifth Avenue, took care of my wardrobe. The American gig was gold, I'd go,

"Charge?"

Flash the plastic and they even delivered the shit to my hotel. Got me all the *GQ* designer crap, and what the hell, a pair of Ray-Bans.

Through the shades, I stared at Hartmann's, an old-time family jewelers with a sign to light me up

EXCLUSIVE ROLEX DEALERS

I like a touch of tradition

The cops, called guards, were unarmed

I fucking loved Ireland

Third night, I was in the pub, one of the ones advertising the *craic*.

Not the dope, the Irish term for a good time, party on. I had a table by the wall, tipped the waitress and she protested, placing a pint of black and Jameson back before me,

"You don't need to do that."

Dragging up that boyish smile, I said,

"But I want to."

Bitch lapped it up

She wasn't bad looking, had that Irish colleen vibe going. Good legs, good breasts, and nice pert arse . . . shit . . . ass . . . gotta focus. Her age, late twenties I'd hazard.

She'd do

Her name was Aine, pronounced, you ready for this,

Awn-neh . . . Jesus, I thought maybe she was Hebrew. I've no beef with them, you understand. I asked her what it meant, like I gave a fuck, she said,

"'Tis Irish for Ann."

Nearly fucked up by asking,

"So I can call you Ann then?"

Got the look and,

"Why on earth would you want to do that?"

Why indeed-y?

You throw the green around, let that *"gee shucks"* mojo out there and the predators gather, chum in the water. Near closing when a skel made his strike. Slipped into the chair beside me, like a quiet virus, said,

"Welcome to Ireland."

Different country, same species, bottom-feeder. He was late thirties and most of them bad, worse teeth and a worn combat jacket. His hair was in full recession, the eyes, cold and cash-registered.

I put out my hand, said,

"Thanks buddy, I'm Teddy."

Yeah

His handshake was the cold fish school. He said,

"Ah, shure we still love Ted, with all his crosses."

I offered him a drink and he allowed he might try a small brandy, Martell if they had it. Aine brought it and I caught the rapid look between them, double act, just the way I liked it.

Ever catch that Mamet movie . . . *House of Games*?

Man, I studied it, the line . . . *and two to take 'em,* carved on my heart.

I put a fifty on her tray, said,

"One for you, hon."

She gave a radiant smile, not a bad-looking babe after all and gushed,

"Aren't you the terrible man?"

She had no fucking idea.

That Kraut poet, Rilke, got himself a line, *Each angel is terrible* . . . meant me.

The shark gave his name as Seamas. I didn't ask for translation, I knew that was Jim. He worked in communications and I wanted to go,

"You're a natural."

Second brandy in, my shout of course, he made the pitch,

"Well now, Teddy, *cara,* they treating you all right over in that Great Southern Hotel?"

He leaned a little on the *Great.*

Fun guy

I hadn't mentioned where I was staying

Game on

A time, they had me in that secure facility, yeah, the madhouse, the home for the bewildered, and the shrink, he's giving me all these tests, leaned back, said,

"You show latent sociopathetic tendencies."

The shite these guys talk

So I went with, asked,

"Gimme fifty bucks."

"Excuse me?"

"Give me fifty bucks or I'll slice your jugular."

The alarm bell right there on his desk, his hand hovering and he asked,

"Are you serious?"

I stared at his hand, said,

"Depends on how latent those tendencies are."

Ah, for the good times

Seamas was waiting for my answer. I peered at his combat jacket, First Airborne and Paratroopers insignia. I needled a tad, let his balance stay precarious, asked,

"You were in the service?"

Nailed the fuck but he rallied, said,

"My, am . . . own small tribute to the boys doing their bit."

The sarcasm leaking all over the words

Good, I like a player.

Was going to run with

"The grunts in Baghdad, the nineteen-year-olds from Idaho and Montana, I'm sure it helps, knowing you're sitting there, slurping cognac, talking garbage."

But I needed him

He was on the same hymn sheet, went for flattery, smiled, glanced at my feet, his teeth accessorising his jacket, green in neon, said,

"I like your trainers."

I'd briefly zoned

Happens

I go away sometimes, like a white blankness, a space apart, with some episode from the past narrating on the side.

A college broad I was fleecing, trust-fund mama, met her on that spring break gig they do. I was in my professor year-out sabbatical, writing the novel shtick, right down to the leather patches on my corduroy jacket.

Easy role

Crib some Updike, Cheever, sprinkle with Blake, it's a
 lock

Blake I learned from Thomas Harris, *Red Dragon*

Go figure

Blake is a shoo-in, they suck that right up

Took her nine large but it went south

Had to drown the bitch and in the shower, you think
 that's easy, damn soap makes everything slippery
 and you're a bit woozy after the sex. The upside, it's
 a clean kill.

My own reading stretched to Julia Philips, *You'll Never
 Eat Lunch in This Town Again.* She has a story in
 there, hanging with Coppola, him doing forty shots
 of espresso daily . . . the fuck kind of jones is that?

I snapped back, levelled my eyes on Seamas, said,

"Converse Originals, Chuck Taylor endorsed."

They were

He went,

"Who?"

"Never mind, my hotel is good, they're treating me real
 fine."

He finished the brandy, relaxed, said,

"You need anything, anything at all, I'm yer man."

The hook

Before I could launch, he said,

"In Ireland, we speak Irish English, like the Brit version
 but loaded, you with me?"

How complicated was it? I nodded and he continued,

"For example, we say *'They saw you coming,'* means,
 you're ripe to be ripped off. Now I wouldn't want that
 to happen to a nice fella like yer own self."

I said,

"I'm here to spearhead a major distribution deal in . . ."

I gave him the full look, ribbed my nose with my index
finger

He nodded, he was a clued-in guy and I continued,

"And . . . we need some people we can rely on. We ask
them to front a small amount of cash, say two large,
and entrust them with a sizable package to see how
they manage. The profits are enormous. . . ."

I rubbed my eyes, getting that sincerity in there, then,

"The people I select need to prove their worth so we
ask them to come up with the cash in twenty-four
hours . . . most don't, or can't, and we know from the
off, they're not the people we need."

I let him digest this. The guy hadn't seen two large in
one place in his whole lousy life. He asked,

"What's to stop you taking off with the cash, if I could
produce the readies?"

I smiled

"See, you're the kind of guy I feel I'm seeking. You're
thinking outside the box. As a sign of my good faith,
I'll let you hold my passport and driver's license.
Where am I going to go without them?"

I ordered a last round of drinks, let him see a mess of
credit cards and a thick wedge of notes. He gulped
his drink, then,

"Twenty-four hours, Jesus, hard to come by two large
in that time."

I raised my glass, said,

"Well, we move on, you've had a nice evening, we say
good luck and I move on."

His hand was up and he protested,

"No, no, I'm in, I'll get it."

I indicated Aine and said,

"If she can raise similar, you're in for twice the payoff."

Now he smiled, asked,

"What makes you think I know her that well?"

"It's my speciality to know people."

He was impressed.

One, as they say . . . *jarring note*. Apart from the zon-
    ing out that happens to me, I'm pretty much on top
    of my game, I've been doing this shit a long time and
    am, very, like, very good at it. As Seamas and I fin-
    ished off our drinks, a guy who'd had one too many
    nearly smashed into our table. He had that highly
    concentrated drunk walk of watching every step and
    then it suddenly gets away from you and you're do-
    ing a reel and a hornpipe. He hit the table hard and
    as he was that rarity, a good-natured souse, he was
    all apologies and he'd buy us fresh drinks, the whole
    pathetic nine and, being caught unprepared, I said,

"No sweat, guv, don't worry about it, mate."

In full glorious Brit/London voice

Fuck

What it sounded most like was natural, like my real tone

I laughed it off as I got an odd look from Seamas. I said,

"I do a lousy Brit accent, you think buddy?"

A heartbeat, then he said,

"Don't we all."

It nagged at me but then I reasoned, Seamas was a dumb
    schmuck, why I picked him.

We agreed to meet the following evening. I'd bring the
    product and he and Aine, they'd bring whatever cash
    they raised.

He said he had a van and would pick me up on Shop
  Street around seven, we could do our business with-
  out prying eyes.
I clinked my glass against his, said,
"Here's to the Galway connection."
And he said,
"God bless the work."

My basic scam is hit a place, select some skels, lay a line
  of patter, offer a slice of the large pie, let 'em in for
  two, three Gs and five times out of ten, I hook. Mainly,
  I get about half what I asked and four towns later, I'm
  usually ten to the good.
The beauty is . . . who they gonna call?
Sure it's fraught but I relish the edge, love the mind fuck.
Women are best, get a few of 'em, get a bitch-fest brew-
  ing
Next day was R-day, Rolex time. My mouth was dry, I
  was hitting the precipice, going out on the wing, not
  entirely sure if the plastic would take the weight.
But, it went like, dare I say . . . *clockwork*
Walked outa the jewelers, the gold Rolex on my wrist
  and Mont Blanc in my jacket.
I'd pushed it, got cocky, adrenaline roaring in my ears,
  blinding me to the risk. And, too, I was fucking
  dazzled by the watch. You'd shit a brick to hear
  the price. Lemme say, a town's worth of scam.
Sitting in a coffee shop after, wolfing a Danish, double
  espresso to chase, I eased a notch. I was going to have
  to split sooner than planned. The credit card would
  be flagged. I'd, maybe, forty-eight hours to the good.
Maybe

Dublin would be next, do some sightseeing, pluck some
fresh meat.

For the rendezvous, I dressed to impress, my new leather
Boss jacket, Tommy Hilfiger chinos and soft tan
loafers, Italian of course.

That afternoon, I'd arranged some protection, level the
playing field. I'm not too big on trust.

There's a lot of shysters out there

Got me a knife

I had a younger brother, Darren, snivelling little bastard,
always in my face and worse, getting the shine from
my folks. Back then, their attention seemed worthy
of merit.

So, I drowned him

Doesn't take long, you do it right, even looks like you
tried to save them, like you were trying to help.

Tragic accident

Golly gosh, gee whiz.

Backfired

After, the old man got sucked into the bottle and never
came back.

His belt began to appear and my mom, she found mother's little helpers and that's all she wrote. I think of
cute Darren sometimes, the look in his eyes, those
moments before the close. I learned then, a plea is a
piece of shit.

Wished he could have seen the Rolex though

Shop Street, the main pedestrian gig in Galway, they
have a camping store. Got me a fine blade, hand-
tooled and the guy asked,

"You backpacking?"

I'm wearing a fucking Rolex, was he blind? I said,

"Packing all right."

If Seamas had any other alternative, I'd gut him like a Galway salmon.

Learnt the finer points in Brixton, have a scar on my abdomen to prove it.

Hit real low, rip up, fast, steady and then, buddy, pull way the fuck back. Those entrails are going to splash

And Aine, who knew?

This were a novel, the critics would say . . . the female character is only a cipher . . . are they kidding, aren't all women? What's to describe? They nag, end of story.

I could ball her, have me some Irish but it wasn't a priority. She got lippy, well, I'd use my hands, watch the Rolex catch the light as I squeezed.

As you can see, I was primed

They picked me up off Shop Street, in a van that needed a major overhaul, not to mention a decent wash, fucking nowhere people.

Seamas, in the driver's seat, and I squeezed in beside Aine, got a little hip action grinding, she was hot

Aine said,

"Looks like rain."

The micks and the forecasts.

Seamas said,

"We'll drive out a ways, no need for prying eyes."

We pulled up on the outskirts of the city, Galway Bay spread before us. Seamas produced a flask, said,

" 'Tis poteen, we call it *uisce beatha,* holy water and it's a miraculous bevy all right."

He offered me the flask and seeing my hesitation, Aine whined,

"You won't drink with us?"

What the hell, I grabbed it, took a healthy wallop and it
    kicked. I gasped, asked,

"That's what, like Irish moonshine?"

Aine gave me a glorious smile, said,

"More like good night."

Came to with my head on fire, throbbing like a bastard
    and then the cold, my whole body frozen.

My naked body

I sat up and pebbles embedded in my ass. I was on a
    beach, not a shred of clothing and checked my wrist

No Rolex

Dawn was breaking, the light creeping over the bay. I
    began to get slowly to my feet, dizziness and nausea
    hitting in waves, saw the note, wedged under a stone.
    I grabbed it, read,

Teddy, mate, guv
        We saw you coming. We're Irish but
Not green . . .
And that knife . . .
Not nice
We confiscated it, lest you hurt yerself. Now, that
would be no way to treat a Brit, would it?
You better get your arse in gear, rain is forecast.

I crumpled it and said aloud,

"Always with the bloody weather talk."

Slice of Pie
by Bill Cameron

•

Real is the word that immediately comes to mind when stepping into a world created by the exceptionally talented Bill Cameron. The landscape he illuminates is one we've seen before, but never with such focus or appreciation. Bill shines a light on real life, and suddenly we recognize an object, a person, an emotion. *Yes, that's exactly the way it is . . .* He brings clarity to private spaces, and helps us see the familiar with new eyes. Bill's short story, "Slice of Pie," is a wonderful slice of life, a small and intimate world as immediate as a whiff of mothball, urinal cake, or Tabu.

—Anne Frasier,
USA Today bestselling author of *Pale Immortal*

Blue ceramic fish on the wall, three on a diagonal, with gold bubbles. *Blub blub blub.* They used to be in the bathroom off the rec room in the basement. She moved them upstairs after Dad died. Said they felt homey, and it was her house now, for golly's sake. The other thing she moved up was the framed sampler, hung above the toilet. Its colors had faded over the years, but its message was still clear.

If you sprinkle
When you tinkle,
Be a sweetie
And wipe the seatie.

Goddamn thing never ceased to piss me off. Ever since I was a kid. Bugged Dad, too, which was why it had been consigned to the dungeon. I guess the sampler's what had me in such a foul mood. I was staring at it—captive audience, if you follow my stream of self-consciousness—when the doorbell rang. The sound jolted me out of my irritable reverie and I sprinkled on the seatie.

I heard the *tump* of Ma's Keds across the living room. The front door opened as I zipped up. Muffled voices. I swiped toilet paper across the seat and flushed, washed my hands. By the time I got to the living room, she was already handing him the twenty dollar bill.

"What's going on, Ma?"

The disheveled fellow at the door—dark brown jacket missing half the buttons, greased-back hair—tossed me a look when I came in, a *fuck you* glint in his eyes. He exuded a funk laced with tobacco and sweat. Ma squeezed the bill against his palm with one hand, patted his arm with the other. I thought it was awfully hot out to be wearing a coat.

"This is Mr. Franklin. He lives in the apartments up the block. He locked his keys in his car and I'm loaning him some money for a locksmith." She looked at him and smiled. He tried smiling back. I doubt he'd brushed his teeth this century.

"You ever seen him before, Ma?"

She looked at him and opened her mouth, but he horned in. "I live up the street," he said. "In the apartments." He gestured vaguely with the twenty dollar bill. "In 3257. Up the street."

"Good for you. Why don't you go bum your dope money off someone who isn't on a fixed income?"

"Raymond!"

"This guy is running a scam on you, Ma."

She sucked air and drew herself up to her full five feet, four inches. Her capri pants and sunny, open-collared shirt belied her attempt at fearsomeness, but the crisp edge to her voice was clear enough. "Raymond, I will not have you speaking to a guest this way—a guest in need, no less. You will apologize to him immediately."

"Ma! He's conning you. Probably doesn't even have a car."

"Listen," Franklin muttered, easing back into the doorway, "I'll get the money somewhere else."

Great idea, but Ma was having none of that. "Don't be ridiculous," she said. "Take the money. Pay no attention to my son. He learned his bad manners from his father, bless his soul."

"What a bunch of crap." I turned on my heel and stalked away, headed to the dining room, the kitchen, anywhere. Ma jawed some more with Franklin, the sound chasing me through the house. More apologies and whatever. Him wheedling. Then the front door closed. The bells she'd hung from the doorknob jingled.

She found me in the kitchen, bemused by doilies and trivets. Everything had changed since Dad died. The sampler in the bathroom, the goddamn bells on the door.

"Raymond, your behavior out there was appalling. I won't tolerate it. Mr. Franklin was my guest."

"Your guest scammed you. It ain't the good ol' days anymore, Ma. People are scumbags." I nosed around on the countertop, looking for something to distract me from her indignant glare. I didn't really want to get into it with her, but I couldn't help but bristle at her ongoing foolishness. I lifted the stainless steel cover off a dessert plate on the windowsill, discovered an apple pie underneath, neatly cut into eighths. Two eighths already gone. I got a plate out of the cupboard, then started to open the silverware drawer for a fork. Ma pushed the drawer shut, almost catching my hand.

"What do you think you're doing?" she said.

"What do you mean? I'm getting a slice of pie."

"No, you're not. Your behavior has been reprehensible."

"Don't be ridiculous, Ma."

"Perhaps next time you think you're going to throw your weight around in my house, you'll think again."

"Ma—!"

"Mr. Franklin was my guest. You shall have no pie."

She locked her eyes on mine and set her jaw. I threw up my hands. "Fine. Whatever. When you never see Mr. Franklin again, don't whine to me about it."

I left her frowning among the trivets. Rather than go straight to my car, I walked up toward the apartments where Franklin claimed to live. Three boxy quad-plexes called the Linda Loo, probably after some shoddy developer's daughter. Warped green aluminum siding, circa 1963, and torpid arborvitae formed the unifying design theme. One of the buildings was numbered 3257, so give Franklin credit for doing a little research before running his scam. I didn't see him or his mythical lock-smith anywhere.

I went back to my car, drove home. Tried not to think about it.

Since Dad died, I didn't come around Ma's much. All the knickknacks and tchotchkes that materialized out of nowhere had turned the house into a granny museum. Ma moved the TV out of the living room and hid it under a blanket in the basement. She converted my old bedroom into her sewing room, and covered the pool table with a sheet of plywood so she could spread out her quilting projects.

My sister, Kathy, says I have no business being up-set. It's not like I live there anymore. Ma had to live in a man's house until my father died, a house ruled by power tools and televised sports. She's just now finding her own way, Kathy tells me. A sixty-five-year-old woman finding her own way? What the hell was that supposed to mean? I'd have been content to go my whole life without ever learning what an antimacassar was.

But the next day I drove by after work. Didn't stop. I looked up at the house, then drove past the Linda Loo, rolled through the neighborhood. I was searching for Franklin, I realized. No idea what I would do if I found him. Demand Ma's twenty back, I suppose.

But I didn't see him that day, or the next.

Kathy called me the following afternoon at work. "Mom says she's seen you driving past the house."

"That's ridiculous," I muttered.

"Ray," she said, "I know Dad is gone, but Mom doesn't

need you to look after her. She can take care of herself."

"She handled that scammer real well the other day."

"That's none of your business." Her voice was sharp,
but then she continued more softly, "You've got to let
go, Ray. I loved Dad, too, and I miss him, but in a lot of
ways he could be a real prick." I had no response to that,
so she added, "Come over today. You and Mom can talk,
clear things up. I'll be there to help."

I rolled my eyes, but agreed to stop by when I got off
work.

Ma and Kathy were scrapbooking when I arrived.
The coffee table was covered with colored paper, bottles
of glue, three or four pairs of scissors, and a scattering
of old photos. I recognized some shots of Kathy and
her husband with her kids, a few of Kathy as a child herself. Kathy was five years older than me, and by the time
I arrived on the scene the camera had lost its allure.
There wouldn't be any pics of me in the mix.

"What's going on?" I said, as if it weren't obvious.

Ma looked up at me, her lips a tight line. Since I was
last over, she'd gotten her hair cut into a bob better suited
to a woman half her age. "I hope your attitude has improved today, Raymond," she sniffed.

"Mom," Kathy said, "you promised you wouldn't do
this."

I waved Kathy off. "Gotta use the bathroom," I muttered. I didn't, but after that welcome I figured any
excuse to get away. In the bathroom, I closed my eyes,
refused to look at the goddamn sampler. Why I gave a
shit about Ma and her twenty dollar bill I had no idea.
To hell with her, I thought. I'd go out and make some

small talk, glance at some pictures, then get the hell out of there. Let Kathy deal with it when Franklin or someone else ripped Ma off for serious green.

I flushed the toilet like I'd gone in there for a reason, then rinsed my hands and drew a breath.

"Raymond," Ma said when I returned to the living room, "I didn't hear your water go into the toilet. If you piddled on the seat, you better have cleaned up after yourself."

"Oh, for Christ's sake, Ma—!"

Her eyes flared. "Don't use that tone with me, young man! And don't you ever take the Lord's name in vain in my presence."

My hands clenched at my sides. "What, I'm supposed—"

"I think you need some quiet time alone to think about your attitude." She folded her hands across her chest.

I opened my mouth, a retort on my lips, but instead turned and plunged out the front door and down the front steps. I heard my sister follow after me. "Ray? I'm sorry! Ray?" I didn't see any point in answering. I'd been grounded, no longer allowed to watch TV or play with my little friends.

"Ray!"

I stopped and shook my head, turned without looking. "I'm gonna take a walk. I'll be back in a little while." I could see her feet on the top step of the porch.

"You're embarrassed," she said. "And I'm sorry. You didn't deserve that. It's not fair, I know, but she's just trying to tell you she doesn't need looking after anymore."

"Yeah? Well next time it might not be twenty bucks,"

I said. I turned and headed up the street. The air was so
dry it crackled. The goddamn sampler was stuck in my
head—*If you sprinkle when you tinkle, be a sweetie and
wipe the seatie*. Like a tune, it ran over and over again.
I shook my head, tried to think of something else. Tried
to look at the sun-browned lawns I passed, the drought-
hammered flower beds.

> *If you sprinkle*
> *When you tinkle*

She should have left the damned thing in the basement.

I turned the corner near the market a couple blocks
up from Ma's house, head down, and bumped into a figure coming the other way. Smelled old cigarettes and
pomade.

"Excuse me," a voice said. I looked up and the first
thing I noticed was the dark brown jacket missing half
its buttons. Then I looked into his face, into his eyes. He
recognized me, started to smile, but that same *fuck you*
glint was there.

"Hey, man—"

I punched him, that quick. Didn't even think about it,
just *pop,* and a thin line of blood appeared on his lip. His
eyes got wide, but the *fuck you* didn't go away. I hit him
again, in the chest this time.

"Jesus—!" He turned and started to run, but I grabbed
him by his piece-of-shit coat and spun him down onto
the sidewalk. He started to curl up, but then tried to get
tricky and launched a foot at me. I caught it with one
hand, tossed it off to the side. Kicked him in the ass. His

eyes bulged as I popped him in the soft spot between his cheekbone and lower jaw. A sharp spear of pain shot from my knuckle to my elbow. I didn't care. He groaned, tried to crawl away. I grabbed his jacket, pulled him to his feet.

"How's that for wiping the goddamn seatie, asshole?"

He cringed in response, one hand raised in defense. I pushed him back down, hard. His head bounced off the sidewalk, made a sound like a melon struck by a baseball bat. His eyes rolled back and tears welled and he pulled his hands up in front of his bleeding face.

"Jesus, man—what's yer problem?" he whined.

"You know what my problem is, you fuck." I heard a sound like an insect in one ear. "Scamming an idiot old woman. It's only because it was just twenty bucks you're still breathing." I kicked him once more and left him to ruminate on that thought.

It was a couple blocks back to Ma's house, far enough to give me a chance to calm down a bit and rub the blood off my knuckles before going inside. Kathy was still there, sitting with Ma on the sofa, the two of them looking through the scrapbook. Kathy gave me a tight little smile, then turned her attention back to the pictures. Ma just looked at me and said, "I hope your attitude improved during your walk. You're too old to not know your place."

"Yeah, well, I ran into your friend Franklin." No reason to get into the details, but I was feeling proud of myself, inspired by the raw, rubbery feeling in my bruised hands. "You won't have to worry about him scamming you ever again." I thought that would shut her the hell up.

But she only pursed her lips. "Raymond, you're no better a judge of character than your father was," she said, her voice tinged with a mix of disappointment and satisfaction. "Mr. Franklin paid me back this morning, plus five dollars extra for my trouble. I gave him the last slice of pie."

A Failure to Communicate
by Toni McGee Causey

•

Only the South could've produced Bobbie Faye Sumrall. Maybe only Louisiana. The distinction's too fine for me because I'm not from the South, but I can tell you that Bobbie Faye could not have been born on the laconic plains of the Midwest, or the cold streets of Boston, or the freeways of the San Fernando Valley. She is a heat-seeking missile, a Technicolor heroine rising out of the humidity with a vocabulary as explosive and a past as checkered and abilities as stunning as any you'd find in Marvel Comics. The same can be said for her creator, the extravagantly talented Toni McGee Causey. In "A Failure to Communicate," a motley trio of bad boys picks the wrong Feng Shui Emporium to hold up and discovers that Bobbie Faye is the last woman on the planet you want on the other end of a gun.

—Harley Jane Kozak,
author of *Dating Dead Men*

One hour and forty-five minutes ago . . .

If she got out of this one alive, he was just going to fucking kill her. It would be much easier that way. She was his ex, she was a raving fucking loon, and here she was, holed up inside Ce Ce's where she worked (an outfitter store, with the dumbass name of Ce Ce's Cajun Outfitters and Feng Shui Emporium, though he was surprised Ce Ce didn't include the whole voodoo aspect of her business—probably couldn't cram that on the small wooden sign).

Bobbie Faye Sumrall, who was supposed to have been his wife by now, was a hostage. God help them all. And he was the fucking detective who had to somehow get her to come out and quit terrorizing the hostage takers so they could end this standoff.

This was not going to go well.

He knew it, he could feel it in his bones. He hoped like hell she didn't blow something up. Again. Especially not while she was in there.

"Detective Moreau?" a rookie cop asked.

"Cam."

"Uh, Cam, the newspeople are asking—"

"Quit talking to them. Do not speak to them again. And move the perimeter back five more feet. If they ask you another question, move it back another five. Got it?"

"Yessir." The rookie cop ran off.

Media helicopters jockeyed above them. The news was all over this—because of course, she was the Contraband Days Queen. Unofficial, but you'd swear she was fucking royalty, the way their little industrial city of Lake Charles, Louisiana, treated her. If one freaking hair on her head was injured when all of this was done? He would have death threats.

Her future ex-fiancé (if Cam had anything to do with it) approached, stripping away the firefighter gear he'd borrowed: Trevor Cormier, FBI, former government-sanctioned mercenary and clearly as insane as she was. Trevor was older than Cam's thirty years by about six, though maybe more. Cam wasn't sure. He had Trevor on height, but then, he usually had most people, at six four. Trevor was a measly six foot.

"She's not coming out," Trevor said, pissed off, which satisfied the hell out of Cam. Not that she didn't come out, but that she didn't listen to Trevor any more than she'd listened to him.

"She's still armed?"

"Yes."

Fifteen minutes ago . . .

"Get down get down *get down!*" she shouted, sliding along the aisle like she was heading into home plate, rolling onto her side as she slid, sweeping the aim of her compact Glock across the counter, hoping like hell the customers would listen to her before they got themselves killed. The fat one called Avery—twenty-three, he'd told her—blubbered into a cell phone, begging the cops to just take him away, anything to get him away from *her.*

He wasn't the problem.

The other two were. Kip, blond mop top, raggedy jeans drooping off his skinny hips, and Van, the so-called brains behind this operation.

Kip had lost his mind, the pressures of being made to take hostages when all he really wanted was Romy. Kip, who screamed obscenities even Bobbie Faye hadn't

used or heard, and that was a new record. He waved
around a Sig he'd gotten from the broken display case,
loaded, she knew, by the rounds he'd found there, intent
on shooting Mr. Maynard, the balding, bandy-legged
old man standing between him and Bobbie Faye. Mr.
Maynard's arthritis meant he moved so slowly, Bobbie
Faye didn't know if he could hit the floor fast enough to
avoid being shot. Romy stood where she'd left her, frozen, paralyzed by fear and, if the flat, resigned look in
Kip's eyes was anything to judge by, if he made it past
Mr. Maynard and her, Romy was dead.

Which meant she had to take the shot.

The real problem was Van. Older, scarier. And nowhere to be seen.

Kip made a decision, tears streaming down his face,
shouting at Mr. Maynard that he would kill him, too. He
aimed.

She aimed better.

Kip saw her Glock at that last second, his eyes going
wide, and he turned into the shot as she chanted, "Get
down!" and Mr. Maynard slowly dropped to his right,
crashing one knee into the floor.

And then Van stepped up behind her, put a gun to her
head, and laughed.

Five and a half hours ago . . .

Ce Ce waddled around to the gun counter, her long
chocolate braids swinging against her honey skin.

"I'm taking this." She nodded toward the bank bag.
"You got the place?"

"Sure, Ceece. It's a Monday; it's usually pretty slow."

"Yeah, but you're still recuperating from that last thing. You're looking kinda pale."

"I'm fine, really. Go on."

"I've gotta run a couple of errands. I'll bring you back some lunch."

"Rosie's?"

"You betcha, hon."

Five hours ago . . .

"Where did all these people come from?" Allison, one of the identical nineteen-year-old twins working the front counter, asked. "We don't usually have this many on a Monday."

Bobbie Faye shrugged, wishing Allison hadn't streaked her jet-black hair. Until she had, Bobbie Faye had been the only one who could tell her and her sister, Alicia, apart, and they'd had fun messing with some of the more pain-in-the-ass customers. Drove Ce Ce right up the wall, though, so Allison had obliged.

"I think Ceece's been talking up those crystals," she answered. "I've had at least six people ask me for the 'sale' rack because they're too embarrassed to admit what they really want."

"Think she's been telling 'em they're great for sex again? She's still got at least two dozen crates in the back to move," Alicia said, joining them.

"She didn't do so good using the whole 'peace and harmony' thing," Allison added.

"Kinda hard to sell that idea while you have a gun and knife counter, too," Bobbie Faye said.

"Yeah." Alicia grinned at her. "Especially when the woman behind the counter has blown up half the state."

"Only parts of it, smartass. Look, you have a customer."

"Oh, that's Romy," Allison said. "Girl we graduated with. You need anything back here?"

"Nope, got it, go visit."

Bobbie Faye leaned on the gun counter, her particular special area of the store. She knew the weapons and taught firearm safety and marksmanship at the firing range Ce Ce'd had constructed out back behind the store. Well, old ramshackle Acadian-style-house-turned-store; with so many add-ons that made no sense, it looked like an architect had hiccuped and scrambled multiple plans into one old place. She watched as the twins wove through the precariously stacked merchandise, everything from cammo to scented candles to board games to deer scent, and they greeted their friend, a slip of a girl who had the saddest eyes Bobbie Faye had seen in a long time.

"Is this a good gun?" a blond mop-topped boy asked her. Technically, a young man. She was twenty-nine and probably only four or five years older than this kid, but he looked so lost in his baggy clothes, she had to quash the need to see how on earth he had them held up on his body. He tapped on the glass countertop, pointing to a double-action Sig Sauer on the top shelf.

"Sure," she said, and she began explaining the handgun to him.

Two hours and fifteen minutes ago . . .

Trevor stood there with a gun to his head, suited up in firefighting gear, dirt and sweat smeared on his face as if he'd had a hard time with the burning car.

"Look man," he said to Van, who was shouting obscenities and pressing the .357 into Trevor's skull, "I just came in to see if the place was okay. I didn't know. Really."

"You're lying!" Van said. "You're a cop! You ain't fucking takin' me to jail, man."

Bobbie Faye's entire gut knotted, and Adrenaline had not only woken up every single cell (not that they really needed further alerting, they were jangling so loudly, she was surprised she hadn't deafened everyone in a three-mile radius), but Fucking Pissed Off knocked at the door, because if anything happened to Trevor . . .

"He's just a fireman, Van," she said, as calmly as she could. "Cut the poor guy a break. If he was a cop, he'd have come in here armed or something. Let him go."

"No, keep *me*," Trevor insisted. "Let the women go."

"Nah, man, we gotta keep us some good hostages. I know how this works."

"They're going to get on your nerves," he said. "I have a crazy fiancée and, man, her head would be spinning about now."

Bobbie Faye gave him a slit-eyed glare. "Probably because she'd rather you not be stupid and argue with the man with the gun at your head. I'm sure she'd prefer you to come home tonight and do that whole 'happily forever after' thing, so don't be an idiot."

"I'm keeping the girl," Van said, pointing to Romy. "That bitch is the reason why I'm here."

"Then give me the Contraband Days Queen," Trevor said. " 'Cuz man, they're gonna go ballistic on you, if you hurt her."

"Sure, take her. She's driving me batshit anyway, always arguing."

"No!" Kip pounded his skinny fist on the counter. "She's our ticket out."

"Please take her," Avery whined. "Please? She scares the crap outta me." Avery had retreated to the farthest point in the room.

"She tends to have that effect on some people," Trevor agreed, and she rolled her eyes.

"I'm not going." Bobbie Faye could hear Romy sigh. "You can take the other women, but if Romy has to stay, I'm staying."

"You're only going to get yourself hurt." Trevor's expression begged her to reconsider. "And I think you have a fiancé, too, right?"

"Holy fuck," Van said, "you mean there's some moron out there who's willing to listen to you argue with him for the rest of your fucking life?"

"Yep," Trevor said. "I heard he's got it bad, too."

"Geezus, point me at him and let me put a bullet in his brain and put him out of his misery."

Three and a half hours ago . . .

Bobbie Faye saw the car, just like Romy had described it. A classic '69 Mustang fastback, and the car gods were soooo going to strike her dead for what she was about to do.

She didn't have time to hesitate; she maybe had two minutes before they realized she was missing, had slipped out a door off the weird little bathroom she'd gotten permission to use. The car was out of the line of sight of the front windows, parked over on the side street, a potholed one-way affair that most people avoided. She slim-jimmed the lock, one of her talents learned when she had dated a couple of criminals. She wasn't entirely sure if that was past tense or not, because Trevor skirted that fine line. From the little she really knew of him.

The door lock popped and she eased it open, placing the candle inside the Styrofoam cup she'd brought with her. She poured the Coleman fuel on the brand-new carpeted floor, laid the fire wick against the seat, poured a little more fuel from it to where the candle sat inside the cup, now with an inch of fuel inside.

It was hard to light the small votive candle without lighting the fuel around it, but she had to—she needed the minutes. She carefully closed the door—it wouldn't really matter later if it had been open or closed, but she didn't want a random breeze blowing out the candle or, worse, setting the fuel on fire too soon.

There was a moment when she was finished that she knew she could run for it. Head to the right, to the busier street, go inside somewhere safe, make the phone calls that needed to be made.

But they were listening, and if she made that phone call, people might die.

She could walk away. Walk to freedom. Trevor would show up, Cam would show up, other people would take care of it, and she could just walk away, perfectly safe. Self-preservation shouted to go for it, Bravery whined in the corner that really, it had been on overtime for the last few months and fuck it, it was *tired*, and Common Sense begged her to listen, for once.

She turned back toward Ce Ce's.

Four hours ago . . .

"What do you mean, it's not here?" the young guy the others had called Van asked.

"Pretty simple," she said. "It's. Not. Here. Means *it's somewhere else*."

"You're supposed to have a lot of cash from the weekend!" he shouted, pointing his .357 in her face.

"Yeah," the fat kid they'd called Avery piped up from behind Ce Ce's computer, "a lot of cash. Right?" He turned to the mop-top blond. "You did the research, you said there was a lot of cash."

"There is. There's always a lot after the hunters and fishermen come through here on the weekend."

"Which is why," she tried to explain patiently, refraining from pantomiming and pissing Van off even more, "Ce Ce brings it to the bank on Monday mornings. She left a little while ago. It's probably already in the bank by now."

"No!" Van said. "You get her back here!"

"Uh, sure thing, I'll just get right on that."

"I'm fucking *serious,* dude."

"Well, gee, *dude,* I'll call her up and say, 'Hey, Ceece, we've got a couple of genius thieves over here whose timing kinda sucks. Would you mind terribly bringing the money back so they can have another try?' "

Van cocked the Smith & Wesson, shoving it against her forehead as Romy and the twins screamed.

Eight hours ago . . .

She woke before the alarm, per usual, and she listened to his breathing, his arm curved protectively around her waist. She knew the change in her breathing alone would wake him; Trevor was—almost impossible to believe—a lighter sleeper than she was. He tapped off the alarm before it had a chance to jangle loud talk-radio hosts who were trying too hard to be cheery in the morning. Then he did what he'd been doing every single day for the last three months: he brushed a kiss across the scars, three angry craters just above her hip, almost healed completely.

"I'm going to marry you," he said, for the hundredth or so time. She'd lost track.

"You're going to be late for work," she teased, still not having given him an answer. She wasn't trying to be coy, wasn't trying to torment him. She just didn't have an answer to give. "Besides, you have enough grief in your life."

"One of these days," he said, "you're going to look in the mirror and see these and realize you stood in front of bullets for me. And you don't just do that for anyone, Sundance."

But she had, she'd started to tell him. It was, actually, a lot easier than promising a heart. She'd take the bullets any day.

"One day," he whispered, teasing her body wide awake, the humming sensation in her skin almost loud enough to hear, "you're going to realize you want me as much as I want you."

"Cocky bastard," she said, and he grinned.

Twenty minutes ago . . .

Van paced, his greasy hair having fallen out of its hair band, demented wings now flapping around his face.

"I'm gonna fucking kill her, man," he shouted at Kip, but pointed the .357 at Romy. Well, at Bobbie Faye, because she stood in front of Romy, and had made Romy stand behind a stack of metal deer stands; they weren't solid, but they might deflect a round or two. "You and your stupid ex-fucking-girlfriend! We were coming in here for *money*. We were gonna be set! The police are dragging around, they're waiting us out! They're not gonna give us another car *or* the money. I'm gonna fucking kill her."

"You have me," Bobbie Faye said, "and they'll give us a car and we're going to leave and I'll take you to a friend of mine. He's a gunrunner, and he'll get you out of the state. You can let all of these people go."

"I'm not going to no fucking gunrunner friend of yours!" Van shouted, working up to a froth. "You don't think I know he'll kill us! We need money. Someone's gotta pay a ransom for you."

"Sure thing," she said. "I'm sure the governor will pay you to get me out of the state. He's been kinda wanting me gone for a while now."

Four and a half hours ago . . .

Bobbie Faye hadn't liked the look of the guy loitering just inside the front door, with his sneer and dark hair slicked back into a ponytail and unlaced army boots paired with tight jeans that showed off his entire package, as if he was the only man on the planet who had one. Everything she knew about reading body language said "bad intentions" and she had the cell phone to her ear to call Cam. He always chewed her out for not calling him to help, and this time, she was going to do it.

She hesitated, mid-dial. She didn't know what she felt for Cam, didn't quite know what the hell to do about it, either. Best friends, almost enemies, then lovers, then definitely enemies, then a weird truce when she'd realized just what had happened between them, what he'd intended. That he'd wanted to marry her. That he'd been so stupid, he'd screwed everything up. Loyalty split down the line between him and Trevor and she couldn't think about it; it made everything hurt all over again.

It was the hesitation that cost her.

The guy loitering at the door drew a gun. She stood there, knowing her Glock was a mere two inches away, but he was watching her, shouting. He turned the lock in the door while the blond mop top ran to lock the back.

"Everybody down on the floor. And get your cell phones out, now!" the guy at the door shouted. "If I find one on you, I'm shooting you, you got that?"

Mr. Maynard leaned a little toward her and whispered, "I can tackle 'im if you wanna shoot the other ones." Mr. Maynard was at least eighty-five and stiff as a brick from arthritis.

"Not just yet, Mr. Maynard."

"You let me know when."

She nodded as the fat kid—someone called him Avery—hacked into Ce Ce's computer.

"There," Avery said, "we're tied into the 911 computer dispatch. Anyone calls the cops, we'll know first."

"Anyone here stupid enough to call anyone, like on some other phone somewhere, I'll start killing some of you."

"He's done it before," Avery said to the crowd, and from the about-to-piss-himself expression he had, Bobbie Faye was pretty sure he was telling the truth.

Kip ran back in, sauntering past her and taking her cell phone out of her hands, then proceeded to scoop up the other phones and pat down every customer in the store.

"Everybody against the wall," the guy at the front door instructed.

"Everybody except Romy," Kip said, swaggering over to where Romy huddled with the twins. "She's mine."

Two hours and forty-five minutes ago . . .

"Definitely arson," the fire chief said. "Unofficially, of course," he told Cam, who'd just arrived, "but they didn't bother to hide it. But you gotta see this."

Cam followed the man over to the smoldering car, and, nearby, there was an arrow burned into the ground. Pointing at Ce Ce's.

Which, come to think of it, was dark, with not a soul moving around.

"Did y'all evacuate the store?" he asked and the chief looked over there, scratching his head.

"No, as a matter of fact, it was dark when we got here. We had the fire contained, and there's a sign on the door—'Closed for Lunch.'"

"Ce Ce doesn't close for lunch."

Cam looked at that arrow, then realized at the bottom, there were initials: "BF." Bobbie Faye.

Oh, holy shit, this was bad. If she couldn't call, if she'd had to do this?

Trevor appeared, just like that. Cam would have sworn under his breath that the man had Bobbie Faye tagged with some sort of electronic device, but she'd have killed Trevor if he even thought about it. Maybe the man had a finely honed sense of impending doom. The kind he'd developed when *he'd* dated her.

"I want you to keep up the fire fighting," Trevor said to the chief, an eerie calm to his voice. "Keep everything looking normal. I need to get into some fire gear—do you have an extra jacket or something?"

"I'm sure I can scrounge something up."

"You're not going in there until we know what the hell is up," Cam told him.

"Wanna bet?"

Twelve minutes ago . . .

"I'm not going with her," Avery whined. "She blows things up. I don't want to be blown up."

"You're going with me," Bobbie Faye said to him like

she would a third-grader, "because if you don't, Avery, I will make sure the nice cops outside shoot your ass."

Avery started crying and Van kept pacing.

"And we're taking that fucking bitch, too," he said about Romy.

Bobbie Faye heard Romy gasp.

"No, Van, you're not. You try to take Romy, I'll kill you."

"You don't fucking have a gun anymore!" he shouted, stomping over to her. "Miz Fucking Big Bad, whatcha gonna do? Talk me to death?"

"No," she smiled sweetly. "I'm going to do *this*," and she moved, glad he'd finally gotten close enough.

Ten minutes ago . . .

SWAT and Cam and Trevor swarmed the place. A girl screamed incoherently on the other side of the room and two officers moved in her direction to calm her down. Two men down, a scrawny one over by the counter, bleeding, but alive, from what Cam could see, and a second, bigger guy, writhing and screaming in pain, holding his crotch. Bobbie Faye on the floor, sitting against a display case, looking completely exhausted. He wanted to go to her. Jesus, he wanted to go to her, but when she looked up at the two of them approaching, she focused on Trevor, who knelt by her side, checking her out, making sure she wasn't hurt.

It was his own fucking fault, he reminded himself. It wasn't over yet. Not by a long shot. Not even if she thought it was, and he had a plan. Probably a stupid one, but he had a plan.

"Cam?" one of the officers called him over to another young man, bawling his eyes out.

"Please arrest me," he said. "And take me where she can't get to me." He shuddered uncontrollably, barely able to bring himself to look in Bobbie Faye's direction.

"She's not that bad."

Avery gaped at him. "Did you *see* where she put that fish hook?"

Cam flinched, glancing back at the man writhing, the paramedics having a rough time getting him to lie still on the gurney. "Well, if it's any consolation, I don't think she's real concerned about you right now."

"I don't want to take any chances."

Three hours and ten minutes ago . . .

"You did what?" Van yelled, smacking Kip across the face with the gun. "What in the hell is wrong with you?"

The entire storeful of customers inhaled and froze there as Kip pulled out the Sig he'd gotten out of the display case; no one noticed Bobbie Faye had slipped back in.

"Don't fuckin' mock me, man, you just don't know how bad it is." Kip practically vibrated in place with fury.

Romy hid as much as she could behind the twins.

"We said we were getting our big break," Van seethed.

"Big score. Lots of money. I was gonna start out some-where new. We didn't come here for no stupid fucking love potion that some ditzy stupid voodoo priestess sells for ten bucks."

"It's not stupid," Kip said, "and it's real expensive. I couldn't afford it."

"So you what? You set us up, man? You get us to break in here when you know the voodoo woman ain't even gonna be in here? Did you even *think* about the fact that she was taking the money to the bank this morn-ing? Huh? I should fucking kill you right here!"

"She's powerful, and I didn't want her to do some-thing weird to me, like turn me into some sort of warty frog or something. She can do that shit. But I looked back there and none of her stuff is labeled. I don't know which one is the love potion."

"You're out of your fucking mind," Van said, tapping the .357 against Kip's chest for emphasis.

"I just want Romy *back*," Kip yelled, tears flowing down his scrawny, dirty face, and Romy hid even more behind the twins. "She broke up with me and she be-longs to *me*. She's *mine*, and I'm gonna keep her."

"Love isn't something you can buy, you fucking idiot," Van shouted. He waved the pistol and everyone flinched, ducking. "You think some lame potion is gonna make her *love* you? Are you *sick*? You think it's gonna make her love you enough to stand in front of this gun for you? Huh? C'mere," he shouted at Romy, and sev-eral of the customers stood in front of her, and Bobbie Faye in front of them.

"See," he said to Kip, "total fucking strangers stand-ing in front of a gun for somebody they don't even know,

and they don't love her. And she don't love you enough
to come out from behind there and stand in front of this
for you," he said, tapping the end of the gun barrel. "You
gonna get shot for her stupid ass? You gonna get killed
for that shit?"

"Yeah," Kip said, with a little too much bravado. "I'd
take one for her."

Van kicked over a tall rack, smashing it, and the sink-
ers and fishing tackle and artificial baits scattered. "That
ain't nothin', man. Hell, that ain't even hard." Spittle
formed in the corners of his mouth and he paced, his
movements jerking with each syllable as if the muscles
were determined to independently express the pain.
"People out there, they'll use you for the stuff they can
get, like flowers or jewelry or stupid curtains with big
pink teapots on 'em that don't go with any of your shit,
and then one day, there ain't nothing else big you got,
you can't do nothing big enough and then, bam, they're
gone and you got to stare at them *fuckin'* curtains. Goddamned fucking teapots!" He raked an entire shelf of
kitchen supplies onto the floor, his face red, tears stain-
ing his cheeks. Every customer shrank as far away
as they could without moving, without attracting his
attention.

"That real kind of love," he ranted, kicking the uten-
sils out of his way, "that going home every day to the
same person, wantin' them to come home to you for the
rest of your fucking life? You can't buy that, man, not
with your stupid fucking love potion. It ain't about the
big things, it's about what somebody does, day in and
day out, whether or not they stick. And she ain't gonna
stick, man, not even with some fucking potion.

"I needed that money," he shouted, wanting to aim at Romy and having to settle for aiming at Bobbie Faye. "I needed to start over, to get away from them fucking teapots!"

Bobbie Faye stared at Van, so into his rant that his face had turned red, his hair flapping with each word as he rocked his body hard, and it amazed her how even crazy people could have a moment of brilliant clarity. Why was it always the psychos who understood love best? The universe had a real perverse sense of humor sometimes.

The sudden, concussive *whoomsh* of the Mustang exploding outside rattled the windows, set off car alarms all across the neighborhood and Bobbie Faye knew that it would take exactly two minutes, forty-three seconds for the fire department to arrive (because, unfortunately, she had in-depth experience at this), and it would take longer than that for Van and Kip and Avery to wrap their minds around the fact that their getaway car just left.

Five minutes ago . . .

Trevor checked her over, making sure she wasn't hiding any wounds, and then he rechecked her.

"Quit," she said. "I'm fine." She was tired, but okay. "Let's go home." She opened her eyes to see him grinning, dead sexy, and she felt the humming in her skin again. "What?"

"You answered me, finally."

"I've *been* answering you, you idiot."

"I didn't think you realized you were."

"So much for you being the brilliant FBI man, huh?" He didn't need to know she'd finally figured out that she'd been answering him every time she thought of him as home.

"Am I going to have to make sure you're taken hostage every time I want you to make a major decision?" he asked as he stood and helped her up.

"Don't push your luck, Butch," she said, grinning for the first time that day. "I still know where the spare fish hooks are."

One Serving of Bad Luck
by Sean Chercover

•

Once every decade a novel comes down the pike, heralded
    by stunning reviews, blurbs to kill for and you go,
"Hype."

Not with *Big City, Bad Blood*.

It's even better than the lineup of top mystery writers claims
    it to be

If ever there was a shoo-in for the Shamus Award, here it is

Sean not only is one hell of a writer, he used to be a PI, so
    you're truly getting the real deal

But was it a one-off, a kid gets lucky, writes the one amaz-
    ing debut and sayonara?

Here is a short story, featuring Ray Dudgeon from the
    novel, and damn, it's almost better.

The short story is notoriously difficult to pull off, and to
    capture all the wondrous sides of the character that made
    the novel sing is a daunting task

Sean does it effortlessly. . . . . damn him

Ray is trying to get justice—and more important, serious
    money—for a woman left paralysed from a botched car
    repair job

His dogged pursuit of the shady characters involved brings
    him to the very bottom rungs of the American dream

What makes Ray so compelling is his humanity and

compassion; he hints at the traumatic events from Big City but never dwells on them, a masterstroke of plotting

And his way of ingratiating himself with pool hall hustlers, trailer park losers, people whose dream is beyond dead, is as moving as it is compelling

The final scenes, when Ray is attempting to pull off a massive bluff, is edge-of-the-seat stuff, you can smell the sweat that is dribbling down Ray's cheeks as he squares off against the goons of big business

It's Ray's own humanity that makes this story sparkle

Cheap whiskey, air conditioners that have to be rationed in a trailer park, and Ray's own heartfelt response to this, make the story so much more than just a mystery

As a companion piece to Big City or even an introduction to the flawed but wondrous Ray Dudgeon, it works on every level

And you know what, I think we've seen nothing yet, this is a series that is going to become one of the essential annals in PI fiction

One thing is for sure, if you read this short story, you'll run to the nearest bookstore to get hold of the novel and it might be the very best mystery you'll read this year

Sean Chercover is not only the real deal, he's a hell of a nice guy, too

That can't be fair, can it?

The least he could do is be arrogant

But no, not one iota in his whole body

He is that rarity, a writer's writer that the public loves

Does it get any better?

I was supposed to be Sean's mentor; I'm just delighted to be his friend

—Ken Bruen, Galway, February 2007

The phone on my desk rang, and I stared at it. Thinking, *Don't be so surprised; it's a phone, it's supposed to ring.*

Only my phone hadn't been ringing a lot, lately. Not since I'd taken that bodyguard job that turned into something bigger and some people ended up dead and others went to prison. They say that there's no such thing as bad publicity but they don't know what the hell they're talking about. The case generated a lot of press and I'd gotten the reputation of being stupid enough to go up against Chris Amodeo and the Chicago Outfit. And my clients melted into the ether.

Surviving a showdown against the Outfit had earned me a lot of undeserved street cred, but it didn't pay the rent. I'd been staying afloat with modest gigs like process serving, background checks, and divorces. Divorce work is bad for the soul, but when the phone is quiet you take what comes your way.

I picked up the receiver and said, "Ray Dudgeon."

"Say, Ray, how you been?"

"Good. Fine. You?"

"You know, I can't complain. But I'd be even better if you'd do a job for me."

I wasn't going to say anything about Rik losing my number for half a year. How could I blame the guy? Anyway, he was the first of my A-list clients to return and I appreciated it.

Rik's client was a librarian in Springfield. A woman in her mid-forties, single, no children. Her name was Sarah Shipman. At the end of a long vacation in Chicago, she took her car to a Juno Auto Center for an oil change and tire rotation. An hour later, she picked up the car and pointed it south on I 55. Forty miles out of the city, her right front wheel fell off and the car swerved into a bridge abutment at sixty-eight miles per hour. Something bad happened in Sarah Shipman's spinal cord and she was paralyzed from the waist down.

Obviously Juno's advertising slogan, "Done in an hour—and done right!" was only half true. The company offered $600,000 to make her go away.

"Hell, her bills are already near that," Rik said. "On top of medical, she had to have her bungalow retrofitted for a paraplegic, there's physio and occupational therapy to teach her how to live the rest of her life in that goddamned chair. And as she ages, she's going to have even more medical needs—"

"I get it, Rik. Six hundred thousand isn't enough."

"Six hundred thousand is a bad joke," Rik said. "We're asking for ten million. Which, I might add, is extremely reasonable."

Rik was an ambulance chaser, but I dig through people's garbage for a living, so he didn't have to justify himself to me. "Extremely reasonable," I said. "I wouldn't give up the use of my legs for ten million. And it's not a lot of money to avoid some nasty publicity."

"You'd think. But my client's history is somewhat less than pristine. You know, a few speeding tickets and a couple of smashups over the years. So they're challenging the accident report. Truth is, her insurance benefits have maxed out and the kindhearted bastards at Juno figure she'll fold under pressure and settle on the cheap."

Rik needed to apply pressure the other way. He needed to interview George Garcia, the mechanic who'd worked on Sarah Shipman's car. But Garcia had quit his job and his phone was disconnected. So my task was to find him and take a witness statement.

"We don't have the luxury of time," Rik concluded, "and you're the best I ever met at coaxing a witness statement, Ray." I figured the compliment was his way of apologizing for having ignored me so long. Or maybe he meant it. At the risk of sounding immodest, I am pretty good at coaxing a witness statement.

George Garcia's last known address was a trailer park in Bensenville. Situated directly under the flight path of O'Hare, it was not a quiet place to live, but everybody's got to live somewhere. Some of the trailers had little Astroturf front lawns, complete with pink plastic flamingos and folding chairs. But the late-July sun was oppressive and the chairs were empty and I didn't see a soul as I wandered around the lot. In the relative quiet between the deafening roar of planes taking off and landing, I could hear air conditioners humming. Some residents were home. These were not people who could afford to leave the AC running while they're out.

I found Garcia's double-wide and knocked on the door. Nobody answered. His air conditioner was silent. The lock was easy so I let myself in. The air inside was hot and close. Old air.

I flicked the light switch next to the door and searched the place. No towels or soap or shampoo in the bathroom, medicine cabinet bare. No clothes in the closet, drawers empty. Sweat trickled between my shoulder blades and I decided to step outside and then I heard

someone pull back the hammer of a revolver behind me.

"I'm in my rights to shoot you where you stand.
Where You Stand!" The voice was angry, or scared, or
maybe a little crazy.

I raised my hands beside my head. "Please don't point
that at me with the hammer cocked," I said evenly. I kept
my hands up and turned to face him.

He was about five foot eight, in his late fifties. His
face was full of ragged old scars. One scar began at his
hairline and ran down over his left eye and continued
on the cheekbone, all the way down to the jaw. The skin
below the eye was stretched down and a lot of pink socket
showed. Another scar ran sideways from his flattened
nose to his right ear, which was missing the lobe. He
wore a T-shirt that had once been white, stained blue
jean cutoffs, and green flip-flops. Blue tattoo art covered
his arms like sleeves. The gun was a stainless Colt .357
and it was pointed at my chest and his finger was on the
trigger. His hand shook. With the hammer cocked, there
was a distinct possibility that he might shoot me by accident.

"Please point it to one side," I said. "You can always
point it back at me if you feel the need. I'd hate for you
to make a terrible mistake." Another river of sweat ran
down my back.

"You don't give me orders!" But he pointed the gun
to one side. "I'm the property manager here. Who the
hell are you?"

"My name is Ray Dudgeon. I'm a private detective.
A lawyer hired me to find George Garcia."

"Yeah?"

"Yeah."

"You still got no right to be in here." A stream of tears erupted from his mangled left eye and ran down his cheek and tumbled onto the linoleum. He didn't seem to notice. Using only my index finger and thumb, I fished my badge from my breast pocket and held it open for him to see. Then I smirked like we were old buddies.

"Listen, why don't we go to your trailer and have a drink and I'll tell you all about it. If you don't like my story, then you can call the cops. There's a pint of bourbon in my car."

He eyed the badge for a while and then uncocked the hammer with his left thumb and lowered the gun. "Got ice in my trailer."

"Name's Phil," he said as we entered his mobile home. A thermometer by the door read 105.

"Say, you get the ice and I'll crank the old AC here—"

"Don't touch that!" he barked. "Your hooch buys some talk. It don't buy air-conditioning."

I fished a twenty out of my pocket and dropped it on the coffee table. "Twenty bucks."

"Deal," he said, and opened the freezer door. I cranked the AC to high.

"You're no pushover, Phil. I respect that. Gotta be careful, look out for yourself."

"Fuckin' *A*," said Phil. He ran his fingers through his greasy hair, wiped his hand on his back pocket, and grabbed a fistful of ice cubes. He dropped the ice in two grubby mugs and deposited the mugs on the coffee table. I poured bourbon over the greasy ice and we sat and drank. Phil outpaced my drinking three-to-one.

And he made it clear that I wasn't going to hear what he had to say about George Garcia until I'd first heard the life story of Phil the property manager.

Phil had left home at fifteen and drifted from Florida to Chicago. He became a hardcore biker—a member of the Outlaws. He was a pretty bad dude once upon a time and he offered plenty of details to make sure I believed him. But his biker days ended twelve years ago when he lost a high-speed argument with an eighteen-wheeler. Which explained the face.

Brain damage was also evident. As he spoke, his left hand occasionally flopped around on his lap like a sunfish on the deck of a boat. He didn't seem to notice. He also didn't notice when, every minute or so, he let out a loud vocal tic that sounded like, "HEEP!" I tried not to notice, either.

As it turned out, Phil was aware of the problem with his tear duct, which spilled salt water down his face every few minutes. "Fuckin' duct," he said, wiping his cheek with the back of his fish-hand. "Fuckin' bad-luck duct."

I refilled his mug and nodded at a wedding picture on the side table. "Your daughter?"

"Yeah, last time I seen her was eight years past. She got this nerd she's gonna marry, so I get ready when I hear they was comin', HEEP!" Phil opened the drawer of the side table and handed me a bullet. "See that? Read it." I inspected the bullet and found an inscription on the side of the casing: *Gavin Brooks*. Phil pointed at the photo. "So my little girl brings the nerd to meet her old man. She goes shopping and, soon as she's gone, I hand the kid that thing and tell him to look at it real close. I say, 'You ever do anything to hurt my baby girl, I'm gonna plant this slug right between your eyes. That's a promise.' HEEP! And the kid just about craps his pants." Phil laughed himself into a choking fit, got it under control, wiped his leaky eye, and swore at his malfunctioning tear duct. I handed the bullet back to him.

"And I bet he never hit your daughter," I said.

"Damn straight."

"So you're a man who understands that there's a right way and a wrong way to treat people," I said. Thinking, *Let's get on with it.* "My client represents a woman who is paralyzed from the waist down. No fault of her own, a wheel fell off her car. And George Garcia rotated her tires just an hour before the accident."

"That's a real shame," said Phil, now into his fourth bourbon. "But I don't know . . . A couple of tough guys in fancy suits come calling and suddenly George moves away. And now you. George is a good man, and I don't want to see him hurt anymore."

Tough guys in fancy suits.

"I'm not trying to hurt George," I insisted. "Juno Auto Center has plenty of liability insurance, and nobody's suing George personally."

"Not yet, anyway." Phil, the skeptic.

"That's exactly right. Not yet. And not ever, if Juno pays the claim. But so far, Juno won't pay. If George gives me a witness statement, the company will have to settle and we can put an end to this whole mess. And I'm sure he'll start sleeping better."

Phil drank some. "You talk a good game, mister."

"I'm not shitting you, Phil. This thing is moving forward, like it or not. If George won't give a statement, the court will issue a subpoena and he'll be compelled by law to testify. He runs away from it, he goes to jail. He perjures himself on the stand, he goes to jail. You say he's a good man and I believe you. He may lose his mechanic's license and he may have to find a new career. But the woman lost her legs. Giving me a statement will let him put this in the past and get on with the rest of his life."

I thought I'd closed the sale, so I just kept my mouth shut and pretended to sip bourbon and waited.

"So what's the cripple want, a hundred million or something?"

"Ten million," I said.

"Still a lot a bread."

"I wouldn't cut off my legs for ten million." I refilled his mug and watched his fish-hand flop around on his lap. And waited some more.

"Neither would I," he said finally. Salt water surged from his left eye and fell down his face. "Fuckin' duct."

Phil told me what he knew, which didn't include George Garcia's current address. I spent the next day in various government offices. I'd learned from Phil that George's wife split a few months before George quit his job. Apparently she intended the split to be permanent. I got a copy of the divorce papers she'd filed a week before the accident. Then a photocopy of George Garcia's face from his driver's license photo.

A variety of other searches came up empty. George hadn't sued anyone or been sued, he hadn't bought or sold property, he hadn't applied for a firearms permit, and no warrants had been issued for his arrest.

I stopped at my office and stuffed an envelope with two hundred dollars, the photocopy of George Garcia's picture, and the address of Sparky's Bar, in Bensenville. Phil had told me that Sparky's was Garcia's favorite local watering hole before he took off. I called Kate Barrett, a uniformed cop I knew. Kate was happy to earn some quick cash and she was on days, so her shift ended at six.

I left the envelope for Kate at the First District Station. The cop at the desk felt the need to inform me that private detectives are pathetic, bottom-feeding wannabes who make a living on other people's misery.

I thanked him for sharing.

Seven o'clock found me at Sparky's, with two pints of beer in the belly and more on the way. I'd lost thirty bucks at the pool table and gained two new buddies. Losing money at pool is an efficient way to gain new buddies who see you as a nice enough guy and a bit of a mark. Definitely not a threat.

My new buddies were Tibor and Nick. Tibor was a crazy Hungarian who looked like Sean Penn and talked like the listener was holding a stopwatch. He spent some time arguing the proposition that *Kiss Alive II* was the greatest live rock 'n' roll album of all time. Nick was a quiet chain-smoker who preferred *Get Yer Ya-Ya's Out!* I sided with Nick and proclaimed my love for the Stones.

The front door opened and Kate Barrett approached the bar and came to a stop at my immediate left. Although now off duty, she was still in uniform. Nice touch. She showed the picture of George Garcia to the bartender and the waitress, both of whom acknowledged knowing

George as a customer but professed not to know his whereabouts. Kate turned my way and handed me the picture.

"How about you, sir," she said. "You know George Garcia?"

"No, Officer," I said, "I've never seen him." I passed the photo back to Kate and she showed it to Tibor and Nick and asked them the same question. They only knew George as a fellow Sparky's regular and casual drinking buddy. She asked if any of us knew where she could find any of George's family. Nobody did. Kate thanked us all and left. So far, so good.

"Cops," I mumbled, opening the door to conversation. "You can't ask a guy's family to rat him out. That's just wrong." *Translation: I'm on George's side.*

"Right on," said Tibor.

"Unless this George guy did something really bad," I reconsidered. "Like, if he's a child molester or something." *Anybody care to defend him?*

"Wait a second," said Nick. "George ain't no child molester."

"Hey, I don't know him," I said, holding my hands up in a "no offense" gesture. "He could be the greatest guy in the world. I'm just saying, *if*."

"There is no *if*," said Tibor. "George is good people. You can ask anybody here."

"That's right," said Nick. "George is solid."

"I didn't mean anything by it," I said. "If you guys say George is good people, then I feel sorry for him, 'cause the cops will get him. That was my whole point." *Care to prove me wrong?*

"Don't bet on it," said Tibor, "unless they get the idea

to look in Indiana. Even then, George's mom has a different last name." *Bingo! You've still got the touch, Dudgeon.*

Nick shot Tibor a look and I knew it was time to change the subject. I made up a story about a friend who got convicted of a burglary even though he was innocent. Then I lost another ten dollars at the pool table and drank another beer, hoping that the subject of George Garcia would come up again. It didn't.

In addition to the two hundred dollars I'd given Kate, I'd dropped sixty dollars on beer and lost wagers. Indiana is a big state, but I considered Rik's money well spent.

The next morning, I phoned Rocky Millwood, the private detective who'd served divorce papers on George Garcia. He looked up the file and told me that he'd served George at Juno Auto Center, at 9:15 A.M. The date of service matched the date of the accident. It was possible that George had slipped out for a few drinks after getting the bad news and before working on Sarah Shipman's car. Or not.

Millwood had no idea where to look for Garcia. The only addresses he had were the trailer home and place of work.

I didn't want to visit George's estranged wife, but you go where a case leads you or you find a new line of work. So I looked up her current address from the divorce papers and arrived at her modest apartment in the early afternoon.

Betty Garcia was a mousey little thing in her mid-twenties. Everything about her—body, face, hairstyle, mannerisms—seemed vaguely pleasant and entirely forgettable. You could ride the same bus with Betty Garcia on the daily commute for five years but if someone showed you her photograph, you'd swear that you'd never seen the girl before. A great attribute for a private detective or an assassin, but Betty was neither.

We sat at a Formica table and drank instant iced tea and she told me about her marriage to George. They'd been high school sweethearts and then Betty got pregnant and they got married. George earned his mechanic's license and they moved into the trailer park. Betty assured me that they weren't "trailer trash," even though I had suggested no such thing. She explained that they had to cut corners so she could go to community college part-time. She studied marketing.

And fell for her teacher.

"George loves me and he's a good father," Betty insisted. "It's just . . . well it's kinda hard to explain. College opened up a whole new world for me. George still likes watching television, but I like *books* now. I mean, I tried to get him to improve himself, but he just wanted to do his job and play with the baby and he wasn't interested in improving himself. Whenever he did read a book, it was either a book about cars or one of those stupid novels where everybody shoots at each other. But Andrew, he's in *public relations* and he's like a genius— his apartment is full of books and not just about marketing, either. Andrew's into *philosophy,* like Plato and stuff. He's really making something of himself. Anyway, so that's what happened. It really wasn't anybody's fault. I guess you could say I just sorta *outgrew* George."

Maybe Betty was an assassin, after all.

I laid down the same line that I'd used on Phil—it was best for George to come forward and give a witness statement and get on with his life. I knew Betty would respond to the idea of George getting on with his life, and she did. But she had no idea where he was. I told her that I had reason to believe he was staying with his mother in Indiana.

"Oh, that's easy," she said. She left the room and returned with a small piece of paper. She handed me the paper, which had an address written on it. "His mom lives in Des Plaines, but she has a dumpy little cottage. It's just a shack, really, in the middle of nowhere. Rural Route 2, about fifteen miles south of Gary."

Gary, Indiana. Some people call it the armpit of America. Which is an uncharitable thing to say but, Christ, it's a sad city. Steel mills with smokestacks belching fire and the air smells like *Mom's home cooking* and potholes in the streets and downtown shops displaying boarded-up windows, padlocked doors and graffiti. Litter and vagrants and abandoned houses and the only shops thriving are the liquor stores that live on every corner like parasites feeding on despair. A city of suburban White Flight and economic gloom. A city on its knees. *God Bless America, Land of the Free and Home of the Very Fucking Brave . . .*

I passed through Gary without stopping and continued south on Highway 41. Near Cedar Lake, Rural Route 2 ran by some smaller lakes. Garcia's cottage backed onto one of them.

I passed the driveway and parked a hundred yards up the road and walked back with a six-pack of beer in my left hand. The property was thick with trees and I could just make out a one-story, wood-shingled building. Behind the cottage, the early evening sun reflected orange off the tiny lake. It was hot and humid and I'd fed about a dozen mosquitoes by the time I reached the top of the dirt driveway that led to the little house.

There was no car in evidence and no lights burned behind the screened windows. But there was no reflection off glass behind the lower half of the screens—the double-hungs were open for breeze. A good sign.

The little cottage sat on cinder blocks. I climbed four creaky wooden steps to the front door, put the beer down, and knocked. No answer. Knocked again, harder.

The door opened and George Garcia stood before me with a week's worth of stubble on his tanned face. His orange T-shirt had an R. Crumb cartoon on the chest, with the slogan KEEP ON TRUCKIN'. He smelled like Brut antiperspirant and body odor, in equal measure. He was long overdue for a haircut and he looked like he hadn't slept in a month.

"Whatever it is, we're not buying any," he said and started to close the door. I stopped it with my right foot.

"I'm not selling anything George," I said, "except maybe a clear conscience." He disappeared inside and I picked up the six-pack and followed him in.

We sat on threadbare furniture and I put the beer on the coffee table between us. Next to me was a floor lamp made from an old rifle. I turned it on. The wood paneling behind George sported a needlepoint wall-hanging that depicted a flotilla of ducks. Mallards. There was an old

cast-iron woodstove at the end of the room and a doorway led to the kitchen. No door, just a doorway with a
painted plaster crucifix hanging above. Looking into the
kitchen, I could see about a dozen gallon jugs of water
lined up on the counter. The place had no running
water.

It was hot inside the cottage but not as bad as Phil's
trailer. The place smelled musty, like my grandfather's
house in Georgia. I always loved that smell.

George plucked a bottle from the six-pack. He twisted
the cap and took a swig and said, "The cops on TV don't
bring beer, so I guess I'm not under arrest."

"You're not under arrest," I said, "and I'm not a cop.
But if you keep running from this thing, there will be
cops soon enough. They definitely won't bring beer."
Then I explained subpoenas and bench warrants and the
perils of perjury. I explained that giving a witness statement might motivate Juno to settle and George might
spare himself the trauma of testifying in a courtroom.
He drank two bottles of beer and smoked half a dozen
cigarettes during my sales pitch. When I talked about
Sarah Shipman and how she'd lost the use of her legs,
the cigarette in his hand trembled and his eyes welled
up, so I closed on the morality angle. "Everybody tells
me you're a good man, George. Phil, Tibor, Nick,
Betty . . . everybody. It's time to do the right thing."

He covered his eyes with his left hand and exhaled
hard through his nose. I opened a new beer and handed
it to him and opened one for myself. I took a mini-
cassette tape recorder from my pocket, pressed record,
and placed it on the table between us.

"You don't understand, man," he said. "I can't. The

lawyers from Juno, they put a lot of pressure on." The
tape was recording and I didn't stop it. He lit a new cigarette and now I wanted one, too. I took a swig of beer
instead. Thinking, *Two months without a smoke, Dudgeon, don't blow it now.*

"The lawyers from Juno . . . ," I nudged.

"Yeah, see, they told me to move out of state. They're
giving me enough cash to buy food. They said they'll
get me a job at a Juno Auto Center in another state, when
the lawsuit is over. California, maybe. All I have to do
is stay here for a year or so and keep my head down,
they said. I didn't know what else to do."

I glanced at the crucifix hanging above the doorway
and said, "Don't sell your soul, George."

"It's not the money. These men are very bad. They
come by every Monday to give me my week's pay, but
really just to check on me. If I back out . . . and they
carry guns." He took a long pull on the beer.

"I appreciate your honesty, and we can protect you.
Just give a statement and you can come with me. We'll
make sure they don't find you." George Garcia drained
the rest of the bottle and stared into space for a while.
Then he nodded his head.

On the morning of the accident, Rocky Millwood
served George with Betty's divorce papers. George
hadn't gone out drinking. He stayed at work and did his
job. But he was an emotional wreck and he couldn't con-
centrate. Images of Betty and their child flooded his
mind and he spent the day fighting back tears. With a
knot in his gut, he went through the motions of his job
on autopilot.

"Honestly, I don't even remember working on the

car," he said. "I'm sure I did and I'm sure I fucked up somehow, but I don't remember. The whole day is a fog, after the divorce papers." He reached for a new beer. "I shoulda taken the day off, even if they fired me. I shouldn'ta been working. That poor woman . . . I'm just so very sorry." Tears ran down George Garcia's face and he let them run.

I found some paper towels in the kitchen and brought the roll back to him. He wiped his face and blew his nose. I asked him a few more questions and he answered them and I clicked stop on the recorder.

"Okay, George, you did very well," I said. "Let's get out of here."

He shook his head. "My mom's coming by in the morning. If I'm gone, she'll worry."

"Tomorrow's Monday. You said Juno's goons come on Mondays. Leave her a note."

"No, I have to speak to her . . . explain things. She'll be here at eight. Come back at nine and I'll go with you."

"You don't want to risk them showing up."

"It's okay," said George, with a failed attempt at a smile. "They never come before noon. Just make sure you're not late. I have to say good-bye to my mom."

A waning gibbous moon above and Bob Dylan's *Nashville Skyline* on the stereo made the drive back to Chicago tolerable. I sang along with Bob to chase George Garcia's sadness away and arrived at my office just after midnight.

I transcribed the witness statement from the audio-tape into my computer. I made sure to include the

coercion by Juno's legal department. Of course they'd
deny it, but with the implied threat of a criminal investigation, a quick settlement was Rik's for the taking. I
printed out the statement and emailed a copy to Rik's
office, feeling pretty pleased with myself. *Three days to
find a witness who was hiding in another state and
didn't want to be found. Not too shabby.*

But the congratulatory pep talk was impotent and
George's sadness returned and I had a hankering to
drink myself to sleep. A bad idea. I tried to focus on just
one of the multiple streams of thought that clamored for
my attention. The voices in my head were doing just fine
without any help from me, so I finally gave up and let
them fight it out amongst themselves. As I sat there,
George Garcia's sadness grew and morphed into Sarah
Shipman's sadness. And mine. And everyone's.

We encounter people like George and Sarah and Phil
(and even Betty) and we say to ourselves: *There but for
the grace of God go I.* Then we are self-satisfied. Look
how grateful we are, not taking our good fortune for
granted. Look how virtuous. We pity George and Sarah
and we wallow in our gratitude, because pity and gratitude reinforce the illusion of a great distance between
us and *them.* We avoid that other thought. The thought
that goes: *Better him than me.* Because we're all just one
bad decision from being George Garcia. One serving
of bad luck from being Sarah Shipman.

And there are nights when the proximity is impossible to ignore. This night, the choice was insomnia or
booze and I had a big day tomorrow so I chose tired
instead of hungover. And made it to bed relatively
sober.

* * *

I pulled into the dusty driveway at 8:50 A.M. No other cars on the property. Which meant George's mom had already come and gone, or she was late . . . or George had been lying to me. The cottage door was unlocked and I let myself in.

The smell of feces and fear told me all I needed to know. George's body lay on the couch, an empty bottle of cheap vodka at his side. He'd opened his wrists with a hunting knife, which lay on his chest. The cushions had absorbed a lot of blood and there was a large puddle, dark and viscous, on the floor beneath his right arm, which hung off the side of the couch. Flies congregated around the blood puddle, like greedy tourists at a Vegas buffet.

There was a note: "Tell the lady I'm sorry about her legs." Signed, "George S. Garcia, Jr."

I snatched up George's cigarettes and lighter and marched outside and lit a smoke and took a deep drag and got a head rush. I paced back and forth from the cottage to my car, thinking, *You've got a dead witness, an unsigned statement, and an unverifiable recording of that statement.* Thinking, *You idiot, why did you leave him alone?* Thinking, *You've still got the touch, Dudgeon . . . not too shabby. Fuck.*

I called Rik Ransom and his secretary heard the tone of my voice and put me straight through.

"I just read the email," said Rik. "Really nice job on the statement, Ray. Outstanding. You may have earned a bonus."

"Things are complicated," I said.

"Complicated how?"

"Trust me, you do not want to know. Just call Juno and read them the statement. Tell them that we have George Garcia in a safe place and he is no longer under their control." Another drag on the cigarette. "And Rik, time is of the essence. We're expecting some thugs from Juno this afternoon."

"So get out of there."

"Can't. And don't ask."

"You're serious," he said.

"Deadly. Look, I know this isn't normal procedure. You're the lawyer and I'm just the keyhole-peeper but you've got to trust me on this, no questions." There was silence on the line.

"All right, Ray. If you say it's complicated, then it's complicated." He cleared his throat. "We go back a ways, you and me. But I have to be frank with you. A rumor went around, after the Amodeo thing . . ."

"Yes."

"Rumor was, you'd become a little unhinged. Maybe more than a little."

I had no idea how to answer that. "It was blown out of proportion, Rik. I'm telling you, I'm acting in your best interest here. Right now you really don't want to know the details, and you'll thank me later."

"I see." Another protracted silence. "Okay, I'm going to follow you on this, Ray."

"Just make the deal fast and call me when it's done."

They rolled up well before noon, in a dark blue Lincoln Continental. The Lincoln pulled into the dirt driveway and came to a stop about fifteen feet in front of me. I held my position—sitting on the top step, cell phone to my left. Pistol in my right hand, pointing casually at the ground about six feet in front of me. They got out of the Lincoln and closed the doors.

Tough guys in fancy suits.

The taller one was a trim six four and pumped iron a couple times a week, I guessed. The shorter one was about six feet and looked like a poster child for steroid abuse. Probably weighed in at a hard 260. I'm five nine. You could call it almost five ten with my shoes on. I weigh about 170. With my shoes on.

But there was a gun in my hand, while they both clutched handfuls of moist air.

"Hi, fellas," I said with a neutral tone. "My name's Ray. I'm a licensed private detective and I've been retained as Mr. Garcia's bodyguard. Mr. Garcia does not wish to have any visitors, and you're on private property. Please leave."

"And if we don't?" said Shorty. His eyes gleamed with a hunger that said he wanted this thing to escalate. But Stretch sent him a glare and I got the picture. Stretch was the boss—maybe Juno's resident tough-guy lawyer. Shorty was a paid goon, probably had some fancy title like "Vice President of Corporate Security."

"Listen, Ray," said Stretch with a rubber-band mouth. "We need to speak with Mr. Garcia. Five minutes and we're gone. History. Out of your hair." He gave me a rubber-band smile and they took a step forward in unison and I raised the gun and pointed it at Stretch and said, "Hands!"

They stopped in unison and raised their hands slightly. They were now a dozen feet—*four quick steps*—away. They'd gained three feet and all they'd given up

was about five inches distance from hand to gun. If
they had guns.

"You're bluffing," said Stretch. I admired his ability
to hold my eyes. Not because my eyes are particularly
intimidating but because when someone points a gun at
you, the urge to stare at the gun can be overwhelming.

"Yeah," said Shorty, "you ain't gonna shoot." His
right leg moved forward a few inches.

"You'll be first," I said to Stretch. Thinking, *Goddamn, this sucks.*

"Stand down," Stretch said to Shorty. A quick glance
at a duly admonished Shorty, standing down as ordered.
Eyes back to Stretch.

"As I said, you'll be first. Whatever happens after that
probably won't make you feel a whole lot better." This
was tough-guy talk, which is not really my strong suit.
I wondered how I was doing. Stretch had lost a half inch
off his smile and now he put it back but it looked unnatural.

"All right," Stretch said, "but we need to hear it from
Mr. Garcia."

Shorty cupped his hands to his mouth and called,
"Hey Georgie, you want us to go? Just come to the window and say the word and we're gone, buddy!"

"He won't come," I said. *Truer words were never
spoken.* "Look, guys . . . we all know that either one of
you could kick my ass around the block without breaking a sweat. That's why I'll have to fire first." I added
my left hand to my right, holding the pistol in a Weaver
stance. "So you have to leave the property now, or I'll
be forced to defend my client." My mouth wouldn't

smile even if I bribed it, so I didn't bother trying. I just sat there, thinking, *This is taking too long . . .*

Stretch made his decision and, by virtue of some sort of goon telepathy, they both stepped back and opened their doors in unison. "We'll just park on the road over there," Stretch jerked a long thumb toward the road about fifty feet away.

"Fine," I said, "you guys hang out over there and call your boss. I'll hang here and call mine. I expect you'll get instructions to leave but maybe I'm wrong. We'll see. Meantime, as long as you're on the public road we're cool."

"We'll let you know what happens," said Stretch.

"I'm sure you will."

They got in the car and backed out of the driveway and parked on the road, blocking the drive. I let the gun point at the ground and forced my hand to relax a bit, to keep circulation to the fingers. I took a few deep breaths, picked up the cell phone, and dialed Rik Ransom.

"It's Dudgeon," I said. "Got company over here. Two very bad men from Juno. I need you to speed things along."

"Jesus, Ray. Don't get killed."

"Doing my best. How much longer?"

"I'm waiting for a call back. They're stalling."

"Until they hear from Stretch, I suspect." Back at the car, Stretch held a cell phone to his ear. "Rik, they're calling it in. Get ready now and make this deal fast."

"Why don't you just get outta there? You've got the signed statement."

"I didn't say it was signed."

"Well get the fucker to sign it . . ." There was a pause on the line. "Oh shit. Don't tell me—"

"I didn't tell you anything. Just work fast. Shorten the deadline." Stretch closed his flip phone. "He's off the phone. If they don't call in a minute or two, you call them." I hung up and nodded at Stretch. He nodded back at me.

And we waited. I was glad to be waiting outside. Inside, I'd have to watch the strange spasmodic slow-motion rigor mortis dance. And smell the exotic perfumes of decay. By comparison, Stretch and Shorty were good company. So I just sat in the hot sun, feeding mosquitoes and waiting for the phone to ring.

An hour and forty minutes later, Stretch got out of the car and walked toward me. I stood and moved off the steps, keeping him between me and Shorty. I aimed at his chest and he held his hands up at about shoulder height but didn't stop. My sweat-covered forearms reflected the afternoon sun. "Far enough," I said at about twenty feet. He stopped.

"We're all professionals, doing our jobs here," he said.

"Right."

"Good. See, my associate needs some toilet paper."

"You are kidding me," I said.

"Swear to God," he said and smiled, almost like a real person.

I felt my own mouth smile. "Really?"

"Hey, don't rub it in." He jerked his thumb back toward the car. "He's gonna be hearing about this for a very long time, I promise you."

"Well, I hate to give you an even better story to tell,

but there's a gas station a few miles up. He can leave you on the road and come back, or you can both go and come back. Best I can do."

"Come on, have a heart. Do it for my sake, I gotta sit in the car with the guy." The rubber-band smile returned and sent me into high alert.

"Sorry, no." I held the gun steady. *Wait him out . . .* We stared lovingly into each other's eyes for a millennium or two.

"You're Ray Dudgeon, right?"

"I am."

"You didn't say so earlier."

"Would it have scared you away?"

"No."

"Didn't think so."

Stretch shrugged and his smile faded. "Thought you'd be taller," he said.

"I'm not."

"No. You're not." He turned around and walked back to the car and got in. I returned to my position on the top step.

Another fifty minutes trickled by while I sat there, sweating and feeding even more mosquitoes. It was in the upper nineties and the T-shirt was now plastered to my back. The Juno boys sat in air-conditioned luxury in their Lincoln Continental. *Pussies.*

The cell phone rang and I answered it.

"Ray, we did it! Whoo-boy, we did it!"

"Close to ten million?"

"Hell, we passed ten an hour ago. Naturally, with our newfound strength, I raised the bar to fifteen this morning. We settled on twelve."

"Done deal?"

"Like dinner. Notarized faxes have been exchanged and couriers have been dispatched with originals. We're official."

"Then why haven't my friends heard the good news?"

"Oh, shit. I thought they'd be long gone by now. That's terrible, Ray. Really sorry about that. I'll make a call."

"Sure would appreciate it," I said, and broke the connection.

Ten minutes passed and then Stretch answered his flip phone and listened and bobbed his head. He flipped the phone shut and Shorty reached down and put the car in gear without looking in my direction. Stretch nodded at me. I held up my hand and nodded back. The car pulled away, down the dusty road and out of sight. I picked up the cell phone and dialed 911.

I'd just found a dead body and it was my duty to report it.

Prodigal Me
by J. T. Ellison

•

Women are great crime writers. They always have been, and for a long time now they have set the agenda and driven the genre. All my favorite writers are women. Why? Are they better writers than men? Not exactly, but somehow they develop nuance and context more effortlessly. Check out this story by J. T. Ellison. It's a classic short, with a great payoff twist in the final paragraphs. But watch how J. T. paints the feel, the context, the background, with deft, subtle, unforced strokes. That's not just talent—it's talent plus total self-confidence, which is a truly winning combination.

—Lee Child,
New York Times bestselling author of
One Shot

He's not speaking to me again.

It's happened before. I think the longest we've ever gone without some sort of verbal communication is two weeks. But that was back when he thought I'd tricked him and let myself get pregnant. I hadn't, but he didn't want to hear that from me. I remember it was two weeks because when I started to bleed, he started talking.

Apologies, for the most part. The black eye had faded away by then, too.

So I don't usually become alarmed when he quits conversing. I'm just not sure why I'm getting the silent treatment. I wonder how long it's going to last? It can actually be quite nice, not having to make conversation. We can sit at the kitchen table, each sipping from our respective coffee cups. I have many cups. I decide which to use based on my mood each morning. Today I have one of my favorites, decorated in loops and swirls of color, abstract, joyful. That's how I woke this morning, content, but feeling a bit out of place. This was the perfect chalice to represent my feelings. Yesterday it was the bone white with the geometric triangular handle. All sharp edges and uncomfortable to hold. No elegance there, befitting the dark nastiness that I'd felt when I got up. But today was different. Better. Happy. Even without speech.

I watched him from under my lashes, tasting the bitter brew. He'd made the coffee before I arose. He'd been doing that lately, and it was unusual. Normally I was the first to the kitchen, the coffee was my responsibility. I certainly made a better pot. I wondered if that was why he'd designated the coffee to me in the first place, because his was lousy.

He was snapping the pages of the paper, passing through them so quickly that I knew he wasn't really reading anything. He knew I was watching him, and he heaved a sigh and laid the paper flat on the wood. He looked at me then, finally. His eyes were bloodshot. Not attractive at all. When we'd first met, he'd had the most beautiful blue eyes, a shade that matched the sky on a crisp fall day. Today, they were muddy, a hint of brown in the azure depths. He didn't meet my eye, just stared at my shoulder. I slid my silk dressing gown down just a bit, enough for the smooth white skin above my collarbone to show. He dragged in a breath, swept up his cup and threw it at the kitchen sink. It shattered, and I rolled my eyes. Typical for him, communicating through violence. For a smart man, he was so very stupid.

I glanced at the clock on the stove; it was well past time for him to leave for work. I sat back in my chair, ignoring him. The sooner he was out of here, the sooner I could clean up his mess and start my own day.

He didn't leave right away. He'd walked out of the kitchen right after his temper tantrum, but went into his study instead of heading out the front door. He generally preferred that I stay out of his study. Even our maid, Marie-Cecile, was only allowed in twice a week to vacuum and dust, but she was never allowed to touch the desk proper. Those were his rules, and Marie-Cecile stuck by them faithfully, even while she muttered Haitian curses under her breath. It always gave me joy to see her in there, hexing him for his transgressions.

It struck me that I hadn't noticed Marie-Cecile's car in the drive. She came every day at 9:00 A.M. like clockwork, with Sundays off. With a house this size, you have to have someone to help with the work. Besides, all of our friends had someone come in. Personally, Marie-Cecile was the best of the lot, but perhaps I'm bragging.

Today was Thursday, and it was already 9:30 A.M. Normally, I'd be at the club; my Tuesday/Thursday golf group would be teeing off between seven and nine. I'd slept later than usual, and I wasn't in the mood to play this morning. I'd join them for lunch instead.

I set about making the kitchen right, wondering where Marie-Cecile was. Not like her to be tardy, to miss a day without letting me know in advance she wouldn't be here. She'd only done that about three times in the three years she'd been cleaning for us. Very reliable, was Marie-Cecile. No matter. I was certainly capable of straightening up. The cup had been made of heavy fired clay, and though it had broken into about fourteen pieces, they weren't shards and slivers, but well-formed chunks that made it a cinch to gather. That done, I wandered back to our bedroom.

Sunlight spilled through the windowpane, enhancing the patina on the buttery walls. I'd designed this room myself. The decorator had commandeered the house, overloading the rooms with her personal touches, but I wanted one small place that I knew was mine, and mine alone. Guests didn't get to venture into this part of the house anyway. It was my own little refuge, even more so now that he was sleeping in his study. Eight bedrooms, and he chooses a hobnailed leather sofa. To each his own.

The bed wasn't made, which was odd. I knew I'd put it together before I made my way downstairs this morning. I always do. It's the first thing that happens when I wake up. I slide out the right edge, pull the covers up, and make the bed. Maybe he had come back into the room after I went downstairs, pulled the covers back to tick me off. Typical.

I made up the bed, humming to myself. That's when I found the hair. It was his, there was no question about it. I must have had too much to drink last night. He'd slept in the bed with me, and I didn't even remember.

Perhaps that was the cause of his silence. Things hadn't gone as well as he'd hoped?

It's hard to explain, but he does come to me, in the night. I let him, mostly because it's my duty to perform, but also in remembrance of a time when I welcomed him without thought, joyful that he'd chosen to be with me. It wasn't that long ago, after all.

Bed made, I showered and dressed in khaki slacks and a long-sleeved Polo shirt. I threw a button-down over my shoulders in case it was still cool out. Layers for my comfort, layers for their perception of how I should look when I walked into the club. The official dress code was undiluted preppy.

He was gone when I passed the study on my way to the front foyer.

It was not meant to be my morning. My Jag wouldn't start. And Marie-Cecile was nowhere to be found, so I didn't have a ride. We lived on the golf course though, so I detoured through the fourteenth fairway and wandered up the cart path on the eighteenth. We're not supposed to do that, but I timed it well—after the ladies' group had finished and before the seniors' group made the first turn.

I arrived at the front doors a little breathless, more from the chill than the exercise. I'm in good shape. As his wife, I have to be. It's expected. Not much of a challenge for me, I'm naturally tall and willowy, but I still work with a trainer three times a week. Like I said, it's expected.

My friends and I have a standing luncheon on Tuesdays and Thursdays. After our round, we gather in the Grill Room, settle our bets, eat some salad, and gossip.

Some of the older ladies play bridge. I've always wanted to learn, I just haven't gotten around to it. There is something so lonely about them, sitting in their Lilly Pulitzer capris, their visors still pulled low, shading their eyes from the glare of the multitudes of sixty-watt bulbs. Sad.

My usual foursome was sitting along the back wall today. Bunny (that's actually her name, I've seen the birth certificate) had the farthest spot, the place of honor. Back to the wall, viewable by the whole room. My spot. She lounged against the arm of the chair, her feet propped on the empty seat facing the window. My punishment for missing the round this morning, I suppose. Bunny glistened with the faint flush of exertion. She always looked like she'd just rolled out of bed, freshly plucked and glowing. No wonder there, she was sleeping with half the married men in the club, as well as most of the tennis and golf pros. Probably a couple of the high school caddies and college kids, too.

Tally and Kim rounded out the threesome, both looking a little peaked. Tally was short and brunette, a striking contrast to Bunny's wholesome blondness. Kim was blond, a little dishwater, but since she'd moved to Bunny's hairdresser, she'd been getting some subtle highlights that worked for her complexion. Kim was fiddling with her scorecard, probably erasing a couple of shots. We all knew she cheated. We let her.

Tally sat with her back barely touching the chair, ramrod straight. Uncharacteristic for her, she usually slouched and sprawled like the rest of us. The chairs were suede-lined and double width for our comfort, and they served their purpose well.

I approached the table, expecting Bunny to see me

and drop her feet off my newly assigned chair. Instead, she was talking about me. I stopped, indignant. They hadn't even noticed I came in. She was so caught up with whatever maliciousness she'd intended for the day that she didn't realize I was standing barely five feet away. I could hear her clearly. Talking about me. Gossiping about me. That little bitch. I started for her, then stopped. Maybe I'd eavesdrop a little more, see what I could use against them later.

Don't get me wrong, I'm not naïve enough to think that a group of women friends aren't going to talk to one another about the missing person. But there's a big difference between talking about a friend who's absent and publicly dissecting that friend's life. We're all *somebody*, the four of us. Which means that there are multitudes of fodder, plenty of grist for the communal mill. There are some things that are sacred, though, and an open discussion of my disastrous marriage is one of them. You just don't do that.

I started toward the table again, ready to give Miss Bunny a walloping with the side of my tongue. A short frizzled blonde with mismatched socks beat me. Damn. Shirley.

Shirley was one of those people. You know the ones I mean. Not to be mean, but they drift around the periphery of any tight-knit group, waiting like a dog for the table scraps. Shirley wanted to be a part of our group, but that would never happen. She was just too annoying. Yet Bunny's face lit up when she saw the diminutive disaster headed to the table. She swung her feet off the chair, rose like Amphitrite from the depths, and hugged Shirley. Physical contact with a barnacle? That was well known to be strictly forbidden. What in the hell was going on today?

I had become persona non grata without a clue as to why. No one would look at me, each woman kept her eyes from mine. Busboys and waiters wandered right past me, no one asking to help me, no one offering me a refreshment. After my long walk to the clubhouse, I could have used a nice Chardonnay. That was it. It was time I let my presence be known to my so-called friends.

I glided to the table, mouth slightly open, deciding which opening I'd use. *Hello girls, waiting for me? You lousy bitches, how dare you speak about me behind my back? Bunny, you look divine today—whose sperm are you carrying? Kim, I think you need a quick trip to Alberto's. And Tally, darling, do try to sit back, you look like you've got a pole stuck up your ass.*

But all my words died in my throat when I saw what Shirley had brought as an offering to my group of friends. The newspaper unfurled, bearing a special edition logo, the headline seventy point. GUILTY, it screamed.

I stormed through the house, looking. How dare he. How could he do it? What was he thinking?

I wasn't finding what I was looking for. I needed to stop and think. I was in a black rage, I couldn't even see straight when I was this worked up. So I sat on the bottom step and took a few breaths. That helped.

My husband was not a foolish man. He wouldn't have left a trail, or a bunch of clues. I had all night to search. The rest of my life, if it was necessary. I'd start in the obvious place. The basement.

I'd had a very difficult time reading the article Shirley had brought to my friends in gleeful attribution. She was a lawyer, one of the few women in our circle that actually worked for a living. A prosecutor, at that. Assistant District Attorney Shirley Kleebel. She paid her dues, if you know what I mean. She wasn't married to or aligned with a man of the club. *She* was the member, one of the few singles to join. That's part of the reason she'd never make it into the right circles. We had nothing to gain by being around her. Really, even meek and mild Tally had her signature on the checking account of the largest footwear mogul in the country. Shirley had nothing, except her name.

So I'd been a bit skeptical when I'd read the article. If I'm being totally honest, I didn't believe it. Not that it was outside the realm of possibility. My husband could be vicious when he chose.

It lauded Shirley as a genius, having resurrected a trial that was not only lost before it began, but achieving a guilty plea from the jury. I ran the article over and over in my head as I searched. According to the reporter, this had been done already. Several fruitless times, in fact.

But it's a big house. There are places no one would think to look simply because they wouldn't know they were there. Passages between floors with unseen staircases, a tunnel in the basement that accessed the freestanding garage. Escape routes. I thought them charming when we'd bought the house, then put them out of my mind. Now, I needed to comb through them, because I knew I'd find the truth in one of those dark, dank places.

Either way, he won't be coming home tonight. There won't be any more arguments, no broken coffee cups, no unmade beds. The bed. He'd slept in the bed last night. And he'd cried. I remember that now. He sobbed winningly, and told me how sorry he was. That he'd never meant for it to go so far. That he loved me, he truly did. He'd cried himself to sleep, then gotten up in the middle of the night and wandered away. I hadn't understood last night. Now, I think I did. But I'd have to see for myself.

The basement reeked pleasantly of cool and damp. I sensed nothing unusual, no odors, no sights that gave me cause for alarm. I crept around the corner, slipping silently through the gloom. If what the article said were true, if my friends' gossip was accurate, I'd have ages to find all of the little passageways in this house. I think there's one that goes all the way up to the clubhouse, but I've never found it.

The one I did know about was just ahead. A false wall, easily misleading without the exact knowledge of where it should be. If you looked closely, you could see a crack in the foundation, like the floor was settling. The fracture ran up the wall, and if you pushed just the right brick . . .

There, the wall swung open to reveal a small passageway. When the house was built, over two hundred years ago, the original owner wanted to be buried in the house. That's right, in the house. The crypt was the logical place to look.

I couldn't describe the emotions I felt when I saw it. It had been a sloppy job. He knew no one would ever find their way in here by accident. He thought he was safe.

So pale. I'd always loved my hands, long-fingered,

smooth-skinned. Sticking up out of the dirt, though, they didn't look quite as nice.

The article said it was Marie-Cecile that testified against him. She'd seen it all. Seen his hands around my throat. I wonder why I didn't remember that part.

Son of a bitch. I hope he rots in jail.

Maybe I'll go visit him.

The Only Word I Know
in Spanish
by Patry Francis

•

When I read Patry Francis's debut novel, *Liar's Diary,* last year, I knew that this was a book worth savoring, and a writer worth my absolute attention. Now she writes a very different story, about violence and young men and what guilt can do to a boy when he thinks too long and hard on what he's done. Once again, Ms. Francis demonstrates that she's one of those rare writers who not only knows how to tell a story, she knows how to tunnel deep into our emotions.

—Tess Gerritsen,
author of *The Bone Garden*

It all started with a crime I didn't commit. But could have. I mean, I've done similar shit in the past; I just never got caught. But that's irrelevant, right? This time, when the cops dragged me and a couple of my friends in and beat the crap out of us, I was totally innocent. From what I hear, a bunch of kids lost it on some old guy who was trying to make a living selling Puerto Rican food on the street. You know—chicken and rice. That crispy flatfish they eat. I've had it before myself; it tastes like their cooking grease, but otherwise it's not bad. Okay, maybe I was in the vicinity. But my friends and me, we were what you call innocent bystanders. Spectators. Kind of like those people who used to hang out at the Coliseum waiting for the show.

At first, they just called him a few names, told him to take his grease wagon elsewhere. Then they circled the block, giving him a chance to disappear. They'd had a few beers by then. Probably some other stuff, too. When they came back and found he was still there—a skinny old man folded over his little flame . . . Well, that's when they got seriously pissed. It wasn't anything personal; they just wanted him off their streets, out of their sight. But no matter how loud they got, the old man just ignored them. It was like they didn't even exist. The next thing you know, they had kicked over his stupid little cart. And then they were kicking him, too.

I was standing a couple of rows back, but somehow the old man on the sidewalk found me and looked right into my eyes like he knew me. Like he'd always known me and always would. I can't describe it, but there was so much sorrow in those eyes, it went right through me. Not hate, not even pain—just sorrow. "Let's get out of here," I said to my friend, O'Toole. I mean, why was the guy looking at me? Out of all the people on that street, he has to stare at me?

I was down on Station Avenue, shooting hoops with O'Toole and Ryan Dawson when the cruiser showed up. From nowhere, the cops are all over us. Talking about this guy—this Mr. Reyes. According to the cops, the guy was down at City Hospital getting his head X-rayed as we spoke. And the worst part about it, this pig who's slamming us into walls, calling us project scum and shit like that, has family in the Heights himself. Officer Monahan, his name tag said. My brother, Chip, actually used to hang out with this Officer Monahan's cousin. They're Irish like me and O'Toole, probably with something else mixed in, the way everyone is these days. But still, there ought to be some loyalty.

That's what Ma says anyway; she remembers the days and all that. I stared up at that name tag from the floor, thinking that if you changed a few letters, his name was the same as mine: Moran. I know it was a funny thing to be thinking about at a moment like that, but after you take a few good kicks to the head, you start getting a lot of strange shit jumping around in your head.

It was all over pretty fast. A few hours later, they put us in the lineup, and the street vendor—that Mr. Reyes the pigs kept yelling at us about—said we were the wrong kids. Monahan was practically screaming at the old man by the time he got through with him. We could hear him from the other room where they were holding us just in case Mr. Reyes wanted to take another look. "The kind of beating you took, and you're going to let these kids walk?" he said, like he wanted to whip the old man's ass himself. "You mean to say you're going to let these punks get away with it?"

The old man's voice was so low that even with his ear against the wall, O'Toole couldn't hear a thing. But I heard it clear as could be, even with the accent. "Can I go home now?" the old man said over and over, like he was the one locked up instead of us. For some reason, I was desperate to get a look at the old man's face. To make sure he was okay. But I never did. Still, when I think about him, the way I do sometimes right before I go to sleep, I can see his face perfectly. Especially those eyes. *Los ojos.* I don't know why, but it's the only word I remember from Spanish class.

Anyway, if it weren't for my mother, that would have been it. Three kids get knocked around a little down at the station, and then tossed back out on the street. Kind of thing happens every day; that's what Dawson said. Afterward, we went out and got ourselves totally wasted, figuring we deserved it. And that should have been the end of it. *But not with good old Ma around.* You'd have to know my mother to understand. It's like the lady sits around her whole life just waiting for a chance to get even. With who or for what—it doesn't really matter, as long as she gets even. Naturally, when she saw my face in the bright light of the kitchen, there was no way she was going to let it drop. Mrs. O'Toole and Ryan's foster parents? They looked at their kids' bruises, shook their heads, and went back to their beers. Probably figured they could use a beating or two whether they needed it or not. But not Ma.

I spent most of the weekend avoiding her, passed out on someone's living room floor. The kid's name was Dougie and I guess Ryan knew his sister. Anyway, his mother was over at her boyfriend's house or something, so we had the apartment to ourselves all weekend. When I woke up Monday morning, it took me a few minutes to remember where I was.

Picture it: there I am laying on someone's dirty rug, picking dog hairs off my T-shirt, feeling like shit, and I'm trying to come up with some story to tell my mother. Even though half the time she doesn't bother to ask.

Sometimes when I hear her talking to the other mothers out in the parking lot, she says she's been through all this shit with Chip before, and he used up all the good stories. I couldn't come up with anything original if I tried.

But this time, when the only thing I really want in the whole world is to be left alone, Ma practically comes running down the walk to meet me. "Where the hell have you been?" she's screaming right in front of this whole pack of little kids who are lined up waiting for the ice cream truck. Course, kids in our neighborhood are so used to people yelling, they don't even bother to look. Not unless the blood starts flowing. My mother takes my face in her hands like it's some kind of specimen, turning it this way and that, poking at the bruises, the cut on my lip. I push her hand away.

"I'm tired, Ma," I tell her.

But of course, Ma's having none of that. "I bet you're tired," she says, her touch turning rough. "How do you think I feel? I haven't had a moment's sleep all weekend."

I was about to ask her why the hell not, maybe mention that I'm gone almost every weekend, and she usually sleeps just fine. But instead, I duck into the room I used to share with Chip. It's all mine now—ever since Chip's girlfriend had a kid and they decided to get a place together. All I want is a chance to bury myself in sleep. With luck, I can sleep till three o'clock when Ma leaves for her job at the nursing home. And by the time she gets home at eleven, I'll be out again.

Most of the time it's an arrangement that works pretty well for both of us. But as soon as I hit my room, I see my clothes laying across my bed. A pair of khakis and a white shirt I haven't seen since I made my Confirmation.

"What—are we going to church?" I say to Ma who has followed me into my room, and is standing there with her arms folded across her massive chest. "Is it a Holy Day of Obligation or something?" It's a joke, because neither Ma nor I have set foot in the church since the day of Confirmation. After pushing church on us all those years, Ma all of a sudden decides the place is full of phonies, and the priests are all perverts anyway. She says they're just lucky none of them ever laid a hand on Chip or me when we were altar boys, or you can bet she would have made them pay.

"Just get dressed, wiseass," Ma says. "We're going down to the court-house."

So there I am, hungover, my face sore as hell from the way Ma pressed her thumbs into the bruises, and I'm aching for sleep. "The courthouse?" I say. "I told you I didn't do anything. They dropped the charges, I told you."

I hate the way my heart is starting to pound at the mention of the courthouse. And the worst part is I know if it were Chip, he wouldn't even blink. Even when he got sentenced to six months a couple years ago, he just stood there with his hands in his pockets, smiling. All he'd needed was a beer, and he would have looked like he was hanging out in the courtyard with his friends. Like it was a summer day, music blasting, nothing special going on.

"Damn right, you didn't do anything; that's the point," Ma says. She's going through my drawers by then, firing clean socks and underwear at me. "They messed with the wrong kid this time, Cody. *The wrong family.* That trashy Monahan and his buddies, they're not going to get away with it. Now get yourself dressed and looking respectable."

Ma's eyes look so angry that for a moment I think she's planning for us to go downtown and kick the shit out of those cops ourselves. Or maybe she's got a gun concealed under her aide uniform. But then that word "respectable" sinks in; and I understand. She intends to beat them at their own game. File a few charges of our own—police brutality, false arrest, or just generally being assholes—anything that will stick.

A couple days later, Ma's got the night off, and she makes me go to the grocery store with her so I can carry the bags. Says her back is killing her from work. So what else is new? Anyway, when we get home, Chip is sitting in our living room working on a can of malt. From the pile of empties on the coffee table, it looks like he's been there for a while. Course, right away Ma knows what's going on.

"I hope you don't think you can come running back here every time you and Allison have an argument," she says. She's putting away the food by then, slamming the cans and bottles around the way she always does when Chip is home.

"It's a little more than an argument this time, Ma," Chip says, after finishing off his malt in one long swig. "It's over. Allison and I are done."

Ma stands in the doorway between the kitchen and the living room. "And what about your son?" she asks. "Is he done, too?"

Chip stares at the television set where a tennis match is on. I know he's not watching it, because Chip hates tennis. "Hey, what can I tell you?" he says. "Girl's a total bitch."

For the rest of the night, none of us says much. Ma makes stuffed pork chops with mashed potatoes. But when it's time to eat, Chip says he isn't hungry; maybe he'll have some later. So there we are in the kitchen, Ma and me, chewing on our pork chops in total silence. I can tell Ma's thinking about the whole thing with Allison and the baby, probably wondering if Chip is really home for good this time. And me, I'm thinking that I'm supposed to meet Mike O'Toole and a couple of other kids in about fifteen minutes, and I'm wondering if O'Toole has any weed.

Then all of a sudden Chip yells from the living room. "I heard about those charges you filed against Monahan down at the court-house," he says. "Big mistake."

"The world's leading expert on mistakes speaks," Ma says, scraping the bones from her dinner into the garbage. She pauses a minute, her plate in hand, waiting for Chip to answer back. When he doesn't, she drifts toward the doorway. "And what was I supposed to do? Let those assholes kick the crap out of your brother—for something he didn't even do? You got to stand up for your own in this world, Chip. That's what I've been trying to tell you."

By then, I'm wishing I didn't eat those pork chops. I'm starting to feel sort of queasy and sick to my stomach. All I know is, if I get the chance, I'm gone. Then, Ma and Chip can sit around and talk about Monahan all night if they want to. But before I can get my Nikes on, Chip speaks up again. "Well, maybe so, Ma. But if you stand up for your own with the cops, your own are going to pay. I'd drop it if I were you."

So even though I don't want to get involved, I hobble in from the kitchen, one sneaker on, the other in my hand. "That's what I told her," I say. "But do you think she'd listen?"

"Shut up, Cody. You stay out of this," Ma snaps. Like this is just some argument she's having with Chip. Like I'm not the kid who's going to have to go out on the street and live with it.

But there's no winning, so I put my other sneaker on and get out of there.

I'm already having one of the shittiest days of my life when I get to O'Toole's. Then he pulls out this newspaper, obituary page.

"Read it," he says, sitting beside me on his bed. After I scan it real quick and see that no one under the age of sixty-one is listed, I hand it back to him.

"Is this supposed to mean something to me?"

That's when he points out the tiny obit in the corner: "Felipe Reyes, dead of a heart attack at age 63."

"Coincidence," I say, still trying to give that paper back. "You know how many Ricans out there are named Reyes?"

But then O'Toole makes me read the whole piece, including the paragraph that mentions that he had been the victim of a street attack a week earlier, and that no one had been arrested for it.

"So the guy died, what's it to me?" I say. "It's not like

he was my uncle or something. Besides, read it. The old man died of natural causes. A heart attack. Had nothing to do with what happened on the street."

But when O'Toole looks at me, it's obvious that whatever the obit says, we know why the guy died. We saw it in his eyes that afternoon on the street.

That night I got so messed up that when I came home I didn't even notice that Chip was gone. Probably back with the girl he was calling a total bitch a few hours before. Anyway, I was glad to find myself alone. Before my mother got up, I went and cut Felipe Reyes's obituary out of the paper. There was no picture, but all the time I'm cutting, it's like I'm seeing that face. Feeling those eyes on me, looking at me like he thinks I can save him. And like some psycho, I'm talking back to a dead man.

"What do you want from me, man? What the fuck was I supposed to do?" After I had read the clipping over three or four more times, I stashed it in a cigar box where I hid my pipe and rolling papers.

The hearing against Monahan was pretty much hell—dressing up in my Confirmation clothes, high-water pants and a sports jacket that Chip used to wear to court, and trying not to look at Monahan. To make it worse, half the courtroom was packed with his relatives, the other half with cops. But that was okay. I didn't need too many seats for my supporters. All I had was Ma—that's it. Oh yeah, don't forget Allison and the baby who squalled his effin head off until the judge had to ask them to leave. So that leaves me with Ma all dressed up in her polyester dress, fake gold jewelry, hair blown into some TV-lady style, trying to look like she's someone else. Trying to look like she hasn't spent half her life on welfare, the other half wiping people's asses. Chip said he would have come, but he was still on probation—why aggravate them?

Then, when I turn around, who do I see but my old English teacher sitting a few rows back. And I'm thinking, what the fuck? But then, Mr. Boyle isn't your average teacher. For one thing, the guy's got to be about a hundred years old. At least seventy. To make it worse, he's half blind, and so deaf that he was pretty much in his own world up there in front of the class. Going on about some effin Shakespeare play like it's the most important thing in the world. Like it's real or something. I swear, sometimes the poor old geezer gets so worked up about these plays, that he goes all misty-eyed right there in the classroom. Makes a real ass out of himself.

But to tell you the truth, some of those plays aren't bad—once you get past the way they talked back then. For a while, I really got into some of that stuff. When no one was around, I'd sit up in my room reading them to myself—sometimes out loud like Mr. Boyle did. It was weird—like this guy Shakespeare, who died about a thousand years ago, was writing about exactly what was happening to me. Like he understood me better than my own mother. Better than O'Toole even.

I even stayed after class to talk to Mr. Boyle a couple times when I had nothing better to do. I'd ask him what a certain line meant or something. Of course, the poor old geezer was thrilled; it was probably the first time in twenty years that someone was actually interested. But then Mr. Boyle started getting weird. He'd look at me with those watery blue eyes of his and talk about my "potential." Why wasn't I doing better in school? he'd ask. Had I started to think about college? That kind of crap. So I figured this guy is totally in the dark. After that, I stopped dropping in on him; didn't even show up for my final. And now when I pick up one of those plays I used to like, it's like they're written in Greek for all the sense they make.

To tell you the truth, I can't even believe Mr. Boyle still remembers me, or that he'd bother to come out to my hearing. I know I should go over and say something to him—thank him for coming, shit like that. But when I look in those watery blue eyes of his, I suddenly feel like I'm going to do something stupid. Like I'm going to break down and bawl or something. So instead, I jam my hands in my pocket and turn away—just like Chip would do.

As far as O'Toole and Dawson were concerned—the other "victims"—they weren't going near the place. Even if my lawyer called them, they swore they'd lie. The night before the trial, Ryan cornered me in the courtyard. "You know what you're going to be if you go through with this?" he said. "A marked man. Everything you do, the cops are going to be on your ass. Everywhere you go." Like I needed to hear that shit, right?

Still, there was that one moment when the whole thing felt pretty good. The moment when the judge pronounced the word "guilty." Telling the whole world that Monahan was the criminal. The loser. The scum. Not me. The shock that crossed his face, and the way the relatives all kind of gasped at once was almost worth the whole thing. I didn't even care that the sentence was so light it was a joke. All he got was a two-week sus-

pension, and six months office duty. And since the suspension was with pay, it pretty much added up to a
couple of extra weeks of vacation.

Of course, Ma was pissed as hell. "You call that
justice?" she ranted to her buddies in the project. As if
any of them knew the first thing about justice. But
me—I was satisfied. No matter how light the sentence,
nothing could take back the word that the judge had
pronounced for all to hear. *Guilty.*

At first, it looked like my brother and Dawson and all
the other kids in the project were wrong. No cops came
out of the woodwork to make my life a living hell like
they had predicted. At least, not any more than usual.
But I have to admit one thing: until the trial, I never actually noticed how many of them there were in the
world. I mean, they're everywhere. Outside the school,
cruising the mall, in front of me on the street, behind
me in my mother's car. They stopped at the same places
I went for pizza, talked to girls Chip knew. Unconsciously, they touched their guns right in the middle of
an ordinary conversation, as if to remind themselves
they were there. And at home in the Heights, only the
cockroaches outnumbered them.

When I asked O'Toole if he thought the city had
added to the police force or what, he told me I better
stop smoking so much weed—I was getting paranoid. I
guess it's pretty bad when a kid whose nickname is
"Chimney" tells you you're smoking too much.

Anyway, it was several months after Monahan went
back on active duty that things began to happen. Maybe
it was those lonely hours driving around in the cruiser,

or the assholes that got away, or just all the people who hated him. Or maybe he had just been laying low those months. Kind of like Chip does when he's on probation. Laying low. Biding his time. The first time I knew something was wrong, I was at a party.

It started off as a typical Saturday night. We're all in this girl's house, having a few brews when all of a sudden the cops show up. Three cruisers, like it's some kind of raid or something. And the thing is, they're acting like storm troopers. Tearing up this girl's mother's apartment like she's some major dealer. For a minute, I thought maybe she was—like we're all about to get busted for possession over this stupid girl's mother.

But then out of nowhere I hear one of them saying, "Are you Cody Moran?" And, "Are you gonna tell us who Moran is or what?" Of course, none of my buddies are about to give me away, but some asshole who was in my home room in seventh grade decides to play the big man; he points me out. *That's him over there.*

Well, the next thing I know this fat fuck grabs me off the couch, lifts me right up by the shirt, and says, "So you're Moran, are you?" And the whole room goes dead silent, like everyone's wondering if this guy is going to kick my head in right then and there or give me time to think about it. But he just tosses me back onto the couch like garbage.

"I just wanted to know what you looked like," he says. And all the cops laugh like it's a huge joke. Of course, I'm scanning their faces for Monahan. He's easy to spot, with his sharp nose and those flinty eyes, but he's not there. Only later did I see him outside in the cruiser. Just waiting, maybe humming a little song. When I walked by, he waved at me kind of cute like a girl would. *See ya.*

All right, so I admit I'm pretty freaked. I run all the way to Chip's house, heart banging like a fool, and when I get there, my brother's not even home. Instead, Allison comes to the door. It's obvious she's been crying—like she does at least half the time. So there I am, half the city police force on my ass, and I'm listening to this girl whining about what a jerk my brother was. As if I didn't know. The last thing she says is that if I see Chip, I can tell him not to bother coming home; then she practically slams the door in my face.

When I hit the street again, I see a cop car parked less than a block away. But I'm determined to walk real slow, like I'm not worried about a thing. By the time I get home, I've decided I'm not telling Chip anyway. What can he possibly do but make matters worse for me, and probably end up back in jail himself? And I'm sure not about to tell my mother. The way I see it, if the woman stands up for me any more, she'll probably get me killed. No, this is my problem now. There's no one who can help me with it. My only hope is that Monahan is satisfied that he ruined our party, shook me up a little, and that will be the end of it.

But that was before I knew Monahan. I mean really knew him. Not that I actually saw the guy much after that party. But I didn't need to see him. I knew he was around. Lurking just outside the Heights in his cruiser, waiting for me to screw up. Though he never showed his face, he never let me forget he was there. He was there when his buddies followed us one night when we went out in Chad Baldini's car, there when every single one of our parties got busted, there that afternoon when a bunch of cops parked their cruisers by the basketball court and just sat there watching us shoot around. Laughing, smoking butts, and flicking them on the asphalt, closer and closer to us.

Though I hadn't seen Monahan since the night he'd parked his cruiser outside that party, I remembered exactly what he looked like. I knew that pointed chipmunk face; the irises of his eyes were like small gray pebbles. A real flat color, like there was no life in them—nothing.

And I was ready for him, too. The very next day, I went to Chip, and asked him to get me a gun. At first, my brother laughed at me like he always did. "What the fuck would you do with a gun—besides shoot your own foot off." But then he turned serious. "Harm one hair on a cop's head, Cody, and you know what's gonna happen to you?"

"Who said anything about going after a cop?" I said. "I'm talking self-defense here."

"You kill a cop, it ain't gonna matter what you're defending; they'll hang your balls out to dry," Chip said.

But the very next week, he showed up with an old .357 Magnum. I didn't even ask where he got it. "Emergency use only, right bro?" he said, and I nodded. After he was gone, I took the clipping out of my dope box, wrapped them both in a T-shirt, and put the Nike box in the back of my closet.

Meanwhile, Monahan kept coming at me. I have to admit it wasn't too hard to bust me for something back in those days. In fact, it was almost like a game I was playing. Or maybe I was just trying to feel for the edges of this thing I had gotten myself into, seeing how far he would go. Every night I went home and checked on my gun, made sure it was still there in the back of the closet. In the span of about a year, I got myself arrested for an OUI, illegal possession of pharmaceuticals, and receiving stolen property. And those were only the highlights.

Each time they threw me into lockup, they would taunt me. "Make sure you treat this one real special now, boys. We wouldn't want him to break a nail or anything. Might haul us into court on police brutality." Eventually, I just gave it back to them. "That's right," I'd yell. "My lawyer expects me to be treated real nice while I'm here." I knew I was only making things worse, but I couldn't seem to stop myself. And besides, what was I going to do—break down and bawl like some little kid?

I spent so much time in juvey that sometimes when I woke up in my own bedroom, it was so quiet I thought I was going to explode. I can't explain it, but it was like I was just waiting for what was going to happen next. Between the deadly quiet and Ma's lectures, I'd almost rather be anywhere than home.

"Go ahead," she'd say, filling the doorway of my room in her white uniform. "Give them another reason to arrest you, Cody. You're only proving they're right, you know. Go ahead." She pushed her chin in my direction the way kids do when they're challenging you to a fight.

By then I had gotten nicknamed "the Magnet." Everywhere I went the pigs showed up. Eventually, people slammed the door on me when I tried to get into a party, and the only people who would even hang out with me were the project desperadoes—junkies and girls who'd blow you for five bucks—people so low that the cops can't be bothered arresting them. And of course, O'Toole, my best friend since fourth grade. Even if I was the Magnet, Mike still invited me over to his apartment to smoke weed while his mother was at work. When we were really high, we would sit and stare out the window, and look for Monahan. He was never there, but Mike would point down the street and say, "Look, there's his cruiser. I'd recognize it anywhere!" Or else I would look out on the one lonely tree in the courtyard, and pretend I saw his feet dangling from a branch. Then we'd laugh our asses off. To tell you the truth, those hours when Chimney and I were high out of our minds, playing Where's Waldo? with Officer Monahan were the only times I really felt relaxed in those years. The only time I felt free of the two guys who were following me—one an asshole with a badge, the other one a dead man.

There's no telling how long this might have gone on, or how soon I would have ended up facing adult charges, but one Saturday afternoon things came to a head. Picture it: I'm walking home from the store with a pack of butts, minding my own business, when I see this black BMW parked on the side of the road, the window open just enough. And right away, I'm aggravated. I mean, there is this guy with everything, a Bose player, a pile of discs laying all over the floor, leather seats—you know, the whole works. And he doesn't care about any of it. It's almost like he's saying, here—take it; I don't want it anyway. And being me, I can't let him down. Not because I want his stupid box—I don't. I don't even have a car to put it in. And with all the addicts selling shit like that in the project, it's not like I'm going to get any serious money for the thing. In the end, I guess the only reason I pulled that box out of the car was because the asshole who left it there deserved it. And like Ma, I believe in giving people what they deserve.

The crime was so easy I felt like I was sleepwalking. No rush at all. But as soon as I pull the box out and I'm standing there with it in my hand, this cruiser shows up out of nowhere. Like he was always there. Like maybe the whole thing was a setup—the open BMW, the box just waiting for me to grab it. And though I can't see the cop's face, I'm pretty sure it's Monahan. I can feel those flat eyes on me, cutting through me like the siren as I run down the street, the useless piece of shit I had stolen slowing me down. My only advantages are that I'm on foot, and I know the neighborhood. But when I duck down the alley next to Our Lady of the Angels, the cruiser pulls over and I hear someone behind me. Hear their feet thumping like mine on the pavement. And then their breathing—heavy like mine. We're both running so hard, I can almost hear his heartbeat in my ear. By then, I know it's Monahan.

Even though the voice that is yelling for me to stop gets closer and closer, I'm surprised as hell when my face slams the pavement. All of a sudden Monahan is on top of me, screaming, cursing as loud as he can in my ear. But as close as he is, I can't hear what he's saying, can't decipher the words. All I hear is my own heart; all I feel is the sudden gush of water on my face. At first, I think, Shit, what am I doing—crying? But then I taste it and realize it's blood. Though I'm facedown in the alley, tasting dirt and looking at nothing but concrete, I can see Monahan's face as clear as can be.

That's why I can't believe it when the guy pulls me

to my feet and starts reading me my rights. And it's not him at all. It's this black cop I've never seen before in my life. When I realize he doesn't know me, I tell him my name is Fred. Fred Monahan. It's not like I even think about it. It just comes out.

So there I am, sitting in a cell again, staring at those cinder-block walls. Fred Monahan. The black cop comes in and tells Fred he can make a call, so I go to the phone and dial home. But while it's ringing, I see what's about to happen as clear as one of those psychics on TV. I see Ma dragging her tired ass out of bed because it's not even noon yet. And then when she hears my voice, I see that disgusted look she'll get. The way she kind of twists her mouth. "What the hell've you done this time, Cody?" she'll say. Then she'll tell me that she's not coming down, that I can sit here and rot, even though I know she'll be starting to wake up by then, running her fingers through her wiry hair, mentally adding up the money in her checking account to see if she can make bail.

Before any of this plays out, I slam down the receiver. "You got a phone book?" I say to the black cop. His name tag identifies him as Officer Wainwright.

"What—you forgot your mother's number?" he asks.

"I don't have a mother," I tell him. "She died when I was five. Got stabbed by one of her johns." I figure if I'm making up a life, I might as well make it interesting.

Apparently I've done a good job because while I scan the phone book, Wainwright stands there watching me, his hands on his hips, like he finds me real fascinating. Or maybe he's just wondering what I'm trying to pull. "Would you mind? I'd like a little privacy here," I say. But the truth is I can't believe I've got my finger on the number of my old English teacher. And that I'm actually thinking of calling him.

While I'm waiting for him to answer the phone, I'm wondering if the old man still remembers me. I mean, it's pretty strange calling a teacher you had two years ago to bail you out of jail—even if he did show up at that dumb hearing. But who else am I going to call?

Anyway, Mr. Boyle practically hangs up on me when I ask him real politely if he'd mind coming down to the station and bailing me out. But I'm not surprised when he shows. I mean anyone who stands in front of a class and cries over people who don't even exist has to be some kind of a sucker. Not that I care what the cops think, but it's pretty embarrassing when the old man walks into the station with this fussy little white dog on a leash, wearing a pair of jeans that look like they've been ironed. Or when he pays my bail, counting out the bills like he's in the checkout line at the grocery store. Wainwright looks from me to Mr. Boyle and back as if he's wondering what the connection could possibly be.

And I'm wondering, too. I mean, it's kind of awkward, the two of us just gawking at each other when I come out. After he pays, Mr. Boyle stares at me real hard for a minute. Then he turns and leads his little dog out. Not that I want a lecture or anything, but the guy doesn't even say hello.

"Well, what are you waiting for? You're a free man," Wainwright says when I stand there like I don't know what to do. "Until the next time anyway."

By the time I hit the street, Mr. Boyle has a couple of blocks on me. It's a pretty pathetic sight: a hundred-year-old man wearing ironed jeans and walking his little poodle through a neighborhood like ours; poor guy's just asking for a mugging. I don't know why, but I follow him. I mean, he could at least say something. *Hi Cody, how you doing? Good luck with your court case* . . . something.

When I run up behind him, he looks over his shoulder. "Good morning, Mr. Moran," he says, the way he used to talk in class. *Mr. Moran. Miss Phillips.* Even the whores, he talked to like that.

So there I am, out of breath from chasing a guy who's moving at nursing home speed, and I say, "I . . . I just wanted to thank you for coming down. And to let you know that you'll get your money back. I'm not going to skip out or anything."

That's when he stops dead right in the middle of the sidewalk, takes off his glasses, and gives me a long look with his water-colored eyes. "It's not my money I'm worried about, young man," he says. Then he puts his glasses back on and resumes his walk.

Of course, I'm forced to follow him again, to find out what the hell that's supposed to mean. When he asks me if I'd like to stop somewhere for a cup of tea, I tell him I'm not much of a tea drinker, but I wouldn't mind a Coke or something.

Don't ask me why, but the next thing I know there I am sitting in McDonald's having a Coke with this English teacher who's so old he probably knew Shakespeare personally. And to make it worse, I'm spilling everything—the whole story about the crime I didn't commit and everything that followed. I even tell him about Monahan's pebble-colored eyes.

The only thing I leave out is the part about how Felipe Reyes looked at me that afternoon on the sidewalk. Believe me, I wanted to tell Boyle about it. Maybe being so smart, he could explain why the old man let me go. Why he looked right at me in the lineup and shook his head. But there are some things you just can't tell anyone.

Anyway, all through the whole stupid story, Mr. Boyle's studying me, the way he used to study those ancient plays. When I'm done, I figure he's going to say something really deep like he used to say in class sometimes.

But instead, he just looks at me a while and says, "Well, Mr. Moran, it sounds like everything you touch turns to shit, doesn't it?"

And I'm thinking—what the fuck? Does this old geezer think he's cool or something, talking to me like that? I'm dehydrated as hell so I take a huge gulp of my Coke; then I get up to go.

"Thanks for the soda," I say. "But I just thought of something I have to do. Some more shit I've got to get into."

He lets me get all the way to the door before he says, "You can leave if you like, but it sounds like the way you're living isn't working out terribly well. Maybe it's time to consider the alternative."

All right, so he's got my attention. And to tell you the truth, I'm pretty aggravated with the old man—even if he did just bail me out. "And what's that?" I say, standing in the middle of this restaurant like a fool. "Going to church on Sunday? Running for student council, maybe? You don't know anything about me, Mr. Boyle."

He narrows his eyes like he did sometimes when he was reading a play out loud. "I know you better than you know yourself, Mr. Moran," he says.

"Oh yeah—how's that?" I say. By now I'm figuring this guy isn't only deaf and blind; he's senile, too.

"You have no idea how bright you are, for one thing," he says. "Whereas I—I knew it the first day you walked into my classroom. Even before I went down to the office and saw it confirmed on your records."

"Didn't you hear a word I just said to you?" I say. "My problem is what's happening in the neighborhood. All that school shit—those tests they do on you and all—that's irrelevant."

"I heard every word; it's you who's not listening, Mr. Moran," Mr. Boyle says in that dramatic way he talks. "What I'm trying to tell you is that if the neighborhood is the problem, then maybe you need to remove yourself."

"My family's been in the Heights for twenty-five years," I say. "Where the hell do you think we're going to go?"

"Stop thinking so narrowly, Mr. Moran," he says, repeating one of his favorite lines from class. "I'm not talking about a change of address, but a change of focus. For a start, I want you and your mother to make an appointment to meet with Miss Curtain. I'll come, too, if you don't mind."

"Miss Curtain—my guidance counselor? What's she

going to do—call Monahan and ask him if he'd please leave her student alone?"

"Forget Monahan," Mr. Boyle says with a wave of his hand. *Like it's that easy.* "A change of focus means taking your mind off this Monahan character, and directing it toward your future."

That's when I know the old geezer is totally clueless. But for some reason, I don't walk away. I sit there and listen to him talk about focusing on my strengths, and addressing my weaknesses. About college and scholarships and maybe getting a part-time job down at the Y where he knows the fitness director. I sit there and listen for close to an hour—almost like I believe this shit could actually happen. Mr. Boyle even says that if I make the effort, he'll testify in my behalf when my court case comes up.

Since I've got nothing left to lose, I drag my mother out of bed a week later on Monday morning, and show up at this meeting he's set up. Mr. Boyle thinks I'm all excited about this college thing, but that's not it. I'm just wondering if what he says is true: If I stop thinking about Monahan so much, will he disappear? And if he does—what does that mean? Was he just a figment of my imagination all along?

Anyway, for a while, I really gave it a try. I kept both my focus and my body away from any place Monahan was likely to look for me—in the courtyard where the desperadoes hang out getting high, on the street, at parties; I didn't even go to O'Toole's apartment.

At first, Ma was suspicious as hell. "What's this Mr. Boyle taking such a big interest in you for?" she'd ask.

"Calling the house. Going for meetings with the guidance counselor . . . What does he want from you?"

But when she saw me working out, or studying at the kitchen table for the first time since sixth grade, she shut up. "Cody just needs to get one C up in Math, and he'll be on the honor roll," she bragged to her cronies in the parking lot. "His guidance counselor says if he can do that, he'll get a scholarship for sure."

If kids in the project didn't want to know me when I was the Magnet, they wanted to know me even less when I became the Great White Geek. Only O'Toole came around, looking through my books for the home- work papers, and holding them up like relics.

"You did this?" he'd say, looking at the neat rows of math problems like he couldn't believe it.

Every now and then, to prove I wasn't totally lost, I would smoke a bowl with him. Or maybe drink a cou- ple of the beers he was always stealing from his drunk uncle. But for some reason, I couldn't enjoy being buzzed anymore. Instead of relaxing me like it used to, it made me feel kind of edgy and nervous. The way I used to feel when I was waiting for Monahan to show up out of nowhere.

For a while things were so good that I started to be- lieve that Mr. Boyle was right. Maybe I could be some- one other than the person I was born to be. Maybe I didn't have to be the Magnet. And even more amazing— for a couple of months, I didn't see Monahan at all. I started thinking he had lost interest; maybe he was even bragging to his friends that he had "scared me straight." There were days when I didn't even think about him. Not once. But other nights, I'd wake up in my room, my heart pounding like it was the day that black cop chased me down the alley. And it was like Monahan was right there in the room with me, sitting on my chest. Sometimes I thought he was the only person who really knew who I was.

Then, a couple of months ago I get out of work, and I'm heading for Ma's car in this dumb good mood when I spot Monahan's profile in the cruiser. That sharp chin, kind of hunched-up shoulders. This time he didn't send his buddies; it's *him*.

So I walk real fast, trying to tell myself it's a coincidence. Even though, deep down, I know there are no coincidences between Monahan and me. Never were. It's not a coincidence when I see him three or four times in the next week, once parked outside of school, then just outside the entrance of the project, and finally near Mr. Boyle's apartment when I stop in to visit him. And though I want to tell someone, I know there's no use. Even when I didn't see him, I knew he was there. Watching from some-place where I couldn't see him. Waiting for that one moment when I would screw up. The moment he knew was bound to come.

And today was it. Payday. The day Monahan was waiting for all these months. It all started when O'Toole asks me if I want to shoot a few hoops on Station Avenue. But when I get there, he's not on the court. He's sitting in Chad Baldini's car.

I have to get to work in an hour, but I figure what the hell; you can't play the geek all the time. So we sit there for a while, smoking a couple of bowls, listening to some tunes, laughing about old times. Before I know it,

I look at my watch and I'm fifteen minutes late for work. And I don't know why, but I panic; I tell Chad he's got to take me home right away. Then, when I realize he's too messed up to drive, I take the wheel.

Maybe it's the herb, but I feel like my whole life will be over if I don't make it to this stupid job. So while we're driving, I'm all revved up, cursing, practically riding on curbs. And when we get stuck in traffic, I yell out the window so loud I can feel every vein in my head.

O'Toole and Baldini are saying shit like, *Calm down, man. You're losing it. What's wrong with you, Moran?* But they don't understand. They never did. It's not the job; it's getting out. *Getting out.*

So all right, maybe I'm speeding a little. Maybe I'm on edge. But when I came to the stop sign right before you turn into the project, I swear I looked. And it's not like people actually stop at that corner anyway—not if it's clear.

As soon as I saw the blue and white of the cruiser, I knew it was him. I mean, who else? And what's more, I knew it was all over for me. Even before he dragged me out of the car, screaming all up in my face, I knew.

"You think you're going to get away from me, Magnet?" he was saying. "You think you're going to go to *college*? Well, it ain't gonna happen; it's never gonna happen."

He said a lot of other things, too. But that was all I really heard, all I remember.

It was as if this whole dance we'd been doing these past couple of years finally put us face-to-face. For a minute, I thought Monahan was going to kill me right then and there he was so out of control. But instead he just threw me onto the hood of Chad's Hyundai. "Go back to the Heights," he said, spitting out the words.

By the time I got home, I was crazier than he was. I was kicking things, screaming, blubbering, saying the same shit over and over again no matter how hard my mother tried to calm me down. "Wherever I go, whatever I do, he's gonna be there," I scream. "Don't you get it, Ma?"

At that point, I'm not sure whether I'm talking about Monahan, or just about old Mr. Reyes, the guy who's been tracking me with his eyes ever since the day we knocked over his stupid cart. How can I explain that Monahan is the only one who really knows me? And like he says, I'll never get away from it. Never. Anyway, it wasn't like I expected my mother to understand. Not her or anyone else, either.

Eventually, I guess I wore myself out with all my yelling and throwing things around, busting stuff up. I went into my room and got real quiet. A couple of times, I felt Ma breathing outside my door. I felt how tired she was, how tired she'd been for years; her exhaustion was seeping right through the wood. I knew she wanted to come in, see if I was all right. But she probably figured it was best to leave me alone, let me get over this in my own time. And she was right. Besides, there's nothing she could have done to change anything.

Anyway, I guess that's why I wanted to get all this down. So Ma would know it's not her fault. Not hers or O'Toole's or Mr. Boyle's, either. Not even Monahan's. The first thing I did was go into my closet and make sure the gun was still there. After I pulled it out of the Nike box with the clipping about Mr. Reyes's death, I laid them both on the bed beside me and sat down to write in this old school notebook.

Don't call it a suicide note—just the story of what happened. Kind of like what happened to that dark old man the day we started circling his cart. Sure he could have run away. Spent his whole life running. But instead, he hunkered down over his little flame and waited, his eyes—*los ojos*—so black with sorrow that anyone who looked into them would be burned forever.

Teardown
by Marc Lecard

•

Marc Lecard is going to be hot. His novel, *Vinnie's Head*, is a killer, and this new story reminds me of Charles Bukowski meets James Cain who, through some strange quirk of biology, have a love child story. For that matter, Marc may be their love child. He writes clean and lean and swift, all the qualities of a good racehorse and of good easy-to-read prose. Better yet, it's not just easy to read, it's engaging. After the first line, you're in, and you're hooked all the way down to the gullet.

—Joe R. Lansdale,
Bram Stoker Award–winning
author of *Sunset and Sawdust*

"LoDuco, *what* are you doing?"

I wasn't really doing anything, just standing there thinking, but the way the foreman was looking at me that didn't seem like a good thing to say, so I said, "I was about to go looking for you, find out what you wanted me to do next."

Catelle the foreman stared at me, his eyes bulging out. I don't think he liked me. Every time he spoke to me his voice got this whiny, exasperated sound.

"Okay, you found me," he said. "Now how about you

actually do some work today? Pick up all that crap lying around the yard and put it in the Dumpster. You
think you're getting paid to stand around scratching
your balls?"

I scanned the yard. There was a lot of crap. Pieces of
two-by-fours, shingles, fragments of lathe and plaster
wall, little odds and ends of wiring and heating
equipment—all the stuff that gets left behind when you
tear down a house.

I sighed and started picking crap up. The Dumpster
was far away, on the other side of the house out by the
curb, so rather than bringing the crap one piece at a time
out to the Dumpster—I knew that would make Catelle go
mental—I started a crap pile. When it got big enough
I planned to figure out what to do about it.

My cousin got me this job—I had been unemployed
awhile, my benefits running out, and I think he was
afraid I might come to live with him again. So he got
me on a construction crew as a laborer, which mostly
meant hauling heavy stuff around so other people who
knew what they were doing could use it.

This job site was a teardown and rebuild, where the
owners had an old house demolished so they could build
a new one on the lot, usually three or four times bigger
than the old house and built right up to the edge of the
property.

The old house was gone completely, knocked to
pieces and torn out down to the foundations. All that
was left standing was an old garage in a back corner of
the lot. It looked pretty ramshackle, the white paint peel-
ing off all over, the wood gray and rotten-looking un-

derneath. It looked like a few good kicks would bring the whole thing down.

But there was shade along one side of the old garage, and picking crap up is hot and heavy work. It was late afternoon on one of those hot, humid Long Island August days that make you think you're somewhere like Mississippi. I kept looking at the shadow of the garage, imagining how much cooler it would be there. I worked closer and closer to it. That was easy, there was crap everywhere.

When I got even with the back wall of the garage I saw that it was shady back there, too, and out of sight of the rest of the crew. That was a plus.

There was some sort of rusty propane tank against the back wall, bramble bushes all around it. I sat down, smoked a cig. It was nice back there, quiet, cool. I leaned against the wall and closed my eyes, just for a second.

When I woke up it was pitch black out. Something I couldn't see was crawling over my arms and neck. I jumped up trying to brush whatever it was off, tripped over something, and went ass over teakettle into the bramble bushes.

When I thrashed my way out of that, cut to pieces, I sat back down on the propane tank and tried to think things through.

Obviously the crew had left without me. Would they come back when they discovered I was missing? I doubted it very much.

It was a long walk to Montauk Highway and my motel, and a long bus ride back to my cousin's place. It was a little closer to my old house, but I didn't think they would let me in there anymore. I sighed, cursed. There didn't seem to be any other way but to walk it.

When I stood back up I realized I needed to pee, pretty bad. I also realized how close I was to the neighbor's house. A wide-eyed housewife was staring at me out her window as she did the dishes in her kitchen. In the light of her kitchen window I probably looked like some kind of zombie, thrashing around in the weeds.

It was pretty dark out, but even so, I just couldn't take it out with her looking at me, even with my back turned. It would have been like taking a whiz with a spotlight on you. She'd probably call the cops, and I'd get busted for indecent exposure.

So I looked around for a more private place to do my business.

In the light beams from the neighbor's kitchen window I could see there was a door in the back wall of the garage. I thought it probably wasn't locked. It wasn't.

Inside the garage it was completely dark, maybe a little gray where a distant streetlight shone though the one window in the side wall. I took out my lighter, snapped it on, and held it up. There was stuff everywhere, completely covering the floor, piles of old newspapers and magazines, wooden boxes filled with rusty shit, some piles of boards. A kind of ladder made of planks went up the wall next to the door, more piles of rusty stuff humped up at the foot of it. From the smell I was not the first person to think of relieving myself there.

I put my lighter away and pissed in the corner.

Just about the time I finished, I heard a car pull into the yard, and saw headlights cut across the front of the garage. They went out, and I heard a car door slam.

Cool, I thought, they came back for me after all. I got as far as opening the back door, and was about to yell out to whoever it was, when I heard someone say,

"Why don't we just do him right here?"

And I thought maybe I should keep my mouth shut.

"You must be simple," another voice said. "Half the neighborhood'll see us, we kill him outside. Take him in the damn garage."

All right, this was bad. I stepped out of the back door as quietly as I could and was trying to decide whether to jump the fence and risk the neighbor lady freaking out, or sneak around the other side of the garage toward the street, when I heard some cursing, banging, and rattling from the front of the garage.

"These fucking doors won't open!"

"Don't make so much noise! Take him around the back, then."

Maybe it wasn't the best move I could have made. But the fence looked far away, and high, and I could see myself getting shot in the back trying to get over it. I could almost feel it.

I ducked back inside the garage and closed the door.

I backed away in the dark, trying not to trip over the piles of rusty shit I remembered being everywhere. I had my hand stretched out behind me to keep from bumping into things; my hand touched something in the dark.

The boards on the side wall, like a ladder.

I went up them while the back door was swinging open.

When I had got up as far as I could my legs were still halfway down the ladder. I had to hope they didn't look my way, that's all.

Three dark figures stumbled inside and shut the door after them. A flashlight suddenly lit up the floor, roamed around at random, but didn't get over to my legs and high-tops sticking down from the ladder.

"That bitch see us?"

"Nah, she's too busy with her fucking dishes."

The third guy didn't say anything, but I could hear him breathing hard. Myself, I breathed through my mouth, trying to be as quiet as I could.

There were some boards or something laid across the beams, so I couldn't see right down to the garage floor. I could see the beam from the flashlight through the cracks, though. It jumped around a bit, then got steady. I think the guy put it on top of something.

The heavy-breathing guy spoke up next. His voice was all raspy and hoarse. I guessed he hadn't been enjoying himself much lately.

"It's all in here, I'm telling you. All of it," the breather said.

"Where?" said the guy who had been so anxious to start the killing. "Where is it, here?"

Breather actually laughed. "If I tell you that, it's all over. You'll kill me."

"It's a problem, isn't it?" the other guy, the calmer one, said. "If we shoot you before you tell us, we might not find it. But if we say we're not going to shoot you, why should you tell us where it is?"

"Let's cut him some more," Kill Simple said.

"That might work."

"I never meant to take it all, you know," Breather panted.

"Sure. That's why you ditched us and told the cops

where to find us. That's why you ran off to fucking Ohio."

"You were always going to get your share. We could still do that, split it. Three ways. Everyone gets something."

The other guys laughed, or snorted anyway.

"You've got balls, I'll say that for you."

"This is bullshit," Killboy said. "This place is tiny. Let's just tear it apart and find the shit, kill asshole, and get the fuck out of here."

"You'll never find it." The wheezy guy sounded pretty sure of himself.

The calm guy picked up the flashlight and began to slowly shine it around the garage, like a spotlight looking for the actors.

"There's a fuck of a lot of stuff in here," he said. The beam was headed right toward my legs.

I felt with my hand behind me, touched boards, and, as carefully as I could, sat my ass down, pulling my legs up after me. I saw the flashlight beam pass under me, right where my legs had been two seconds ago. I hadn't made a sound. It was hard not breathing, though.

Just then the beams of the old garage let out a groan. It was loud and weird, like some kind of African water buffalo crying out to its mate. I felt the whole business sink a little.

There was silence right underneath me. Even the heavy breathing had stopped.

"The fuck was that?"

Then the whole shebang came down, me on top of it.

Apparently what I had tried to sit on was an old door laid across the beams, because the doorknob tried to go up my ass when it all hit the ground. I hurt in about a dozen places.

Probably not as much as the guy the door landed on, though.

Shaky, I stood up.

The guy with the flashlight was still standing. He shined the light in my eyes. Thick dust and powder drifted through the light beam.

"What the—"

That was all he got out. Suddenly the flashlight beam dove to the floor, and there was a sound like someone playing soccer with a ripe watermelon. With the direct light out of my eyes I could just make out the silhouette of the tied-up guy, his hands still tied behind him, kicking the living shit out of the guy on the ground.

I thought I should give them more room, and backed away. My foot touched something hard. I bent down to move it out of the way, and came up with a gun in my hand.

That was good. I leaned down and picked up the flashlight, which had rolled over toward me. That was better. I put the beam on the kicker, easy to locate in the dark by his wheezing.

He looked like shit, face bloody all over, one eye swollen shut, his shirtfront soaked red. Even so he looked better than the guy on the ground. The guy on the ground looked dead.

There was a stream of blood running out from under the door-and-broken-beam pile on the garage floor. Legs stuck out at the other end.

The voice of the tied-up, blood-covered wheezy guy came out of the dark.

"I don't know what the fuck you're doing here, but untie my hands."

"Why should I do that?" It seemed like a reasonable question to me.

We both considered this statement for a while. Then the tied-up guy said, "Look, I don't know who you are. But if you untie me I'll tell you what I wouldn't tell these assholes."

"Why would I care about that?" I said, thinking, just go, leave the guy and get out of here.

But I didn't go.

"You want to be a rich man?" Wheezy said. "I can do that. I can make you a rich man."

"With what?"

"Diamonds," the guy said. "Diamonds, rubies, emeralds. A shitload of gemstones."

It didn't seem very likely to me.

"Diamonds?" I said. "In a garage in Patchogue?"

"I hid 'em here. This place used to be my mom's."

"Okay, but diamonds? Where did you get them?"

The guy was quiet a while. His breathing had gotten a little less noisy.

Finally I heard him hawk and spit, a full, heavy loogie that hit the garage floor like a pound of beef liver.

"What do you think?" he asked me. "We dug 'em up? From a jewelry store."

"You stole them?"

"They didn't just give 'em to us."

"How long have they been here?"

The guy sighed. When he spoke again I could hear that whiny thing getting into his voice, like Catelle.

"You got a lot of questions, don't you? Ten years, buddy. The stones have been here ten fucking years."

Ten years. I seemed to remember something from ten years back, a jewelry store stickup where the stealers cleaned out the store, which just happened to have a major shipment of jewels passing through. Pretty heavy for Long Island. That's why it stuck in my mind.

That, and I can remember thinking how much you could do with that many diamonds.

The robbers got away with a pile of gemstones. As far as I could remember, the rocks had never been recovered.

I couldn't remember anything else, but it sounded like this guy could fill in the gaps.

"Was that the jewelry store in Bay Shore?" I asked him. "In 1988? Because I remember that one."

"Good for you. Yeah, that's right. Geister's Jewelry, in Bay Shore."

"If you got caught, how did you manage to hide the stones?"

The guy got quiet again. I knew he was adjusting to my habit of only asking questions. I can't help it, but I know it freaks people out.

The situation I was in, though, you couldn't blame me.

"Well, the cops got onto the other guys somehow and pulled them in. I kept my head down for a while, hid the stones for when things cooled off, and left town."

"How did they catch those guys so fast?" I wanted to know. "Didn't you even wear masks?"

"Oh, yeah, we wore masks."

There was a long silence after that, during which I answered my own question and really began to wish I hadn't asked it.

"They thought I dropped a dime on them," Mr. Wheezy said after a while.

"Jesus, why would they think that?" I said. But maybe sarcasm wasn't such a good idea right then.

"Well, it served 'em right. They fingered me as the head guy, the guy whose idea the whole thing was. The judge believed 'em, I guess; they got off pretty light considering."

More silence followed this remark. I could hear the guy shuffling his feet around, like maybe getting himself in position for something nasty.

"Wait a minute," I said, just to change the subject a little. "Where have you been for ten years? Why didn't you come back for the stones sooner?"

"I went down for something else. Hit up a convenience store on the road, got ten years. They never made me for the jewelry store, though."

"What about those other guys?"

"Caught some bad luck there. They were good boys; they made parole and got out early. Before I did. They were waiting for me. I knew they would be, but there was nowhere for me to go, except back inside. I thought I'd take my chances."

"Wow." I considered what he had just told me. "So you never told them where the loot was. No wonder they seemed pissed at you. But why did you bring them here?"

From the little silence before he answered, I could tell

it was costing him. But he said, "It was a negotiation. They would almost kill me, and I would almost tell them where the stones were."

"Why not just give them the jewels?"

"I was counting on the stones. For my retirement. Say, buddy, are you going to untie me or what?"

"If you wouldn't tell these guys," I said, meaning the guys on the floor, "why would you tell me?"

"They were going to kill me, one way or another," he said. "You, you have no reason to kill me. You're gonna let me go, and we'll both be rich."

"I could shoot you, and take all the stones," I said. I would never do that, but he didn't know.

"You don't know where they are," he pointed out. "Just like the dead assholes."

"I could call the cops, turn you in. There's bound to be a reward."

"After all this time? Insurance company's settled that a long time ago. Besides, the stones're worth more than any fucking reward."

He had stopped wheezing, and sounded pretty sure of himself for a guy that was tied up and beat half to death.

"I don't know," I said. "I should just go."

"Go? And leave the diamonds?"

"What would I do with a bunch of diamonds? I wouldn't know the first thing about getting rid of them."

More silence. The tied-up guy had run out of talk.

"I'm out of here," I said, and turned to go.

As soon as I turned around I heard him come after me. I knew he would do that. He didn't want me out there spreading the word, and was looking for a repeat of his soccer match with the guy on the floor.

But I was ready, sort of. I turned around and let him have it with the gun. At least, I meant to. But nothing happened when I tried to pull the trigger. Maybe it was empty, or jammed, or something, or maybe the safety was on. I don't know shit about guns.

Anyway, no big noise, no bullet.

The guy had stopped when I turned around. Now he said sympathetically, "What'sa matter, gun not working?"

I didn't say anything; my thumb was groping around the side of the gun like a caterpillar.

"The safety, that's like a little lever on the side of the gun?"

"On some guns." The guy sounded a lot closer.

My thumb felt something, a little lever, and pushed it forward. I pulled the trigger; the gun went off. A big piece of the roof disappeared. I could see stars through it.

The noise of the gun going off made me completely deaf, so I couldn't hear the guy coming after me. I could see a big black silhouette coming straight at me, though, and tried to swing the gun down on it. I was too slow.

But it didn't matter. Because the black shape suddenly disappeared. The guy had tripped on something coming after me and done a face plant on the garage floor. He was just laying there in the dark. I couldn't hear his wheezy breathing anymore.

When I put the flashlight on him, I could see where his head had caught the sharp corner of some rusty

metal shit lying on the floor, right in the temple. I ran
the beam around, looking for what had tripped him, and
saw a little sparkle, down by his shoes. I bent over and
picked it up.

A diamond. A good size one, I guess. I didn't know
much about diamonds, but it seemed pretty big.

I shone the light around to see if I could find any
more. I did. Quite a few diamonds, big ones and small
ones were lying around. I picked up about a dozen out
of the litter of broken wood on the floor.

Now I was getting excited. There had to be more than
just twelve diamonds. I started digging through the pile
of broken beams, got all the way down to the body of
the kill-simple guy without finding anything.

Running the flashlight over the stuff I had thrown
aside to make sure I didn't miss anything, I noticed
something funny. I picked up one of the broken beams
for a closer look.

The two-by-four was broken off a couple inches from
the end. It looked like somebody had drilled out the end
of the beam, made a big hole six inches deep. No wonder it had snapped off under my weight.

I knocked the beam with the heel of my hand, like a
ketchup bottle. Another diamond rolled out of the hole
and fell on the floor.

I moved the beam around the garage and picked up
lots of sparkle on the floor. A shitload of jewels must
have been hidden in those hollow joists.

It didn't take me long to pull down the rest of the
beams. They were each just held in place with a couple
nails. I even found a rusty crowbar on the floor that
made the job go a lot faster.

Every beam had had its ends drilled. Every beam was stuffed with stones—mostly diamonds, some rubies, emeralds, sapphires, some stones I didn't know the names of. And one string of pearls.

I never worked so hard in my life.

I swung the flashlight across the floor to check and see if maybe one of the other guys would come to and give me shit, but they were still out. They looked like they would be out forever.

Just then the whole world lit up. It looked like an A-bomb test had just gone off in the driveway; beams of light poured through every crack and hole in the garage walls. There were quite a few cracks; it was amazing the building was still standing.

A megaphone voice cracked out: "Police! Put down your weapons and come out of there slowly. Put your hands on your heads. If we see a weapon, we'll fire!"

I can take a hint. I took the gun out of the waistband of my trousers and put it down—a lot of good it did me, anyway—laid down the flashlight—there was plenty of light to see by now—and put my hands on my head.

I walked out of there, nice and slow. I didn't fall down, and I didn't get shot.

As I left I kicked the door closed behind me. It slammed; there was that weird groaning noise again, and the whole building tilted sideways. It didn't quite go over, though.

The cops were surprised to see me, but even more surprised when they saw the pile of jewel thieves and diamonds on the garage floor. I thought of what I could tell them that they would believe, but couldn't think of anything. So I just told them what had happened.

I was right about one thing—they didn't believe me. The hardest thing for them to believe was that I was working a regular job. (Like I said, I knew some of these guys.)

"LoDuco," Sergeant Halligan said to me—I'd gone to high school with him—"*You* have a job? You expect me to believe that?"

But when they called the contractor, the foreman vouched for me. I bet anything he would like to have said he'd never seen me before, but he backed me up.

The housewife at the sink had kept an eye peeled, it turned out. She saw me sneak in the garage, and kept peeking through the curtains, waiting for me to come out. She saw the jewel thieves pull up, and when the ruckus started she called the cops.

The cops couldn't believe I had nothing to do with the jewel robbery, but I didn't, and after a while they let me go. The newspapers had fun with the story. The tied-up guy—he lived, but probably wished he hadn't—was wanted bad for the robbery, which everyone in town still remembered. The guy I fell on went back inside for violating his parole—after he got out of the hospital. And the guy who got kicked pretty good was still dead.

That left me still standing. The papers decided to make a hero out of me, though I notice they never printed my picture. That might have spoiled the illusion. Still, I got some good headlines for a while.

And the wheezy guy was wrong about the insurance company. The reward was still out. The jewelry store came through, too, big time. It seems there was a reward outstanding for the missing jewels and the missing robber, and after some deliberation they gave it all to me.

So between the reward and the big-ass diamond I had pocketed—I forgot to tell the cops about it in the confusion, and then I was too embarrassed to mention it—I made out all right.

Good thing, too, because there was no way that foreman was ever going to hire me again.

Runaway
by Derek Nikitas

•

You know from the first sentence of a story or novel if the writer has the chops to bring a tale to life. Ten seconds after I began reading Derek Nikitas's "Runaway"—which you are about to have the pleasure of reading—I knew I was in the hands of a unique and fresh voice in fiction. As the story lived—because this one is alive and kicking—I no longer thought about the writer, but had opened my eyes into the world of the story itself.

Derek Nikitas is one of the brightest new voices in fiction. From the opening of his short story "Runaway," to its last breath, the mark of great things to come is in every line, every thought. It is like reading Joyce Carol Oates for the first time, or Truman Capote—the story counts, it has meaning, the world it occupies is a world of contradiction, the irrational lives side by side with the reasonable, the dream exists in the open eyes of the awakened.

The centerpiece of the story is a girl named Rhonda, who intrigues and attracts the two boys—Auden and Jeremy—with her mysterious presence. The suburban world looms around them, a growing gothic cathedral of the ordinary. Into this, through their secret hideaway in the earth, Rhonda appears and could just as well be a phantom of mythology as a runaway—first seen "jabbing a serrated kitchen knife at them, baring her teeth, squinting at the summer daylight flooding in," and smelling "like Far East spice and hot asphalt." She is an intrusive force of nature—a wilderness breaking through into the swiftly changing landscape of forest turned to suburban tract.

The world of these two boys has changed in an instant. Their perceptions of their surroundings also transform until the story's devastating conclusion. "Runaway" is intense and brief, and you will not forget Rhonda once you've met her. I hope you will not forget Derek Nikitas's name, either—watch for his fiction. Look for it. Ask for it.

—Douglas Clegg,
author of *The Machinery of Night*
and *The Hour Before Dark*

The two boys pumped their dirt bike pedals, sweating and heaving through backwoods trails and into Jeremy's yard where they found that their fort, rebuilt from treehouse debris that had fallen after an ice storm, had been breached—the blue tarp bunched aside, the padlocked hinge on their secret cellar trapdoor busted. Auden kicked aside the useless padlock and lifted open the door. There in the dark underbelly was a black girl their age they'd never seen before, and she was jabbing a serrated kitchen knife at them, baring her teeth, squinting at the summer daylight flooding in. She was down as deep as a grave, so even her head was underground and the sun didn't shine past her shoulders.

"Holy shit," Auden said, but he didn't budge even when her knife tip sliced across the empty eyelets on his hightops. Behind him, Jeremy gasped at the girl and stumbled back against a flimsy plywood wall.

The boys were both fifteen, three weeks short of tenth grade. Just that morning they'd biked almost five miles out to a construction site, taking one pit stop at the Quickie on Rural Route 104 for tubes of Necco wafers and Slushee ice drinks that they drowned with every flavor until it turned black. Jeremy also bought Junior Mints even though, or because, he hated how much he ate, hated being able to squeeze the blubber around his belly like it was raw pizza dough. In the trees on the edge of a cabbage field they'd drunk their tongues purple, then chewed some tobacco that Auden had stolen from the store and stuffed in a cargo pocket on his camouflage shorts. They spit out the chew and then ate Neccos to kill the putrid aftertaste. For a while Auden told Jeremy that story about visiting his older brother's college for the weekend, how Auden got drunk on Goldschläger and kicked the shit out of this college guy and fingered this chick who thought he was a high school senior. Jeremy had heard it all before, but he liked the details—gold flakes in the booze, meaty punches, the girl's warm wetness.

They stood on the pedals when the canal path got steep and grunted through the pain, both of them— Auden in the lead, shirtless and sunburnt, Jeremy trailing in a drenched-out HARD ROCK CAFÉ ORLANDO tee. The construction site was mostly plain orange earth tilled up by backhoes. Where weeks before there had been forest, now there were twelve cinder-block foundations scattered on twelve acres of ground. It was almost like how the boys had excavated their bunker with spades and then dragged over the old fallen tree-house carcass to conceal it.

With Jeremy as lookout, Auden sat inside a backhoe cab and cranked the gears. He climbed down a concrete wall and scored a wayward nail gun and fired it at the dirt and at the sun. He acrobat-walked a plank laid across somebody's someday basement, and he bounced until the plank bowed and crackled. Auden was all taut-strung tendons, visible veins, and skinned-chicken muscles. He had a rat tail worming down between his shoulder blades and a scar branded where collar meets shoulder—an inch-long slit that whitened when the rest of him got scorched.

Jeremy stood where gravel would soon become an as-phalt rink for street hockey, for darting pets, for SUV tires easing home in the workday dusk. He saw how the road would someday feed into driveways and into homes. He read the contractor's spiel on a billboard—*Your dream house is becoming a reality! Ten rooms! A hundred custom choices! Starting low 200s!*—and he thought about his own house just over the county line, a half mile from the trailer park where Auden lived. It was one floor, two bedrooms, with unpainted siding, no basement, no air-conditioning, oil heat from a tank outside—hardly better than the tree house that Jeremy's dad had built for him one year before splitting from up-state New York for higher pay and warmer winters in Virginia.

Jeremy lifted his bike from where it was propped against a lumber pile. He didn't want to be here any-more. He wanted to leave before one of the sleeping yellow machines sparked to life and crushed him into

grist for making lawns grow green. Auden saw him re-
treating and trotted over, heckling, powdered with sawdust. He aimed the nail gun at Jeremy's head and said,
"You don't deserve to live."

Jeremy collapsed onto the dirt and pressed his face
into his shoulder.

Auden said, "I'm just messing, dude. Look at these
houses not even built and I want to burn them already.
They're gonna all look the same when they're done, just
like all the assholes who are gonna come live in them."

On the way home, they left the canal trail and climbed
down a grassy ravine toward a shallow pond where before they'd seen tadpoles churning like black sperm.
They were trespassing on someone's marshy backyard
where a lopsided swing set was sinking into the ground
and where a dull brown Chihuahua yapped furiously at
them, tearing up grass divots at the limit of its chain.
The tadpoles were now thumb-size frogs that Auden
scooped up from the reeds and loaded into his cargo
pocket. Jeremy watched from the property line. Auden
climbed eight pegs on a telephone pole and hung one-
handed from that height, grabbing handfuls of frogs
from his pocket and chucking them at the Chihuahua.
The dog squealed and flipped and sneezed so hard its
whole head shuddered, even though it was never exactly
hit. Finally, the corkscrew spike ripped from the dirt and
the dog sprinted off through the woods with that spike
on the end of its chain leaping along behind it.

That was just minutes before they discovered that
their safe hideaway had been invaded by this girl from
out of nowhere threatening with her knife and yelling,
"You fuckers back up. I said back up!"

"Hey, chill out," Auden said. He showed her his palms, but he couldn't keep from snickering and tossing wide-eyed nods at Jeremy. He wasn't afraid. He was like a dog made to beg for a treat.

"Who you people?" the girl asked.

"This is our fort, man. Who're you?" Auden said.

"I don't got to tell." She was straining to peer at them over the edge of the hole, and her outstretched arm was resting on the floor now, easy enough for one of them to stomp on her wrist and pry her knife away—but Auden was closer and didn't seem to want this to end fast or simple.

"Look, if you're in trouble we ain't gonna turn you in. Right, Jere?"

Jeremy nodded. He pressed a hand against the plywood wall, against the jutting nails he and Auden had driven in by the handfuls last summer when they'd stitched this broken refuge back together again. He pressed until the nails almost punctured his skin.

The girl said: "You want to know what? I just busted out from juvey."

"Where's that?" Auden said. "Nowhere near here."

"I come all this way walking and hitchhiking. For real."

"It's cool," Auden told her. "We won't say nothing to nobody."

The girl snorted "uh-huh," but she withdrew her arm anyway. Her fingers were empty when they came back up from the dark. She said, "Help me out."

Auden helped yank her onto the fort floor. Jeremy watched as she rose from that trench he'd dug from scratch, that he'd stocked with empty beer bottles and broken action figures, smut mags, a liter jug of Morley's Discount Vodka that he'd bought with lunch money from Auden's older brother, a couple flashlights to browse the magazines with.

She'd been inside there—this girl who was like nobody he'd ever known, not even like the couple of black kids at his school—and now she surfaced in nothing but a pair of jeans and a grimy gray bra, soiled tennis shoes for her bare feet. Her skin was such a deep shade that it was almost purple, much darker than her rusty hair twined in thin cornrows. Her lips were dry brown except where her tongue slicked them moist. She smelled like Far East spice and hot asphalt, and she grabbed him by the shoulder to right her balance. In fifteen years Jeremy had never been touched by anyone who was so alien that only her palms and her fingertips, colored like his own, seemed believable.

"What's your name?" Jeremy said.

"Never mind that. What was I thinking, running off? Might as well turn me in for all I care. Look, I had to steal these pants that's too small." She slapped both sides of her unbuttoned waistband to show where it dug tracks into her skin. Jeremy saw that she'd also stuck her knife through a belt loop on her hip, keeping it close at hand.

He asked, "Are you hungry?"

"Naw. I was drinking some a that hard shit y'all got down there."

"You know," Auden said, "you didn't need to tell us you were from juvey."

"I ain't. I lied. Really I took off from home 'cause I hate my dad. I been on the road five days and—shit—I don't even know where I am, tell the truth."

"You're nowhere, that's where," Auden said.

"I can get you some food, really," Jeremy said.

"Might as well," she said. "And call the cops while you at it, tell them you got Rhonda Peach trapped in your little elf house."

"Don't do that," Auden said, grabbing Jeremy's wrist to prove he was serious.

In his kitchen Jeremy piled leftover barbecue chicken breasts and potato salad onto a paper plate, sprinkled it with vinegar potato chips, then poured a glass of water from the tap. He struggled to carry it all back outside without spilling food onto his yard of parched dirt and pebbles. Over his shoulder he'd thrown one of his mother's oversize T-shirts that she used for a nightgown. He'd rummaged fast because Auden was alone out there with this girl and her knife. Not that it mattered: A threat of violence was something Auden would just drink up like he was dying of thirst.

The girl who called herself Rhonda ate the cold chicken and chips inside the fort, her legs dangling down through the trapdoor into the bunker below, as if she'd been born from there and was still attached to the lower dark somehow. The oversized T-shirt sat in her lap collecting bone scraps and finger grease, and Jeremy stayed wary of anything she might suddenly do or say. He filtered through all the stranger warnings he'd learned by rote, but none of them seemed to apply to her.

She said: "Where I come from, you know, they nothing but dealing down there. My dad he do crack, meth. Y'all got no idea out here with these trees and them birds chirping and shit. One time I seen this dude get popped right in a phone booth. He on the phone and this car roll up and all a sudden, *bam!* right? His ass go down, blood all on the glass. That's why I'm up in here with y'all. Ain't never going back there, feel?" She dropped her last bone down into the hole and balled the T-shirt in her hands and tossed it at Jeremy's face. His eyesight went black for a second, blocking everything but the cold-poultry stench and Rhonda's glassy laughter.

At night Jeremy sat on his living room couch catching breeze from an electric fan. The heat was giving him sores where his flab creased too much, so he ate a package of cinnamon toaster pastries to make himself feel better. While he scratched bug bite welts on his legs, the evening news came on and reported nothing about Rhonda Peach or any missing girl. He wondered if he should explore out back to see if Rhonda had been just some daydream ghost that he and Auden had dreamed up together. When the phone rang it was already in his hand.

"Is she still there?" Auden said over the line.

"I don't know."

"Didn't you go out to see her again?"

"No, not really."

"That's pretty rude, man. Bring her a blanket or some dinner or something."

"My mom'll already notice her shirt is missing. What am I supposed to do?"

"I'm sleeping over tomorrow. Is that cool? Maybe I should come over now."

"No," Jeremy said. "My mom's coming home and she'll bitch."

"So I'll hang out with Rhonda in the fort."

"She's got a knife. We don't even know who she is."

"She's just some kid like us."

"Not like us," Jeremy said. Even with the fan blades thrusting at him full blast he still kept sweating, his thick bangs sticking to his forehead and cheek, itching, as if the heat off Rhonda's body could reach him even from behind locked doors thirty feet away. He'd felt lost and weak like this before—like just a week ago when at the Hammersport Village Library Auden had shown him a secret Web site loaded with authentic forensics files: motorcycle accidents and aborted fetuses, a wedding portrait set alongside the bride's autopsy shots dated three days later, a hunter who'd been hit by a train and whose clean-sheared face had bunched up above his skull like a red toque, vivid in the downy snow. He kept looking, as if those downloads could uncover some kind of truth. Instead they left him raw and hollow and wondering how Auden siphoned up life from that ugliness like it was his main source of fuel. He said: "I want to go out like that. I want to just detonate in a million pieces and totally disappear."

Mom staggered in after midnight stinking of ammonia in her nurse's uniform and carrying a Burger King bag, which she dropped in his lap while she slumped down beside him on the couch. She lit a cigarette and let her eyes swell shut after thirty seconds of Leno. Grueling twelve-hour shifts at the hospital left her too drained to talk, so Jeremy just pulled the cigarette from her mouth and snuffed it in an ashtray. He went down the hall to his bed where he chewed the cold Whopper and fries. He blasted Xbox monsters into gore and watched a mosquito suck his knee and thought of Rhonda out there exposed among the swarming insects. He tried to sleep and thought of Rhonda dozing on the rugged fort floor—or worse, back inside that bunker balled up on the damp soil. He thought of her until her fingernails clicked against his window and startled all the thinking away.

Rhonda pushed upward on the screen and it opened cockeyed. She pressed her face grotesque against that screen and whispered, "Here, here!", groping inside to slap the wall. Jeremy pushed aside fast food trash and scrambled down onto the floor wearing only his boxers. He tried to drag his biggest pillow across his lap, but Rhonda grabbed his hand strong enough to tear ligaments. No ghost about her.

"You damn sweet," she said. "Letting me crash here. You got a smoke?"

"I'll steal some of my mom's cigarettes," he said.

"Ain't got nothing stronger?"

"Naw, just cigarettes. And Burger King if you want some."

It was no sweat swiping a few Dorals from the pack in Mom's purse because she smoked and slept too hard to notice. Even if she caught him or discovered Rhonda, he doubted much would happen. Maybe back months ago when she was dating an Orleans County sheriff's deputy named Randy Coolidge, who'd been over for a steak dinner one night, who'd flashed the Colt .45 he carried for kicks, who'd urged Jeremy not to rush his driver's permit—but that romance had gone stale so fast that Jeremy never even had a chance to fret about it.

Rhonda pushed up the screen all the way, and Jeremy slipped her four cigarettes and a lighter. She took one deep sniff along the length of a cigarette and let her eyes drift shut in satisfaction, humming to herself. "Come up over here a sec," she said, squirming her head under the screen. He leaned closer and she caught his chin and pulled him against her lips for a fast, flinching kiss that left a flavorless slick on his mouth.

"What was that for?" Jeremy hugged his legs against his crotch so Rhonda couldn't see what her kiss had done, couldn't brand him a pervert and run off as fast as she'd appeared.

"You never killed nobody before, right?" Rhonda said, smoking deep drags. " 'Cause I did. I killed this white boy in a pool when I was but six years old. Believe, he was cussing me, poking me, so I drowned him good when nobody was looking. People they got thinking it was a accident. Now you the only one who know—how about that?"

"I don't think I believe you," Jeremy said.

"Damn," Rhonda said, scowling at him and laughing without opening her mouth.

They took to the canal trails with Rhonda standing barefoot on the back pegs of Auden's bike, her dark hands clasped against his naked shoulders as she ducked and screeched whenever the tree branches hung over the path, or when Auden swerved to avoid a root sprouting from the dirt. For a while she was wearing clothes that Auden had borrowed from his mother's closet—a NIAGARA FALLS MAID OF THE MIST T-shirt and a pair of spandex shorts—but when they reached a defunct canal bridge and climbed the concrete embankment, she stripped off those clothes and stood on the bridge grates in nothing but her ragged bra and Hanes boys' briefs that were coming unstitched along the waistband. The sun glinted silver off her back. Except for what made her female, she was all sinew like Auden. Like Auden she was scarred—one raised pink wound on a thigh and the other on her spine above that tattered waistband. Both scars were longer than a finger and neither was fully healed.

Auden and Rhonda had ventured onto the condemned bridge, well beyond the orange detour sign that had been blocking off traffic for years. They climbed the pedestrian handrail where the paint flaked like blistered skin, where a ten-foot drop would send them down into water of unknown depth and blackish pitch. They called it "scum jumping" at school because only fate knew what solid or liquid garbage might flow across your drop zone, and that was the thrill of it. And there were legends, like the boy who'd shredded his stomach open by diving through the rib cage of a floating cow carcass.

"You coming, Jere?" Auden said, dropping his own pants.

Rhonda straddled Auden's back and wrapped her thighs over his hips, and together they leaped like skydivers, howling through a split-second of airtime, still clinging together when they splashed below the water. Jeremy wanted to jump. He struggled to twist a hard knot in his nerves, but his feet wouldn't even step onto the bridge. Still he clapped and whistled through his pinkies when Rhonda and Auden surfaced their heads from underwater and swam to the sandstone bank.

Down at the construction site, the foundations had grown wood structures and fiberglass flesh that breathed when wind came through. Each house was a maze of

door frames and staircases luring you upward to higher
floors that had no floors. Roofs were already laid and
shingled, but underneath was nothing but open voids
waiting for sinks, tubs, window glass, electrical outlets
that would soon juice these houses to life. There were
trenches around the foundations, muddy inside like
moats that had drained, but the boys and the runaway
leaped across them and landed inside hardwood foyers.
Auden found a yellow hard hat on a pile of wrapped drywall packages, and he set the hardhat on Rhonda's head
to make her laugh and swear at him. In the bathroom
Rhonda found a white plastic pipe the size of a baseball
bat and chased Auden with it through invisible walls until he circled back around into the hallway and used
Jeremy as a shield against her. Jeremy grabbed for
Rhonda's swinging pipe. When they ran the floors rum-
bled and the unsettled sawdust misted up to make them
cough. They were hysterical, roaring and choking like
a gas bomb had caught them off guard, like they were
holed-up convicts being raided by a SWAT team.

One house was more complete than the others, this
one with upstairs flooring and some installed drywall,
even electrical boxes and thick metal wires snaking up
the stud beams. In the bathroom, the toilet, sink, and tub
were stark white porcelain, though there was no water
and no faucets to run it. Auden lifted the toilet seat and
threatened to piss, even pulled his dick up over his waistband and aimed it at the bowl, but he quit his bullshit
after Rhonda clasped one hand over her mouth and
slumped into the bathtub laughing and pointing at him.
Auden said: "I'm going to throw you in that basement,
girl," and that was enough to make her sober. In the

basement there was nothing but dark, and Rhonda had kept away from the downward staircases in every house where they'd trespassed—like hiding in that hole had ruined her to darkness forever.

"That ain't funny, needle dick. For real," she said, slapping away his hands when he tried to pull her out of the tub. He reached again and she pulled him down on top of her. Jeremy left them alone that way, knowing Auden would relish her in ways that he himself had balked at. Jeremy's restraint was coiled inside his gut and set to tighten whenever nerves kicked in. But some trick of blood had reckoned Auden guilty of nothing, chained to nothing, sucking up his stolen candy while Jeremy could only follow behind him gathering up the empty wrappers.

Jeremy climbed the stairs to the second floor and headed for the master bedroom where a balcony overlooked wide acres of cleared land. No railing was built yet, so he sat on the edge and wondered if he'd break his legs from a one-story jump. Maybe Auden and Rhonda would drag him back inside and set his bones, and it could be like the end of a battle where they claimed this place as theirs because they'd conquered it fair and square. They could live here while the grass grew long and the moving vans paraded down the road. They could hoard credit cards from the mailbox and charge a big-screen TV with DVDs and pizzas and a couch that folded out into a bed. They could find a way to call themselves a family, even if nobody else had ever lived like that before. Jeremy knew better than to tell Auden about these dreams. Auden only grasped at what couldn't be reached. He wasted no plans on what others judged to be true or right or safe about the world.

They were riding the gravel shoulder on Route 104 past cabbage fields and swampy forest posted against hunters, out past Auden's trailer park and almost to Jeremy's house when they heard a car horn honk from the grape orchard across the street. It was a red-and-white sheriff's cruiser idling on the edge of a blind access road, and Jeremy knew the driver had to be his mom's ex-fling, deputy Randy Coolidge, running traffic for ticket quotas.

"Keep going," Auden said, but Jeremy was already veering onto the road.

Deputy Coolidge rolled down his window and leaned an elbow out. He was wearing his Stetson hat and shades, but Jeremy recognized his blond handlebar mustache and the pockmark scars on his cheeks. After Jeremy crossed, the deputy said: "Hey, Jeremy, how's it going?" Every few seconds a car zoomed by on the road, cueing the dashboard radar to clock its speed.

"Fine," Jeremy said. "Just hanging out."

The deputy lifted his sunglasses and squinted at Auden and Rhonda, who were sitting on the edge of a drainage ditch across the street. He said, "Who're those guys you're with?"

"My friends Auden and Carla."

"Carla, huh?" the deputy said. A woman barked out numbers on the radio clipped to the epaulette on his shoulder, and Jeremy worried it was some kind of coded all-points bulletin against Rhonda, wanted in seven states for crimes that he'd just made himself accessory to with his blurted lie.

"Uh-huh," Jeremy said.

"You guys staying out of trouble?"

"Yeah, I guess."

"How's your mom doing?"

"She's all right. She works a lot."

"She gets tired?" the deputy guessed, adjusting his rearview mirror that reflected nothing but grapevines and farm equipment. A Xeroxed picture of a dog was stapled to a telephone pole near the passenger side of the cruiser. Jeremy now realized it was a bulletin for a missing Chihuahua, the one Auden had goaded into getting itself lost forever in the woods.

Jeremy said, "Yeah, she gets tired."

"Well, tell her I said hi, will you?"

"Okay," Jeremy said.

"I been, you know, tell her I been thinking about her, and she can call me if she gets some free time. If she feels like it. She has my number."

"Okay," Jeremy said, but he was thinking about that dog.

Inside the fort was hot like a car left all day in the sun, hot that scalded Jeremy's sinuses and made him gasp in the blue-tarped haze and the pot smoke billowing out of Rhonda's mouth. She brought the pipe to her lips again as she leaned against Auden's bare shoulder. Auden tilted his lighter upside down into the bowl and thumbed the flame back on. Jeremy had already drunk enough vodka to make his veins alert and his senses jagged. He couldn't remember when or why Rhonda had taken off her shirt, but they were all topless, even Jeremy as he sat across from the other two with the trapdoor shut between them. Rhonda's eyes were fixed yellow stones, warning him while the rest of her shimmered—

her heavy breasts with thin stretch marks shaped like lightning, coal black areolas big as pacifiers. Seeds crackled inside the bowl as she inhaled and drooped her eggplant eyelids. The muscles in Jeremy's limbs wilted. One of his socks was coming off, and it was live wriggling flesh that was molting off.

"My birthday's today," Rhonda said. "For real."

"How old are you?" Auden said. He was rubbing his cheek against her braids.

"Naw, I mean it's today. The first one. My birthday."

Auden cackled and swiped his hand lazily, absently over her breast.

"You fresh, needle boy," she said, sliding away from him. "And I got to piss."

Jeremy didn't know where she was headed—out into the woods or maybe inside his house for a real working bathroom—but after she left, Auden slid forward and reached for the vodka bottle that Jeremy was offering him.

"I want to ask you," Auden said, taking a swig. He crammed his chin into his chest and held his breath while the throat sting passed. "Do you think she's real?"

"What do you mean?"

"I mean do you believe in her? Rhonda. She came out of nowhere, nobody's looking for her. She said she was born today but she was here yesterday. Man, where do you think she came from? Down there?" He hooked his thumb over toward the trapdoor, the darkness beneath it.

"Stuff like that don't happen."

"Maybe not, but come on. How long has Rhonda been here with us?"

Jeremy opened his mouth to answer but he couldn't think of how to clock the kind of time they'd been spending, time that didn't measure in regular hours and days.

"See, you don't know," Auden said. "Neither do I. And what about them houses they're building? Did you stop and think why they're getting done so fast but there's never any workers there—just shit they left behind?"

"Maybe they work at night."

"Nobody works at night, man. And why are they building places like that around here? Did you think about that? Nothing but junk houses and trailer parks. Nobody real is ever going to want to live here or send their kids to our bumfuck school. Something's going on here and you got to pay attention, that's all. You got to follow it. Least I do. Even them frogs grew too fast."

"I want to follow it, I do," Jeremy slurred. But somewhere he'd lost his way in a dream realm where trees uprooted and concrete crumbled and blood trickled from faucets and bridges whipped their suspension wires. The slashed telephone lines were snaking and sparking on the ground and none of the emergency calls were getting through.

Jeremy woke in his own bed with a sheet balled between his legs. Outside the window, rain drizzled through long streams of fog drifting through his yard and the backwoods. His fort appeared through the haze, out beyond the muck field that his yard had become, so he hurried into a pair of sweatpants, grabbed a T-shirt off the floor, rushed down the hallway and out into the yard in his bare feet, slipping and scraping on the pebbly ground. Cold mud spit between his toes.

"Hey! Hey!" he yelled into the fort. "I told you, Auden!"

He yanked at the blue tarp but lost his footing and elbowed the ground strewn with twigs and sharp-edge rocks. Blood on his fingertips, but he didn't know from where—maybe from the way he dug at the nail-riddled walls inside, finding nothing but the empty vodka bottle he'd left there overnight. The empty fort creaked and leaned when he shouldered it, and the second time it overturned, snapping nails and folding upon itself like a box cut down for bailing. There on the ground was the phantom shape of the fort etched in raw earth, crawling with worms and grubs and stunted white roots. In the center of that shape was the naked maw the boys had dug last summer. It was littered with empty candy wrappers and dirty magazines and nothing else but the scattered action figures laying open-eyed like corpses on a battlefield. Jeremy slid down into the hole and pushed at the ground with his fists until he was gasping, until he was convinced that there were no secret gateways to be found. All he unearthed was an old clawed hammer with a duct-taped handle. It was the same hammer he'd used last summer to drive those nails that had kept his hideaway upright for so long now.

"Auden!" he screamed as he rode one-handed. "Auden!"

Bare feet torn apart on the aluminum-traction bike pedals, and his head throbbing with leftover alcohol and too many adrenaline doses by the time he reached the site and coasted downhill across freshly laid blacktop. Doors and windows were pressed into their cavities with brand-name stickers still affixed, fancy doors with coats of varnish and etched-glass portholes. The few houses still without siding wore silver insulation panels, and every acre of ground had been treated with spray-on grass of a shade he'd never seen before in nature. He dumped his bike against a front yard electric box and trudged on foot across the driveway full of gravel shifting underfoot as if it meant to topple him.

"Auden!" he yelled at the second-story windows, though he didn't know why this house over the others, this house with its pastel blue siding and two-car garage like so many of the others. The front door was in place, but it was a petty defense with its routered hole where the doorknob should go. He pushed through the door and screamed up the main staircase, "Where are you?" His voice snapped from the force and now it was nothing but a rasping whisper.

Without speech he turned to other means, first in the living room where a bay window showed a neighborhood vista that curved up the blacktop toward the main road. He smashed his hammer blunt end first into that window and the glass dropped like ice sheets drifting over a waterfall. The drywall he assaulted with the hammer claw, two-handed strokes that punctured and then tore away the paper skin and chalky white chunks. He breathed the white dust and kept swinging until the wound he'd made could be clotted with a Frisbee, then he ripped away the exposed pink fiberglass, handfuls of cottony tufts concealing nothing but solid wood paneling behind it. He punched the wood but it was just as real as the ground below his fort had been.

"Where are you?" he wheezed.

In the bathroom he lifted the ceramic slab off the toilet tank and rammed it through the window. He kicked plumbing pipes with no effect but a record of his bloody footprints. With both hands he grappled the showerhead, snapped it off the wall, tossed it in the corner. He caught sight of his image in the vanity mirror looking wild and wet and electric, and for one frantic second he finally recognized himself. The fat kid in the mirror was him, and he was just that kid's reflection caught in glass, just a shadow. He knew if he just kept smashing he'd break through, and then he could also be in that place where Auden and Rhonda had gone.

He raised the hammer to shatter himself, but the echo of a dog bark stopped him. Back in the hallway, heaving asthmatically, he inched open the basement door and looked down into the pitch-black nothing. The barking was clearer now, set to the rattle of a chain dragging over concrete. It was down there, but distant, much farther than just one story.

Outside, a cruiser siren squawked once. The swirling red-and-blues made Jeremy squint when he looked out the window of his new dream house he'd ransacked. Deputy Coolidge opened his driver door and stepped out onto the gravel. He took off his sunglasses and Stetson hat on his way up the porch steps. In the doorway he said, "Come on, Jeremy. What is this? Why's it have to be you doing this? Why don't you put down that hammer now, will you? I don't like this any more than you, so I'd rather just make it smooth without no handcuffs or nothing. You don't want me to have to use handcuffs, do you?"

But Jeremy didn't answer. Instead, he looked down into the dark and decided for himself that, yes, he did want Randy Coolidge to have to use the handcuffs.

The Crime of My Life
by Gregg Olsen

•

Gregg Olsen's debut novel, *A Wicked Snow,* has stuck with me for well over a year. It's one of those atmospheric, darkly suspenseful stories that hits you hard because it could be true. Gregg's gift as a writer is to set the stage so vividly and create characters so real that you believe you are right there in the middle of the story, seeing what they see, feeling what they feel.

What is truly amazing is that Gregg can bring out the exact same reader reaction in a short story. In "The Crime of My Life" he shares his own story.

I've never met Gregg in person, but through numerous emails over the past few years I feel like I've known him most of my life. His compassion is unmatched, as is his strong sense of right and wrong, his need to expose the truth no matter what that truth holds. And really, what is fiction except shining light on human nature? Sometimes we refuse to look at the dark side. But that doesn't mean it doesn't exist.

I'm certain "The Crime of My Life" will send a chill up your spine just like it did mine.

—Allison Brennan,
New York Times bestselling author of *Fear No Evil*

Book ideas are born in any number of ways. Some come to authors in a burst of happenstance and brilliance. Some come in the throes of a good dream. A few, I'm told, come from God. I have never been so lucky. My books have always been born of the truth. I am a writer of true crime, a much-maligned genre, but one in which I felt I could stake a claim for a career. Or something that resembled a career. It seemed that there were a million stories out there that—given some shaping and research—could make for interesting reading.

The ideas come from television, prisoners who write me, fans who show up at book signings (though I can't say I have enough of those to provide much of a stockpile) and, of course, newspapers.

"The Crime of My Life" is different. This is a story hatched of my own experiences; my own life.

About a year ago my wife, Valerie, retrieved a carton from under our bed amid rolls of Christmas wrapping paper and white and brown tufts of dog hair. She set the box, with its ill-fitting, strapped-down lid, next to the computer where I did most of my writing. She smiled reluctantly and said only three words.

"Honey, it's time."

I understood what she meant. I knew it even if she had said nothing. I had tried to avoid the idea of telling the story contained in the beat-up box. I had resisted it for all the right reasons, though deep down I knew it was beyond my ability to do so. Beyond my need. Beyond the necessity of supporting my family.

I had a dozen such boxes in various spots in my house. In the garage, too. Three that had been stacked and draped with a cheery chintz fabric passed as a bed-side table in the guest room. The boxes were the rem-nants of the books I had written. Inside each were the unspeakable and the unbelievable. I had been writing true crime books for nearly a decade and the memora-bilia I had collected was suitable for a murder museum, if such a place existed. I had letters from Betty Broderick; a signed page of sheet music from Charles Manson. I even had a sketch by John Wayne Gacy (he made a far better killer than an artist). Inside the box of source material I saved about a woman who had killed her husband for insurance money, was the killer's video store card, her purse (a blue and white nautical shoulder bag), and love letters to the man she had conspired with to commit the murder. I even had the convicted woman's shopping list and a brush entangled with her Clairol Frivolous Fawn–dyed hair.

Each was a Pandora's box of sorts, a repository in which I was the keeper, the jailer of little murderous memories. All had been tagged with the name of the book that I had regarded as a potential bestseller.

The carton my wife put near my desk was labeled with the name of a story I had started to write, but had never seemed destined to complete. It read: "The Crime of My Life."

I took an X-Acto knife from Val's art bin and sliced the silver duct tape I had used to seal the box. Even the tape rekindled a recollection of a terrible night. The glint of silver. The flash of steel. A kind of coldness and fear I had rarely known seized me once more. Some things, I know all too well, are too powerful to forget.

I slid the lid aside and drank some coffee before

looking further. The contents were remarkable, not only in their diversity, but in their very familiarity. The top was blanketed by a green leotard, a Halloween costume worn by one of my twin daughters. A small but unmistakable crescent of blood had stained the garment's neckline.

I drank more coffee and pushed the green fabric aside. At first, I used a pencil to do so. Almost instantly, I felt clinical and foolish. Embarrassed. I was the little girl's father. Her blood was mine. I had carried her and her twin from the delivery room like two peachy footballs; one in each arm. I was the daddy who saved her spit-up cloth because I knew that the smell would always remind me of my baby.

I gently folded the leotard and peered deeper inside. The contents had come so close to being the province of someone else's collection; some other writer who made his or her living out of the anguish of others. It had been too damn close. The interview tapes, the photos of the players in the drama, a photocopy of fingerprints done up like a black-and-white rendering of a row of Chinese lanterns. Everything was in there. Everything that had nearly cost me all I held precious in my life—the lives of every member of my family.

And so I agreed with Valerie, it *was* time. I fiddled with the yarn-covered pencil holder little Teddy Bundy had made for his mom for Mother's Day in 1964. (I purchased it along with other personal belongings from the Bundy family's garage sale after Ted was electrocuted in Florida for the murder of a schoolgirl.) I had reglued the uncoiling rainbow yarn twice before, as if keeping it intact somehow mattered. And I wondered.

I have always been fascinated by crime. I have always wondered what brings a child like Teddy to seek the dark side of murder. How a child, born seemingly perfect, is transformed into the embodiment of evil. Before the events took place in the book you are now holding, I pondered the *why* of a crime from a distance. A safe distance.

I'll never forget that summer day when the wheels of homicide had been set in motion, when my own story would become enmeshed and entangled and, ultimately, *greater* than *Love, Lies and Murder*—the crime I thought I was chronicling.

Once I opened the box, I knew that I had to see the perpetrator, face-to-face. Maybe through the smudged glass that separates the free from the trapped, held there like one of those hothouse flowers under a dome of turgid air? Maybe in a cafeteria-style visiting room? I wrote a letter addressed to the inmate and waited.

Two weeks later, word came that the perp would see me and I parked the only luxury I'd ever allowed myself, a white BMW, in the dusty lot of the prison. I'd ended up using the car almost as much for storage as for transportation. File folders, tapes, and the kind of ephemera that true crime writers collect without even trying: a high school annual that I needed to return; family photos that always looked like they'd been plucked from the nicest family in the world—that is, the nicest family that spawned a killer—and reams of MapQuest printouts that led me from trailer park to suburbia and back again.

I was processed with the other visitors. We all stood there—moms, dads, girlfriends, children—and blinked back the shame of having to come to visit someone in a place like this. I always acted a little smug, just because I could.

"Working on a book," I'd say.

This morning I filed in with the others. I had a pencil and four sheets of notebook paper—ostensibly allowed for tallying Scrabble or some other time-filling game. The best games were always the ones that allowed for more concentration and less small talk. Gaps in conversation during a prison visit were always chilling. They allowed the visitor that moment of reflection that ultimately came in a burst: *I'm in a fucking prison talking to my husband, brother,* whatever. Games that commanded attention put the focus on a triple-word score, and not, say, a double homicide. In the prison visiting room, no lulls are welcome.

I saw him from across the room. Being a writer, I was never good at math sans calculator. Nevertheless, I computed the age he'd been when charged and the years that had passed since then. It made him about seventy. I realized at that moment that I should know his age, birth date, and the simple info that create the framework of character.

I didn't extend my hand when he offered his. "You don't look like your picture," I said, taking a seat on a bolted-down bench across the table.

"Neither do you," he answered, puzzling me for a moment, before I remembered I'd actually sent him one of my books years ago. It came from my publisher directly because no author can send a book into a U.S. prison. Not since someone soaked pages in meth.

An inmate review came to mind: *"An intoxicating read. It kept me turning the pages well into the night."*

I always thought of my books as kind of a business card, proof that I was a writer and I was going to tell a real, true story. Like it or not, here I come.

"A Coke?" I offered, knowing that buying an inmate a Coke—with ice—is like giving the incarcerated a whiff of what the freedom might taste like. Or rather, *tasted* like.

"Nice, thanks." His blue eyes were enveloped by crinkly folds, but they sparkled at that moment. He still wanted to charm. He knew he had to.

I got up and put in a few of the quarters of the roll I'd been allowed to bring inside in the institution. The cup fell. Then the ice. I caught his eye and shrugged as the brown foam swelled to the edge of the cup and spilled over. He smiled, but it was forced, slightly unnatural. Like a mimic.

"So, you've finally decided to tell me your story." I winced at my own opening line.

The smile, real or imitation, vanished. "So, you've finally decided to come and see me."

He was being coy, so I returned the affect. "I'm interested in your story," I said. "I always have been. You've been silent. Why now?"

He tilted the paper cup and poured the cola down his throat. I noticed he wore dentures. I wonder if that's why the smile seemed so false.

"I guess now's time. Obviously you're the right author."

A baby from across the visiting room started to cry.

"I wish they didn't bring babies in here," he said. "Doesn't seem right to me."

I nodded, but couldn't resist taking a chance by giving the man a little jab. "I guess you know a lot about right and wrong."

His stare was hard. The crinkly lines around his eyes looked like snakeskin, not the result of happier times. *If he ever had any.* That is, before he did what he did.

With the door ajar to allow him to speak, he started unloading. He wanted to make sure I wouldn't "screw" him over. I almost laugh out loud whenever a killer makes such a request. I've written about women who've tossed their kids off freeway overpasses; men who've raped the babysitter; or the occasional gold medalist of the true crime genre, a serial killer. Whether A-lister or D-lister in the annals of true crime, almost all seem worried about their image. They worry that someone like me—someone with a keyboard and a mouse— could actually screw them over.

"I'll write the truth," I said, knowing those words always sound so pretentious, no matter how many times I've uttered them. The truth was, of course, my version of it. My Magic Bullet–machine with all the condiments of the crime set on high speed and morphed into the pages of the book that I'm writing. "Always, the truth."

But this one was different, and I knew that it was from the moment I'd finally had the courage to open the box after Valerie uttered:

"Honey, it's time."

I peppered the man across the table with questions. This wasn't the real interview, of course. This was my way of gaining trust, scoping out what he might actually tell me.

"You don't deny that you did it?"

"It?"

It felt like a kind of stare down, but I didn't care. He had it coming.

"Killed her," I said, not saying her name. Killers never like you to say the person's name.

He doesn't miss a beat. "No. But there was a reason for it. One no one knows. One you don't know."

"Really? For instance?"

"I'm not ready for that."

They think they are so smart, so cunning. What the killer never considers is that they are in prison and no one cares about them. Their power is only a blip, not a tsunami. You don't need them. *They need you.*

"Okay. Fair enough," I said, a little too rotely. The meeting, the preinterview, was coming to its conclusion. The sizing-up was over.

He crunched the last of his ice. "Okay. I'll see you next week."

He puts out his hand. I grabbed it in a quick surge that I wished transmitted all my mixed feelings.

The TV was playing an episode of *Law & Order* and I saw the blond heads of my daughters riveted to the screen. It passed through my mind that my girls were as fascinated by crime as I was. They grew up on *Judge Judy, L & O* in all its incarnations, and the work of their father.

"Hi, Daddy," they chimed. "This is the episode about the man who kills his wife for insurance money."

I kissed the tops of their heads; the scar on Melinda's neck has faded. She was so young when she'd got the injury that she almost never brings it up.

"That's like saying you're watching an episode of *Gilligan's Island* where they almost get off the island."

They nodded, but they don't get the reference. Sabrina, the serious twin, rolled her eyes, but actually gave me a hug before planting herself back on the couch.

I threw my jacket on a chair and found my wife standing in front of the kitchen sink. She is lovely and she always has been. I am reminded in that instance— Valerie, Melinda, Sabrina have made me a very lucky man. Valerie heard me come in and had a serious look on her face and I knew it wasn't about the dishes that she'd been transferring into the dishwasher, in that perfect, ordered way that I could never duplicate. Her eyes drank me in and I wanted to cry.

"How was your father? Did he talk about your mom? Did he talk about that night?"

"He will," I said, falling into her arms. "When I'm ready."

The Point Guard
by Jason Pinter

•

Like Jason Pinter's debut novel, *The Mark,* this story is a searing look at youth gone awry, as we witness two young boys' robbery of a neighborhood convenience store, and the tragedy that ensues. One youngster yearns to fit in, the other is the gatekeeper who might hold the key to that longing. It is a frightening portrait of childhood envy, desire, and malice. Like Pinter's protagonist in *The Mark,* Henry Parker, young Kevin wants merely to do the right thing, but ends up committing an unspeakable sin. Pinter is a terrific young talent in crime fiction, and this story shines another light into the darkness of our youth. The events within take place in mere minutes, but their aftereffects will haunt the two characters for a lifetime.

—Jeffery Deaver,
New York Times bestselling author of *The Cold Moon*
and *The Sleeping Doll*

Here's how it goes down," Big Tim said. "I walk in there first. Calm as shit, you know? I go to the back, pour myself one of those Slurpees, check out the goods, look at the expiration dates on the milk, whatever. I'm gonna have your cell number plugged into my phone. As soon as I see one of the counter bunnies head for the bathroom, I'm gonna press send. When you feel your phone vibrate, that's your cue to bust in there and make shit happen. No sitting outside with your thumb up your ass, and I don't want to hear it took you a while 'cause you were chatting up some chickenhead outside. Far as I'm concerned, today you're asexual. Reproduce like a spore and shit. Bottom line, when Quik-E-Mart man heads to the john, you walk in there and stick your piece in the other guy's face. Then we're out in less than a minute. Think you can handle that, dipstick?"

Kevin looked at Big Tim. His eyes showed no lack of confidence, if anything they showed that Big Tim would kill himself just to get you. The kind of guy you always wanted on your team, only because you knew he'd put himself in harm's way just to get the job done. Until this week, Kevin had always had a gentle respect for Big Tim. Tim had always protected the neighborhood kids, sometimes taping a lead pipe to the inside of his boot so he'd be ready for battle in case one of those head cases from Marionville decided to hop on the bus, steal some pocket money, head back with wallets stuffed with one dollar bills.

Big Tim was always on their side, sometimes sending those pricks back with bruised shoulders, maybe a broken finger, one time sending a kid back with a concussion so bad the newspaper picked it up, ran a pic of the kid on page seven. Kid never came back, and Big Tim walked around showing off that pipe to anyone who looked, saying that tiny scratch on the end came from denting that Marionville kid's thick skull. You were never in danger as long as Big Tim was around. When he was younger Big Tim lost plenty of fights, but would always come back with a stick, a rock, or a bat to even the score. Pretty soon kids stopped picking on Big Tim. Even if they won the scrap, walked away with a few bucks, Big Tim came back with a vengeance. If you won the fight, you slept with one eye open that night.

Right now Kevin wasn't thinking about that. Big Tim was standing in front of him, wearing a plain gray sweatshirt, gray sweatpants. Usually Big Tim wore a throwback jersey—Bill Russell, George Gervin, Moses Malone—and jeans baggy enough to hide a pipe or whatever instrument he decided on that day. His usually spiky hair was free of gel, neatly combed back, though it looked ready to spring free at any moment. If Kevin didn't see that gleam in Big Tim's eye, that pupil ready to explode, he wouldn't have recognized Big Tim at all. And that was the idea.

Big Tim had given Kevin the gun the day before yesterday. Big Tim had approached him after basketball practice, pulled Kevin aside. He spoke in a hushed tone. It frightened Kevin. Big Tim never spoke softly. If anything he spoke in exaggerated barks, making sure anyone with decent hearing would pick up on it.

"Listen, Kev," Big Tim said. Big Tim kneeled down on the pavement, checking once around each shoulder to make sure nobody could hear or see them. Kevin's heart beat fast. For a moment he was worried that Big Tim might be pissed at him, might take out that pipe and hurt him. Kevin could only imagine what his dad might say if that happened. Then he wondered if his dad might use Kevin's injury as a reason to call Kevin's mom in New York. Then Kevin wondered whether getting beat up would be such a bad thing if it meant his mom might come visit.

When Big Tim reached into his tattered blue knapsack and pulled out a small gun, holding it out to Kevin butt first, Kevin knew a beating was the least of his worries.

"Take it, little man," Big Tim said. Kevin looked at him for a moment, worry in his eyes and his heart. "Go on little sucker, take it. It ain't loaded."

Tentatively, Kevin reached out and took the gun. It was lighter than he thought it would be. It was all black, small round bumps on the handle. There were scratches along the muzzle, and what looked like remnants of a number.

"Serial's been filed off," Big Tim said. "Ain't got to worry about anyone tracing this shit." Kevin nodded, as though that made perfect sense.

"Why . . . ," Kevin said, unable to finish the question.

"That's a .380 Bersa Thunder," Big Tim said. "Sweet-ass gun. Got a combat-style trigger guard and an eight-shot mag. You can tuck this baby into your sock, unless some fool is Superman they won't notice a thing." Again Kevin nodded.

"Why are you . . ."

"Take it home tonight," Big Tim said. "Sleep with it under your pillow. Get used to the look, the feel. Don't be scared, like I said, it ain't loaded, so you don't got to worry about blowing your two-inch dick off."

Kevin wanted to tell Big Tim that his dick was bigger than two inches, but now didn't seem like the best time.

"Saturday," Big Tim continued. "You're going to meet me on the corner of Elm and Winwood. Three o'clock on the damn dot. You know what's on the corner of Elm and Winwood?"

"The 7-Eleven?"

"Damn right. Knew I picked the right kid to help me out."

For a moment, a spark of pride leapt up within Kevin. Not too many people received compliments from Big Tim, and they usually came after a beating, with phrasings like, *Your face can't get any uglier and I can't fuck you up any worse than your mommy already did.*

"So you gonna meet me at that corner at three. If your dads ain't passed out drunk, tell him you going down to the park to play ball. Not like he'll notice, but I know some cats down there'll tell anyone who asks you played all day Saturday. Even scored some nice buckets. S'what they call an alibi, little man."

Kevin nodded.

"At three o'clock, you and me, we're going to rob that shit. We should come away with ten grand, easy. We split it seventy-five, twenty-five. Means you take home two thousand, five hundred dollars."

"What do I do with two thousand five hundred dollars?"

"Bitch, I don't care! Give it to your pops to pay rent. Buy some manga books and shit. Do whatever you want. But that's a shitload of money. You're just lucky I'm being nice and letting you in on my deal."

And that's where they stood right now, outside the 7-Eleven. Big Tim in his gray sweats, Kevin in jeans and sneakers. Just like Big Tim had instructed, Kevin was wearing a T-shirt under a brand-new fleece. Big Tim had bought the fleece for ten bucks on the sidewalk. That way, he said, Kevin could toss the fleece away and any descriptions would be wrong as hell.

"They'll be looking for some chump in a blue fleece, not some cool kid with a T-shirt." Again with the praise. Kevin soaked it up, loved it.

"Let's go over this again," Big Tim said. "When Towelhead goes to take a shit, I call you. You bust in with the gat, stick it in Mrs. Towelhead's face. I'll be in the back by the ice cream. Don't look at me, talk to me, even *think* about me. That way people won't think you had an accomplice, screw the whole investigation up." Big Tim handed Kevin a brown paper bag. "Say you want the register. The whole register. Give 'em this and tell them to fill it up."

Kevin looked at the small bag, saw a tiny piece of turkey at the bottom. He looked at Big Tim.

"I used it for my lunch yesterday, you got a problem with that?" Kevin told Big Tim he didn't. He also wondered how ten thousand dollars could fit in such a small bag, but he didn't say anything. Big Tim probably knew better, and if there was anyone at their school who could have ever seen that much money it was Big Tim.

Big Tim lived in a nice house, much nicer than Kevin's. Big Tim's parents were still together, and Kevin heard a rumor that they owned a thirty-four-inch television. Big Tim would sometimes come to school in a different throwback jersey every day. He bragged about owning a jersey from every team in NBA history, even the ones that didn't exist. Once Kevin saw Big Tim's dad drop him off at school in a black car. It looked clean, didn't have a scratch on it, and Kevin could see through the windshield that Big Tim's dad was wearing a nice suit with a bright red tie. Kevin had never seen his dad with a tie, and the families in the neighborhood that did own cars tended to buy them at a place owned by an Italian named Sal who had a mustache and didn't accept returns.

"Now if Towelhead number one comes out of the john before you're done, wave that gun at him and tell him not to move a muscle. See, these stores got security buttons behind every register. If he's in the john, you only got one to worry about. You watch him like a hawk, make sure he doesn't make any funky movements, you'll be golden. Once you get the money, run like a fucking asshole."

Big Tim pointed to the alley behind the 7-Eleven.

"I opened that Dumpster so you don't have to waste a second. Toss your sweatshirt in there, take a left at the fence, run like hell and you should get away before anyone sees you changed your shirt. Tuck the money into your pants. We'll meet up at four o'clock behind the church in Riverside. If I find out you're holding back on me, I'm gonna get my pipe and bash your skull in."

Kevin shook his head, telling Big Tim not to worry about it. He'd never do such a horrible thing.

"Okay, little man," Big Tim said, smacking Kevin on the shoulder. "You ready to become a big man?"

"I think so," Kevin said. His stomach felt like it was about to leap out of his throat. The gun felt so heavy against his waistband.

"I know what you need," Big Tim said, smiling a frightful grin. He reached into his pocket, then took the gun from Kevin's waist. Kevin heard a small clinking sound, and watched as Big Tim popped out a long black compartment and shoved several small pellets into it. He then clicked it back into place, and thumbed a small lever on the side.

"Loading her up," Big Tim said. "Don't want you going in there naked."

"Am I supposed to shoot someone?" Kevin asked.

"Not unless you have to," Big Tim answered.

Big Tim looked inside the store, nodded to Kevin. "About that time, friend. You ready?" Kevin's heart surged, and he nodded emphatically. "Then let's do it."

Big Tim opened the door, eliciting a jingle from inside. Kevin took several short breaths, gathering himself, feeling the gun in his waist. It was heavier now.

Kevin waited a few minutes. It was getting colder outside. Summer turning into fall. For a moment, Kevin wished he were playing basketball. JV tryouts were coming up, and he needed work on his free-throw shooting. The last point guard had gotten the call from the varsity squad, so Kevin knew there was an opening at the one. If only he was good enough.

Then he felt it. The vibration from his pocket. Big Tim was ready.

Kevin reached in his pocket and turned off the phone. He took one more quick breath. He was nervous, but Big Tim had called him "friend." Big Tim didn't just say that to anyone. If he was man enough to do this, he was man enough to run Coach Raskin's basketball team.

Kevin opened the door. He didn't step inside immediately, instead waited to see if anyone looked at him, noticed him. None did. He was just another kid stopping in for a Slurpee, a stick of beef jerky, maybe he'd get crazy and try to steal a Kit Kat. But not Kevin. Kevin saw one man at the counter. His complexion was dark and he wore a neatly trimmed beard. He smiled as he handed an old lady some change. Kevin looked around, saw the sleeve of a gray sweatshirt in the corner and knew Big Tim was watching.

Without another thought, Kevin walked up to the counter.

"Hello, my friend, what can I get for you?" Kevin didn't know what to say. He fished into his pocket and pulled out the brown paper bag. He placed it on the counter.

"I'm sorry," the man said. "I do not understand."

Kevin reached into his waistband, and with the confidence of Big Tim thrust the gun into the man's face. The smile disappeared like it had never been there. He hands instinctively raised.

"What are you doing?" the man asked, his voice quivering. Kevin noticed a small piece of turkey on the counter. It must have fallen out of the bag.

"Put the money in the bag," Kevin said. He looked back at the corner, tried to see the expression on Big Tim's face.

The man nodded. He pressed a button and the cash register rang open. Kevin watched as the man pulled out a combination of bills, forty or so, and stuffed them into the bag.

"Now please, please leave."

"How much money is that?" Kevin asked.

"I don't know," the man said, shaking. "Two, three hundred dollars."

"I want the whole ten thousand," Kevin said, deepening his voice, trying to sound as intimidating as possible. It was working; the clerk looked ready to pass out from fear.

"I don't have that money here," the clerk said. "It's in the safe."

Safe? Big Tim didn't say anything about a safe.

"Could you open it?" Kevin asked, feeling a slight crack in his confidence. He looked again for Big Tim, saw nothing. He heart hammered. He wanted to get out. He wanted to practice his free throws. He didn't care about the money anymore. But Tim . . .

"I don't have the combination," the man said. "They come every night and open it and take the money. I only have what's in the register. Please take it and go."

"Tim!" Kevin yelled. The store went silent. "Tim, do you have the combination for the safe?"

Kevin heard nothing for a moment, then a subdued, *"Shut the fuck up"* was uttered from the back of the store. Big Tim.

"Tim, the money is in the safe. He doesn't have the combination. Do you?"

"Goddamnit kid, shut your fucking mouth."

Kevin didn't have ten thousand dollars. He had three hundred, tops. Big Tim would beat him with the pipe. He'd have to go to the hospital. His father would frown at him. He wouldn't call Kevin's mother for help. And everyone would laugh at him in school.

Then Kevin heard the opening of a door, and the second clerk, a heavyset man with a shaved head, appeared.

"What the fuck!" he cried out. Without thinking, Kevin turned to the second clerk, remembered what

Big Tim said *(Not unless you have to)* and pulled the trigger.

Thunder shook the store, and the gun leapt from Kevin's grasp. He heard a scream, saw a spurt of red that had to be blood and the second clerk fell into a heap, clutching his chest. The patrons made a mad break for the door, the jingling disappearing amidst the chaos. Kevin saw Big Tim in the corner, his eyes wide, a look in them Kevin had never seen before.

Sheer terror.

Kevin reached down and picked up the gun. It was warm. And still heavy.

He pointed it back at the first clerk, who was frozen behind the counter.

"Please," Kevin said. "Open the safe."

"I . . . I can't," the man said. "For the love of God, don't shoot me."

Kevin pulled the trigger again. There was another explosion, and the clerk clutched his shoulder, red seeping out from between his fingers.

"Tim!" Kevin yelled. "Can you come up here and help me?"

His eyes wide as dinner plates, Big Tim slowly walked to the front. His mouth was open. Fear and confusion in his eyes.

"I need you to open the safe. They didn't have the combination."

"I don't have it," Tim said.

Kevin felt tears well up in his eyes. "I can't get you the ten thousand dollars," he said. "Please don't be mad. I didn't know they would have a safe. I promise I'll get it somehow, just don't hurt me."

"I won't," Tim said, but there was no emotion in his voice. Kevin picked up the brown paper back, dots of blood sprinkled on the sides. He extended it to Tim.

"This is all I got. Take it."

Tim took the bag. Stood there holding it. His eyes fixated on the gun.

Just then Kevin heard another jangle. The front door opened again. Kevin turned around to see three police officers inside the store. They were all holding guns. More guns than Kevin had seen in his life. And all the guns were pointed at Kevin.

The one closest to him, a woman with her hair tied back in a ponytail, yelled, "Put the gun down now, son, and step away."

Kevin nodded, but held the gun.

"Tim?" he said.

Tim said nothing. Just stood there with the bag.

"Tim?"

Again, nothing.

Kevin looked at the police officers. They didn't look like they wanted to hurt him.

"Come on, kid," the lady officer said again. "Put the gun down."

Kevin's mother used to wear her hair in a ponytail. Kevin used to lie in her arms, smell her hair, that shampoo she used with a hint of jasmine. He wanted this woman to pick him up, hold him. Kevin felt hot tears streaking down his cheeks. He mouthed a word, wasn't sure what it was.

"Goddamnit, kid!" It came from a male voice, rougher, deeper, from behind the woman. "Drop the gun!"

Kevin looked at Tim, who stood there like a statue. Tim wouldn't help. He couldn't. It was all up to Kevin.

"I just want the money in the safe," he cried. "Do you have the combination?"

The lady cop looked at the other officers. Then she said, "Sure we do, kid. Put down the gun and we'll give it to you."

"Really?"

"Really," she said.

"Really," said the man cop.

Kevin looked at the man. Looked at the woman. She looked honest. The man did not. Kevin looked at the gun. Looked at the man cop again. Looked at Tim.

"I'll get you your money," he said. Kevin raised the gun. Pointed it at the man cop. Then he heard another explosion, and before the darkness hit he wondered if this would be enough to get his mom to finally come visit him.

Gravity and Need
by Marcus Sakey

•

Debut novelists sometimes have trouble getting noticed. But not Marcus Sakey. His first novel, *The Blade Itself,* seemed to get noticed everywhere and in wonderful places (*CBS Sunday Morning,* the *New York Times Book Review, Entertainment Weekly,* on and on). I've seldom seen so many uniformly enthusiastic reviews. He has been compared to Dennis Lehane, Elmore Leonard, Laura Lippman, and Quentin Tarantino, while fellow authors Lee Child, T. Jefferson Parker, and George Pelecanos praise his talents. And they aren't exaggerating. Sakey's work has a fascinating "you are there" quality that explores gripping character dilemmas and intense moral issues. In *The Blade Itself,* the main character becomes trapped by the demons of his past and discovers that the more he has, the more he has to lose. Now, in his new wonderful short story, "Gravity and Need," Sakey explores a similar compelling theme, the difference between what a person wants and what that person needs, with an emphasis on "want" and the extent to which a person will go to achieve that goal. It's a beautiful, haunting tale with a hypnotic first sentence that made me lean forward, confident that I was in the hands of a terrific writer at the start of what will be a spectacular career.

—David Morrell, *New York Times* bestselling author of *First Blood, The Brotherhood of the Rose,* and *Creepers*

Here's how Pamela introduced herself to me: "Candle wax washes out of sheets. Did you know that?"

People talk about love at first sight, but what they really mean is recognition. You look in someone's eyes, could be anyone, a childhood friend or a stranger waiting for the bus, and in an instant, things are different. Like they've pulled aside a curtain and let you look deeper than flesh.

What you see depends on who you are. Maybe it's peace and plenty. Maybe it's grandchildren bobbling on your knee.

In Pamela's eyes, what I saw was a reflection. And more than that, I saw her seeing her reflection in *my* eyes, the look bouncing back and forth like an endless loop of mirrors. Then she smiled, those lips turning up at only one corner, a hint of teeth, and the next thing I knew we were going at it under the humming fluorescents of the stockroom, her legs wrapped around my back, her ass up on the packing crate of a forty-inch plasma screen.

In retrospect, everything that followed seems obvious.

It hadn't been easy getting the wheelchair up the hill and onto the embankment above the river.

Late sun spilled through the trees and set the steel tracks on fire. A hum of crickets rose loud and steady. The railroad bridge was lonely in the same way as the back side of a strip mall. It's a part of civilization you aren't supposed to see; there's graffiti but no people.

"What are we doing here?" I watched the light rouge her cheeks, highlight her black hair. She looked away, and I thought of the day we met.

* * *

The guy was ideal. Late twenties, outfit by Banana Republic, cheap shoes, and a good haircut. Two years ago he probably had a goatee, and two years hence he'd have a BMW. Ideal.

"I need a new stereo," he'd said.

I shook my head. "You don't."

"Huh?"

"You don't need a new stereo. You need water. You need food and clothes and shelter." I held up my hands and smiled like we were buddies. "I'm not going all grammar Nazi. I'm just saying the things you *need,* they aren't any fun. They're just things you need. What's fun is the things you want. Right?"

He snorted. "Sure."

"Okay. So what kind of stereo do you want?"

The guy walked in thinking about a boombox. He walked out with a 5.1 surround-sound system, a hundred-watt-per-channel receiver, and a progressive scan DVD. Understand—I didn't con him, and I didn't pressure him. Hell, I didn't even sell him. I just told him that it was okay to want something.

Everybody wants. Without that, what are you? Just an animal taking care of needs.

But I didn't waste a lot of time pondering it, because all the time I was talking to him, I saw this beautiful girl staring at me, one side of her lips raised in a secret smile.

After you have sex with a total stranger on top of a three-thousand-dollar television, what you're supposed to do is zip up, exchange fake numbers, and never see each other again.

We went for Thai.

You know that moment on a first date when the conversation hits a lull? You'd been scoring points with the classics—the story about an old roommate's dog, the day you tried to quit your job but were fired first, one about your wacky-but-beloved sister—when suddenly the rhythm is lost. You laugh a second longer than her joke is worth, and fiddle with the chopsticks while the silence beats against your temples. It's unavoidable; after all, you don't know each other. The trick, though, is what comes next. Usually it's banal, a question about her job or yours, a reflection on the décor or the food.

What Pamela said was, "Do you think you could kill everybody in this restaurant if you needed to?"

I narrowed my eyes. Leaned back, looked around the room.

Her words spilled fast. "I'm not a psycho. I'm a writer. It's my job to think about things like that." She paused, brushed a lock of hair behind her ear, then looked down and bit the corner of her lip. After a moment, still staring at the table, she said, "Did I just blow it?"

A waiter came by and splashed water into our glasses, then sulked away.

"Well, it's like this." I scooped gomae, chewed slowly. The peanut sauce was delicious. "I think if I surprised the big guy at the end table with a chopstick in the ear, I could handle the rest of them with a chair. It'd be messy, though."

When she looked up, it was with that smile, and I felt something squeeze my chest.

* * *

Pamela's smile.

I used to babysit my little cousin when he was four or five. A good kid, but he got into stuff. One time, I found him in his parents' room. He'd gotten hold of my aunt's lighter, and was holding the lace curtains in one hand and the Bic in the other, the pale flame just inches away. He had a look of intense concentration, like he was doing math problems in his head.

I shouted, and he dropped the lighter and looked up, caught between the joy of his private world and the panic of the real one. He explained, without a hint of guilt, that he was trying to make more lace—he thought the intricate holes must be made by fire, and he wanted to poke some more.

Pamela's smile is like that. Like she sees a secret the rest of us don't, a dangerous, wondrous secret. And every time she smiles, you think this time it might break free.

Only it never does.

The dying sun made the river sparkle like blood, warmed the metal of the wheelchair.

"Our place." Pamela turned to look at me. "Do you remember?"

Do I remember.

After the gomae, after the pad khee mao and the red curry, after the bottle of wine and the sweet Thai coffee, Pamela wanted ice cream.

"I know this shop," she said. "They have gelato, the real stuff like you get in Italy."

I raised my eyebrows and the collar of my jacket. "It's fifteen degrees out."

"Have you ever had real gelato?"

The place was out on Division, a twenty-minute ride. I kept glancing at her just in time to catch her glancing at me. The third time it happened, we both broke into laughter, and then she reached over and took my hand, our fingers interlacing as though we'd done it a hundred times.

Gelato is smoother than ice cream, and comes in more flavors. I had a scoop of white chocolate and one of pistachio. Pamela ordered espresso, sour cherry, and pumpkin.

"You're kidding, right?"

"Why?"

"That's the weirdest mix I ever heard."

"I want them all. Why choose?" She worked her cone like a project, licking in small, steady strokes to maintain the shape, rolling it around her lips.

It was a little distracting, yes.

Afterward, we went for a walk. A walk, in the middle of January, the streets buried in dirty sludge, the concrete icy, the wind cutting. We went for a walk and I put my arm around her and she fit her body into mine and neither of us shivered. She told me about her writing, how she'd sold one book, a mystery novel, and had a second almost finished. Told me about childhood, her parents splitting up when she was young. How that had never made sense to her, the idea that they changed their minds. If she ever got married, that was it, all or nothing, till death parted. She told me that she danced ballet when she was a teenager, and that her favorite color was avocado, and that her first kiss was with a ten-year-old girl-friend, and I held her and could have listened all night.

But it would have been better if I didn't.

My apartment was too small and hers was too far from my job, so we found a new place, a bungalow pulled back from the street, large and private, the ceilings at Wonderland angles. Pamela turned the second bedroom into a writing den, hanging photographs of crime scenes and a dry-erase board that traced the unhappy fates of her protagonists.

We played house. On the weekends, we built a nation of two and ruled it from the king-size bed. Dirty breakfast plates piled on the floor beside paperback thrillers and the *New York Times*. We'd watch the Spanish channel and make up our own stories. Once we spent all day pretending I was a pilot down behind enemy lines, and she was the naughty interrogator trying to make me talk. She giggled while we shopped for shiny boots and leather gloves, but didn't break character after she put them on.

It was spring when we found the bridge, and by then, Pamela was all I wanted.

We were taking a walk. Funny, a lot of the milestones in our relationship involved walking. Sometimes irony is so neat you just want to shoot yourself.

The park was one of those pleasantly fake spots where the paths wander but the trees are well disciplined. We must have been through it a hundred times. But that morning was the first we spotted the trail. Pamela took one look at it, smiled, and then bet me I couldn't catch her.

It was a thin dirt track that wound under branches and around bushes, the kind with something always snapping out to catch your face. She ran like a little girl, a doe, light on her feet and quick, and it was all I could do to keep her in sight, much less catch her. But every time I heard her laugh, I pushed a little faster through the tangle of woods.

Then, suddenly, sunlight. I slowed as I stepped from the line of trees. A ridge of gravel ballast crested in front of me, dull steel railroad tracks running along it. I shaded my eyes against the sudden brilliance.

Pamela stood on the very edge of the bridge, arms out, chest forward, blue horizon behind, nothing but the breeze and my prayers between her and a thirty-foot plummet to the brown river below.

Like she were cut from the sky.

"Of course I remember." My voice sounded harsher than I meant for it to. But lots of things don't turn out how we intend.

Pamela acted like she hadn't heard, her eyes locked on the river below. She squatted, then sat on the edge of the bridge, her legs dangling. "It was a beautiful day. Spring."

"I know." My hands shook, and I wasn't sure if it was due to effort or memory.

"It was like something from a myth." She reached in her pocket and took out her cigarettes. The smoking was new. I hated it, but under the circumstances, I couldn't begrudge her. With her right hand, she snapped a lighter, held it to her cupped palms. Took a deep drag and then blew a stream of smoke. "We burst out of the forest to this place, and it was like nothing else existed. Just you and me at the end of the world." She shook her head, took another inhale. "You came up behind and put your arms around me and pulled me away from the edge. We made love"—she looked around, pointed—"there, right on the tracks. Waiting to feel a train coming. You had gravel burns on your back for a week. And when we were done, you asked me to marry you. You remember what I said?"

I choked back battery acid. Looked down at my hands, folded in my lap, atop my ruined body. "I remember."

We'd been married for almost a year. The morning it happened, we had been screaming at each other. We didn't fight often, but when we did, you could have sold tickets.

It made sense. All we wanted was everything all the time.

I slammed the door as I left for work, but the battle kept raging in my head. I marshaled arguments to defend myself, launched the imaginary salvoes I thought most devastating. I was right in the middle of saying how tired I was of her divorce issues when the number seventy-two bus sheared off the back half of the Chrysler.

It's not like TV, with attractive doctors and snappy banter. In truth, I don't remember much. The rotting-flower stink of antiseptics. A bright light and a sense of motion around me, like a rock in the midst of rapids. Opening my eyes to see Pamela in a cracked orange chair at the foot of the bed. Her fingers squeezing my toes, eyes a million miles away. And then noticing that I couldn't feel her touch.

Funny thing is, I don't remember what we'd been fighting about.

I could still have a fulfilling life, the doctor told me. True, I would be in the wheelchair. I'd lost my spleen and one kidney, but my lungs, my heart, they were in fine shape. My dick didn't work and my legs never would. But I had the use of my arms, my mind. There were people worse off.

I said, Aren't there always? Is there one poor, crippled, disease-ridden bastard out there that suffers worse than everybody and is *allowed* to be pissed about it?

The doctor's lips went tight as he said that bitterness was a natural part of the healing process. Then he checked his watch, wished me luck, and held the door for Pamela to wheel me out.

"We can make it, baby," she whispered. But I swore I could hear a question mark at the end of her sentence.

This is the bad part.

Before the accident, our world had a population of two. You know those disgusting couples that just draw into one another, that don't seem to even realize other people exist? We were them. And I'm not talking about the early flush of the first months. I'm talking about two solid years. More.

Funny thing about words. You always think you know what they mean, until life kicks the context out from underneath you. Same way every pop song turns into poetry when you're in the middle of a breakup— you see all that pain that you never connected to before.

Take the phrase, "I need you." There was a time those words might kick off a romp that could get us arrested in some states. We said "need" when we meant "want." Same as the kid looking for a new stereo.

It was only after the accident that I learned what "I need you" really means.

I need you to tie my shoes.

I need you to drive me to work.

No. Please no.

I need you to help me off the toilet.

Here's an ugly little home movie I'd rather not remember.

Establishing shot: A man sits in a wheelchair. His fingers clench nervously.

A door opens. A woman in a parody of a nurse's uniform struts in. A preposterously short white skirt reveals pale lace stockings. She closes the door with a theatrical flourish. "Good morning, Mr. Johnson."

His expression twists with desire.

She sways over and puts a hand against his forehead. Zoom in on her blouse, barely buttoned, breasts straining against the fabric. "Oh, Mr. Johnson. You're burning up!" Makeup exaggerates her pout. "I need to cool you down *immediately*."

Red fingernails unbutton his shirt. He touches her neck, traces the curves of her chest. Hoists himself up enough for her to tug off his pants.

"I should give you a sponge bath." Close-up of her nibbling on the tip of a finger. "But I forgot my sponge. Whatever will I do?" She begins kissing her way down his torso. He can feel the light pressure of her lips, the warmth of her breath. So sweetly familiar. It's all he wants. He can feel it at his collarbone. At the hollow in his chest. At his navel.

And then he can't.

To her credit, she spends a long minute trying anyway.

When she looks up, he realizes he's not the only one crying. There's a terrible moment when they stare at each other, and then she covers her mouth with her hand, jerks to her feet, and rushes for the door.

The camera pulls out slow on the man alone in his chair.

The bloodred in the sunset had given way to the pastel colors of those candy hearts you see around Valentine's Day.

"You said that if we were married, it was all or nothing." I took a deep breath. Afraid of what was coming. "That you didn't want to go the same way your parents had."

She nodded, still not looking at me. With a flick of her forefinger she sent the cigarette spinning bright into the shadows below.

The muscles of my chest tightened. All I'd wanted, and I'd had it for so short a time. "Has that changed?" I bit my lip, took a breath thick with fecund river smells. "Do you want a . . . a . . ." I couldn't say it. That word, it's like a home invader, a ski-masked freak in your living room. Once the possibility has been acknowledged, it never goes away. It becomes part of your reality, and you wake up sweating at night sounds forever.

She spun. Her eyes flashed, and I could see beads of sweat on her upper lip. "No. I don't want a divorce. You know better than that."

I let myself breathe. Our relationship had been forged of desire, a fantasy kingdom of want. But since the accident, we'd lived in a world of one-sided need. Selfish or not, there it was. "Look. This place . . . it hits a little too close to home."

She shook her head as if to clear it, and moved behind me to take the handles of the chair. "Maybe it'd be better if I did want a divorce. Easier on both of us. But I'm"—her voice caught—"I'm just not wired that way."

"Me either." Was I telling the truth? Would I stick with her if our roles were reversed? I really don't know. I just know I was relieved.

"Do you love me?"

"Of course." I struggled to turn around and touch her hands. The easiest way to see someone pushing your wheelchair is to tilt your head backward, but there's no dignity in it. You're always staring up their nostrils. "Of course I do."

"I love you too, baby." Pamela smiled at me, that secret laced with darkness, the secret she never shared. Then she took a deep breath and shoved the chair toward the edge of the bridge.

On our wedding night, the bed rocked and shuddered halfway across the room.

When we were done, Pamela flopped on top of me, her dark hair draping my chest. I lay motionless, still inside her, feeling her every breath like it was me drawing air. Our skin pressed tight, our sweat ran together, our bodies connected, and I literally couldn't tell where I ended and she began.

Gravel popped as my chair lurched forward. "Stop!"

The front edges of the wheels hung in open air. Vertigo squeezed my stomach. Thirty feet below, the concrete base of the bridge struts loomed. Even if I missed them, the water was deep. I couldn't keep myself afloat, not with half my body waterlogged and useless.

Behind me, I heard her sob as she bent forward, braced herself, and pushed.

The chair jumped four inches before my flailing hands found the tires. Hardened rubber burned my palms. Gravel slid over the side, hung in silence, and then clattered against the concrete below.

"Stop!" My fingers locked like steel clamps. "Jesus!" The breeze seemed to tug at my dangling feet. My arms were strong from months of maneuvering the chair, and I forced the wheels to reverse, but they skidded ineffectually in the loose ballast.

Fuck dignity. I looked backward, staring at her upside down, trying to understand what was happening, hoping for some answer in her eyes, some hint that this was a joke.

People talk about love at first sight, but what they really mean is recognition. You look in someone's eyes, could be anyone, a childhood friend or a stranger waiting for the bus, and in an instant, things are different. Like they've pulled aside a curtain and let you look deeper than flesh.

What you see depends on who—and where—you are.

When I saw what was in her eyes, I let go of the wheels.

In the sudden absence of resistance, we leapt forward, the chair cresting over the rim of the bridge and starting to fall, the river rushing upward. Just as it went over, I thought, *Forgive me, baby,* and then I twisted my torso as hard as I could and flopped sideways out of the wheelchair, my body slapping against the bridge edge like meat.

Pamela's momentum propelled her. She let out a startled cry and, still clutching the handles of the wheelchair, hurtled off the bridge.

I scrabbled and fell, clawing at gravel that tore up in handfuls. My dead legs swung free. As my body slipped over the side, I made a desperate grab and caught the corrugated edge with both hands. The metal bit cruelly, and my heart slammed against my ribs. I clenched my teeth and heaved, wriggling forward, rocks jamming into my ribs. When I finally felt the tug of gravity ease, I gasped for breath, muscles on fire, as I spun and wormed back to look over the edge.

She lay splayed on the concrete. Apart from the disconcerting angle of her pelvis, she looked almost relaxed, as if she were lounging in the shallows to battle the heat. Her left foot and arm bobbed with the current. Something sparkled just below the waterline. Her ring. Sometimes irony is so neat you just want to shoot yourself.

Pamela's eyes were open, and locked on mine. An eternal moment passed. Then she coughed, and said, "I think I need you."

And through the blood, I finally shared the secret behind her smile.

It's a funny thing, needing someone. If it goes one way, it's a burden. If it goes both ways, it's a bond.

Our breakfast table is higher now, and there are rails fastened beside the bed. Maybe we don't laugh as much as we used to, and everything comes a little harder. After all, not all secrets are pretty. But Saturdays are still our favorite. And though there are now two wheelchairs parked beside our bed, the man and woman in it are committed—all or nothing.

Death Runs Faster
by Duane Swierczynski

•

You wouldn't have worn your best T-shirt if you knew you were going to die today.

But you put it on first thing this morning, not really thinking, other than it was Friday, and you've been saving it all week.

This T-shirt fits best under your uniform. Doesn't bunch up at the top, or sag down near the top button.

You hate your uniform. You hate it almost as much as your job. So you take the small pleasures where you can get them.

Getting to work is a fifty-five-minute hassle, each way, because home is a dark one-bedroom apartment in the shadow of I-95, way too close to the river. This means a cold lonely walk, then a SEPTA bus ride, then a twenty-five-minute trek on the Frankford El to 13th Street, which, if you can hop on the very first car, spits you out near the end of the station, the closest to City Hall.

Which is where you work. City Hall.

You guard it.

You get nine bucks an hour to guard the City of Philadelphia's $24 million (circa 1901) showpiece, originally meant to be the world's tallest building, but now has to settle for the dubious title of "world's tallest masonry building." All granite and brick holding it up; no steel. Of course, it dawns on you that maybe you're not actually guarding the building itself but the people inside of it. Which would really depress you, because most of them are assholes.

But yeah, you. City Hall. You answered an ad one morning, came downtown to the building across the street, filled out some paperwork, watched a forty-five-minute video, and boom, you were qualified to guard the world's tallest masonry building.

What a country.

You're cynical, but you're thankful for the job. You hate your job, but you like having a job. At least it's a job. There were eight months there when you didn't have a job, and that was miserable.

The worst part is right now. End of the day on payday. Because you've got to take the Frankford El back across town to 2nd Street and wait for your paycheck.

This wastes another bus token. Because you then have to hop back on the El, burn another token, plus sixty cents for the transfer. Two tokens cost $2.60 right from the machine. Machine busted? That's four bucks. Plus the sixty cents.

When you make $9.01 an hour, that's like a half an hour's pay burned on just getting paid and getting home. No wonder it pisses you off.

But that's the deal, because the outfit that got the contract with City Hall—it's called Sherlock Holmes Security—has some extremely fucked-up ideas about employee relations.

Get this: There are only two ways you can get your

paycheck. You can go to 27th and Allegheny to Sherlock Holmes Security headquarters and ask Shenice at the front desk. Or you can go to 2nd and Market to Ritz Checks and Money Orders. Direct deposit?

Your ass, direct deposit.

Two choices: burn a token and a transfer taking the subway and bus to the middle of the North Philly badlands, or burn only a token going across town to Old City.

You weren't born brain dead. You ain't going to the Badlands for a paycheck. Even if Shenice were hot. And she's not.

Of course, Ritz Checks takes 4 percent of your check before you see a single buck.

"Financial services," indeed.

The line usually snakes out the front door.

On a good day.

Sometimes, though, like now, like today, fucking Christmas Eve, there's an absurdly long wait for the checks. Because this afternoon Sherlock Holmes Security had a holiday party for upper management, and Shenice—whose job it is to drive the checks down to 3rd and Market, because nobody ever fucking goes up to 27th and Allegheny for their fucking checks—is a little drunk, and a little late. She can't drive, so some accountant guy offers to take her down. You don't know it, but Shenice decides to spread a little holiday cheer in the parking lot first. She blows the accountant, who can't come, because he's had too many pills and too much to drink, too. Since he can't come, he asks Shenice about other options. She suggests letting her finger his asshole, which promptly grosses him out, and doesn't help the problem one bit. The accountant asks about fucking her pussy, but Shenice demurs. She's got a boyfriend, and that wouldn't be cool. Not on Christmas Eve. They are at an impasse. The accountant says, "Fuck it, drive yourself." Shenice says, "What about the checks?" The accountant is already up the stairs, back to the party. So Shenice goes back upstairs, asking around, and finally Mr. Applegate agrees to take her down, thinking he'll be able to get into her pussy afterward. Boy is he mistaken about that.

By the time Shenice arrives with the checks, the sun has long set, and it's well past five, and you told Petty you'd meet him in Fishtown by six.

There's a long line ahead of you.

All so you can get your biweekly check for $547. Wait. Minus the 4 percent. Which is more like $525.12.

It's Christmas Eve.

Good thing you wore your best T-shirt today.

Your buddy Petty thinks he's a gangster.

Maybe he is.

He's probably full of shit, but maybe he isn't.

Anyway, he promised you something tonight. A job. An easy job. Easiest job you'd ever heard of.

Usually Petty *is* full of shit, but it's Christmas Eve, and you want to believe him, because you need the money, and if you can't believe on Christmas Eve, when can you believe?

"You're a security guard, right? I got a guard job for you. Hour of your time. Five hundred bucks."

Petty thinks he's a gangster because *he* has a friend who says he has an in with the Polish mob.

The Polish mob?

"Don't laugh. They're serious as fucking shit. They're worse than the Russians."

The Polish mob.

"Hey. Seriously now. They've been making inroads in this town for years, and nobody knows about them except the people who need to know about them. It's a war waiting to happen."

Who's this friend?

"Ernie Cifelli."

Sounds Italian.

"He is."

With the Polish mob?

It all sounds loopy, but Petty swore to you it was the truth, and it sounded good over Yuenglings at the Long-shot Lounge, so what the hell. Petty finished college. Even a little bit of law school. Your Christmas Eve plans were kind of fluid anyway.

It's tomorrow, Christmas, you've gotta sweat.

And that five hundred dollars would come in handy.

You don't know this, but Petty is telling the truth. There is a Polish mob, and it's growing stronger by the day in Philadelphia.

They're like Santa Claus and the Tooth Fairy and Satan: they're incredibly powerful because nobody believes they exist.

Except the Russians, of course.

Even the Russians are scared of them.

You don't know any of this, and you don't care right now, because you're standing in line at the Ritz Checks place. You're almost in the door, but not quite there. The rest of the guys are all bunched up, trying to keep warm. You're too far away from the TV to see it, but they've got *Action News* on, and the temperature is in the lower right-hand corner. It's got to be close to thirty. Maybe even upper twenties. A cold Christmas is in store for the Delaware Valley. It's colder since the sun set.

It's past 5:30 P.M. now.

Where the fuck is Shenice?

You're not wearing the right boots for this weather. Sherlock Holmes requires black lace-ups, doesn't matter which kind. You found these at Payless, but the outer shell is too thin for the cold arctic air Philly gets this time of year. Bad enough standing in City Hall, feeling the freeze creep up through the soles of your boots. Out here on the sidewalk it's worse. The cold is like a battering ram against your feet.

If only you could be inside and wait. Even if the heat's not on, it's got to be better than outside.

People with much better jobs pass you by on the sidewalk. You can tell they have better jobs because they're not wearing fucking guard uniforms. The people making the most money wear jeans. The new-style jeans where you can see the threads. You want to save up to buy a few pair yourself. You never can seem to save up.

"Smoke?"

The guy behind you.

You shake your head.

"No, man."

You turn around.

"Smoke?"

He's not asking to bum one. He's holding.

The check-cashing line is a smart place to deal. You know you've got money coming. You've probably got a long nothing night waiting for you. A little weed could even things out. Let you think again.

You don't have money for weed, though.

You need it all for Christmas, and where the fuck is fucking Shenice?

There's Shenice.

Climbing out of the back of a Lexus.

She's got the checks.

Suddenly you're not thinking about the checks. You're thinking about the Lexus.

You need to buy a Lexus by 9:00 A.M. tomorrow morning.

Your kid has always been into cars. You bought him his first Matchboxes when you and Lora were still together, even though Lora was worried he'd bite off a rearview mirror or something and swallow it. They were only ninety-seven cents at Target. Sometimes you could get a ten-pack for five bucks. They made him happy, so what was the five bucks?

But you and Lora had no idea you had an auto savant on your hands.

He's only five, yet can name any car down to the make, model, year—on sight. He'll still shock the living shit out of you, walking down the street, headed to your apartment for a Saturday-night sleepover, naming cars as he goes.

Chevy HHR.

Subaru Forester.

Pontiac Solstice.

Chevy Cavalier.

And he's never wrong.

One day you got tickets to the Philly Auto Show. You ran to the nearest phone, pumped in a quarter, and ended up gushing to Lora's answering machine. By this time you were split up, so she wasn't exactly rushing to return your calls. The show started the very next day. A Sunday. Family Day. She didn't call you back until the middle of the week. You'd tacked the tickets to the corkboard above the wall phone. She said Friday might be good, but Friday you had work. She *knew* that. She offered to let you have him Friday, Saturday, and Sunday, but seemed unable to understand that you couldn't get off work on Friday.

You hung up on her.

A month later, you saw the tickets, and ripped them from the board and threw them in the trash.

A week later, you realized that you could have gone to the show after work on Friday, maybe taken the boy for an hour or so. Not wasted the tickets. At the very least, grabbed an armful of the slick brochures for all of the new cars.

You hate how fucking stubborn you can be.

Now this Christmas the boy wants a model of a new Lexus. The kind that parks itself. He told you on the phone last week:

"Daddy, it parks itself."

How does it do that?

"It goes up, and the wheel turns, and the computer inside tells it to go back, and it goes back, and it parks all by itself."

Wow. I had no idea cars could do that.

"It's an *amazing* Lexus, Daddy."

You did a little research.

It was the LS 460 L.

A hundred grand.

The toy version was $79.95.

It didn't park itself, but the six-year-old operator could pretend.

You told Lora:

I'm getting that for him for Christmas.

Shenice handed over the checks but now they've got to sort them, and it's ten minutes until six, which means there's no way you're going to meet Petty on time. Which means you've got a choice to make.

Stay for the $525.12 check.

Or leave now and meet Petty and make $500 cash. Pick up the check Monday.

Thing is, the check from Sherlock Holmes is a sure thing. It's there, cash in pocket. Take the subway to Allegheny, bus down to Aramingo, walk over to Toys "R" Us and pick up that toy Lexus. Toys "R" Us is open all night on Christmas Eve.

But that would be like throwing away five hundred dollars.

A thousand bucks at Christmas would be a very good thing.

Considering you're going to be spending a lot of it alone.

If you skip the check though, and Petty turns out to be full of shit, then you have zero dollars for Christmas.

Sure, you've got an ATM card.

And if you used it at an ATM machine, you wouldn't

be able to do a damn thing, because the minimum with-drawal at most machines is twenty dollars.

You've got $17.45.

You know because you checked this morning.

You ate a single hot dog for lunch, and washed it down with rusty water from a City Hall fountain, be-cause all the cash you had in the world was four dol-lars. And three bucks of that needed to go to public transportation. You wanted another hot dog.

So there's your choice.

Cash the check now, or cash the check later.

Fucking Shenice.

Why couldn't she have been here at 5:15 P.M. like she always was?

The guy behind you keeps saying, "Smoke? Smoke?" looking for buyers. After all, the checks are here. It's Christmas Eve. The party's just getting started. The line inches forward. You're almost in the door. You can al-most feel the warmth from within.

You make up your mind.

You give Shenice the middle finger and tell her:

"Merry Fucking Christmas."

Not your wisest move.

The job with the Polish mob pretty much involves standing there and looking tough. The Polish mob doesn't have the numbers yet, so for now, they're con-tent with renting numbers. They want to terrify the Rus-sians. Make them crap their dress pants. There are casinos coming to the waterfront, and everybody's play-ing angles. The Poles figure strike early, strike auda-ciously.

They're going to meet the Russians at an abandoned furniture warehouse down near the waterfront.

They're going to tell them how it's going to be.

Take a few fingers and testicles, if need be.

The Russians, though, don't want to mess around. They've already got the warehouse wired.

With enough C-4 to send the roof over to Jersey.

You don't know any of this. You ride up the service elevator with Petty, who's giving you the useless low-down.

"All you got to do is stand there," Petty tells you, "and look like a bad motherfucker."

You get to the floor, join the others.

You stand there.

You look like a bad motherfucker.

Right up until—

A cell phone rings.

"Allo?"

And then—

Ah, you shouldn't worry.

All's well this Christmas Eve.

Your boy, as it turns out, will get his Lexus. Lora's new boyfriend picked it up for him, in an effort to ingratiate himself with your ex-wife.

And what's happened to you isn't even going to ruin your son's Christmas. The police won't notify Lora for a few days, when they find your head on a roof across the street and learn your name from your teeth.

Your body is in the ruined basement.

They'll dig it out eventually.

But hey—at least you're wearing your best T-shirt.

Righteous Son
by Dave White

•

I tease Dave White about his voice. To me (and my wife), he's a dead vocal ringer for actor Paul Giamatti. Especially when Dave gets exasperated (which is sort of often). This is why, in certain small crime writer circles, Dave is known as "Giamatti." Just wait until Dave reads from one of his own novels for an audiobook edition someday. You'll scramble for the cover, thinking, *I didn't know Paul Giamatti did audiobooks. . . .*

But you know the best thing about Dave? His voice. And by that I mean his writerly voice. It was brimming with muscle and maturity in the very first Dave White story I read: "Closure" over at Kevin Burton Smith's Thrilling Detective Web Site. I couldn't believe a young punk barely out of college had written it. And in the years since, Dave's followed that award winner with many fine stories, including the one below. Just when you think you've tagged Dave, he swerves to the left and gives you something unexpected and cool like "Righteous Son."

(As you read this, imagine the voice of Paul Giamatti in your head. I swear, it helps.)

—Duane Swierczynski,
author of *The Blonde*

"Son of righteousness shine upon the west also."
—Rutgers College motto

"Think you're a bit out of place, college boy."

The barkeep put a dirty glass of beer in front of me. The swinging doors of the saloon were unable to keep out the dust, hot air, and smell of horse manure. For the second time today I felt alone, distant. These sensations weren't evident at home.

"How'd you know I was a college boy?" I asked.

"Y'all got that smug-ass look. You know, like you better than this town." He ran his hand along the stubble at his chin. "Where you from, anyway?"

"New Jersey."

I took a sip of the beer. It tasted like gravel.

"No. How smart are you, college boy? What college?"

"Rutgers College."

"Never heard of it. What are you doing so far from home?"

I finished the beer, surprised I didn't have to chew the last gulp. I was in the middle of nowhere drinking beer that was awful. This wasn't how my life was supposed to go, I wasn't supposed to be in Texas or California or Oklahoma or wherever I was. All I wanted was to get this over with and go back home.

"I'm looking for somebody."

The barkeep found a dirty rag and wiped at some moisture on the wooden bar. He didn't appear to wipe it down often; the top of the bar was warped and looked like a hilly road. Like the mountains I had to cross to get here.

"Course you are," he said. "Everyone out here lookin' for someone or somethin'."

A dark spot seemed to catch his eye, and he rubbed the rag hard into the spot. He didn't ask if I wanted another drink. It didn't bother me much, because I didn't.

"You know John Westing?" I asked.

The rag stopped, but only briefly.

"Yeah. I know him."

My hands flinched. I tried to cover it by putting them on my belt. All I found was the handle of my father's Civil War pistol.

"Lemme give you some advice, college." The barkeep gave a crooked grin. "Don't get into any poker games while you're here."

"Don't plan on staying long enough for games."

The grin didn't leave his face. "You're talking real tough, college. Why you lookin' for Westing?"

"If you know him, you know he's originally from New Jersey. I have a message for him."

"He won't be in for a while. He prospects." The barkeep turned his back to me. "You came all the way out here just to deliver a message?"

Sweat formed where my hat met my head. It wasn't from the heat.

"It's going to be a loud message."

My mother sat in the dark in our Trenton house. Her face was silhouetted in front of a pulled curtain. I could see only her profile and it was shaded in darkness. The house was quiet except for the sniffle of crying.

"It was a good funeral. They did Father proud," I said.

"Are you going back to school, Samuel?" she asked.

We were in the sitting room, she sitting on the stool of the piano she used to play when my parents entertained guests. She had pulled the stool away from the piano to the window. I stood in the doorway, watching her.

"In the morning."

The air was still and musty. I wanted her to open some windows, but she refused. She thought that if she let the air in, it would take what was left of my father out.

"How is your roommate?" she asked, her voice hollow.

"He's fine." I thought about the last time we talked. My roommate sitting on the park bench alone, looking at the sky, confused.

"Will he be coming here in the summer again?"

I didn't say anything.

"He's a good boy. It's a shame he has no one. You can't always watch out for him, however."

"He's like a brother to me."

She shuddered at the words.

"Your father wanted you to have something," she said, as if she hadn't heard me. "He told me on his deathbed."

She got out of her chair and walked to me, her arms outstretched. In her hands was a thick wooden box. One I'd seen only once before in my life. She placed it in my hands. She tried to smile, but her eyes misled her face. There were dark circles beneath them, garnished with tears.

I opened the lid and looked at the metal inside.

"It's your father's gun," my mother said. "From the war."

I closed the lid. I was very young when the war raged. I can remember bits of my father before he went to fight, a bright man always quick with a smile. I remember more clearly after the war, the light of the smile no longer gracing his face.

The gun returned with me to Rutgers the next day.

The barkeep nodded toward the door as a group of prospectors came in.

"The one with the beard," he grunted.

I turned on my stool. There were three men with dirt caked on their clothes and their faces. They were loud, swearing and laughing and yelling, until one finally said, "Hey, Red, three whiskeys and six beers!"

The barkeep fished out glasses from behind the bar.

"How'd you do out there, boys?" Red said.

The one with the long gray beard said, "Same as always. A little bit, but nothing major. It'll come." He glanced at me. "Big crowd in here today, Red. Who's the new blood?"

"This is—" Red looked at me.

"Samuel Donne," I said, rising from my bar stool.

"Your accent, it sounds like mine." A grin appeared beneath his dusty gray beard. "New Jersey?"

"Yes, sir."

"John Westing," he said and we shook hands. "What's a New Jersey boy doing way out west? Too hot to be out here for laughs. You're too young to be here prospecting. We got all the gold anyway."

His cracked, dry face shuddered as he chuckled.

"Looking for you, sir," I said, not joining his laughter.

He took his hat off and placed it on the table his friends were sitting at. Dusted off the shoulder of his jacket.

"Me? Where are you coming from? And why would you come out all this way to see me?"

"I'm coming from New Brunswick, sir."

I let it sink in. Let the realization rise through his body until I saw it in his eyes.

"Bartholomew lives in New Brunswick. Goes to the college there."

I nodded.

"I'm Bartholomew's roommate."

"My son's roommate." He appeared to be thinking it over. "Well, why don't you join us for a drink and a game of cards?"

The box rested on my desk. I sat on my bed, polishing my shoes. Across from me, Bartholomew Westing sorted through some envelopes. He'd just taken in the mail.

"What are you doing this evening?" he asked.

These moments were always difficult. Bartholomew rarely had plans and he usually counted on me to make up for that.

"I can't tell you," I said.

Our room was bare, the walls a soft white color, the floor uncovered. We kept the room simple, temporary. A reminder to us that college leads us to a larger goal, it was not a place for us to stay.

"You can't tell me?" Bartholomew smiled. He shifted his frail body toward me to hear me. He looked like he'd just woken up and hadn't eaten in a week. Since I'd been away, it was possible both were true.

I got up, looked into the hallway, then closed the door to our room.

"I saw Harriet near Kirkpatrick Chapel this morning."

"Damn you."

"What?"

"You are lucky and you don't even know it. Every woman you meet falls for you. You have it so easy. I meet a woman and she wants me to help her study."

I shrugged.

Bartholomew's tired eyes were still scanning the addresses on the envelopes. "So you will be with her, then? I was hoping we could go to the pub."

"Not tonight."

"Why not? You're always with Harriet."

"Let me see her tonight. We can go to the pub anytime."

"No. We can't! You have no idea what the world has been dealing me lately. We need to talk. We need to drink. It's time to have fun like the old days. Harriet will still be around for you."

The frustration in his voice prickled my skin. I didn't answer.

"We used to be like brothers, Samuel."

He held an envelope under the light of a candle.

"We still are," I said.

"A woman is dividing us. I'm alone, and you don't care. Soon, I'll lose you as well," he said. "My own brother."

Again, I didn't answer, this time because I noticed the color drain from his face. His shoulders slumped as well.

"Are you going to be all right? This is about more than you and me, it seems," I said.

"Go be with Harriet. I've just received a letter from my father," he said. "I'd prefer to read it alone."

Four of us sat around the table, beers in one hand, cards in the other. As John Westing got more and more drunk, the more he talked, the more he rambled. He seemed to consider me his best friend.

I never played cards before and Red was right, I shouldn't have. The little money I had was draining away before me.

"My son the college graduate," Westing was saying. "It never fit him, it will never fit him. It's not in his blood."

I folded my hand, and took a sip of beer to keep from breaking the man's neck.

"You see, Sam, the thing my son never realized is you can't get away from who you are. Violence is in our family, and it's passed down from generation to generation. He thought by going to school he could become his own man."

He drank an entire glass of beer in one gulp. After the third beer, I had to admit, the taste improved.

Red brought us all another round. Though it had been dark now for hours, I could still feel the heat of the still air on my skin. The temperature didn't seem to cool out here, only settle.

I tried to watch the others play cards, but Westing kept talking, "I've killed men, Sam. I didn't like it, but I've done it. My father killed men. It runs in the blood. I came out here, hoping to get rich, but I knew at some point I would have to kill again. I wrote my son a letter telling him just that. I told him there would come a point where he'd have to kill, too.

"But he wouldn't listen, he's never listened to that. He tries to run from his past. He attends one of the first colleges created in this fine nation. If we go to war, he will not go. But there will come a time where he has to make a choice, and he'll have to kill someone."

The next hand was dealt, and I got three queens, a deuce, and an eight. I bet. The rest immediately folded.

We played a few more hands and soon I was out of money. Red laughed at me, reminded me how he warned me to stay away from cards. I didn't speak to him.

John Westing had his arm around me now, was talking into my ear, spittle flying from his lips.

"So, you've come all this way," he said. "It must have taken you weeks by wagon. Why are you here?"

This was the moment. My hands shook, my throat closed, but I got the words out.

"I'm here to kill you." The words came from my mouth, but they felt as if someone else had spoken them.

Westing laughed. The other cardplayers laughed, too.

Finally composing himself, he sucked down his beer, and said, "Why would you want to do that?"

I put my hand around the grip of my gun and said, "Your son is dead. And it's your fault."

On most occasions, I didn't like taking Harriet to my room. But after we'd had a few drinks at dinner, it didn't seem to matter. We climbed the steps arm in arm, she stopping to giggle, me stopping to nuzzle her neck.

Outside my door, I pressed her against the wall,

kissing her deeply. Her scent surrounded me, the smell of powder on her skin. Her hands ran through my hair, and she groaned softly.

I opened the door and Harriet pulled away from me, stepping over the threshold. She turned into the room, froze, and screamed. I came in behind her only to see my roommate, noose around his neck, hanging from the ceiling.

John Westing drank another beer, confident that I wasn't going to shoot him. He even asked his drinking buddies to leave. They listened. The dirt on his face was now hardened and some of it rolled off as he spoke.

"My son committed suicide? I always knew he was weak."

"Sir, with all due respect," I said, "your son was stronger than you'll ever be."

He balled his fists and ground them into the table-top. "You have no idea what it means to be a West-ing. Bartholomew was an embarrassment to me. His mother, God rest her soul, thought the same thing."

His eyes were glazed over from the alcohol. He couldn't sit in his chair without having to catch his balance on the table. Now was my chance. I reached to my belt and began to pull out the revolver.

"Why don't you just put that on the table, okay, Sam? Where we both can see it."

For some reason, the strength in his voice stopped me. His demeanor hadn't changed, but there was dark-ness in his voice. Something I couldn't put my finger on, but it scared me.

I put the gun on the table.

"Let me tell you a story, so you know where I come from. Then you can tell me what kind of Westing my son was." John Westing leaned across the table and did his best to point a finger at me.

"When I was twenty-five years old, I killed a man in Boston. Drowned him in the harbor. Held his head under water until he stopped kicking and screaming. That's how I met my wife. The man was trying to rob her, you see? And I did what was necessary."

Red had finished cleaning the bar and was now going around and blowing out candles. Shadows crossed our faces.

"Thirteen years later, when Bartholomew was just starting at the local school in Philadelphia, I shot a man. He tried to walk out on a bill in my friend's bar. Again, this was necessary."

Red came and took the last of the empty glasses and whispered to me it was last call. He paused, looking at the gun on the table. He repeated the words.

Westing acted like he hadn't heard. "Get us another beer, will you, Red? Me and Sam here are talkin'."

Red looked at me and I shook my head.

"One day, probably three years ago," Westing continued, "before he left for school, Bartholomew came home with a bloodied nose. One of the boys he was with punched him. I asked Bartholomew what he did in response. Bartholomew said nothing.

"Nothing. Can you believe that? Someone punches you and you don't respond. He wasn't my son. That was not what I brought him up to be. And what he did, he soiled our family's name. I had to find the boy who punched Bartholomew. I went out, found him and his father together." A smile crossed Westing's face. "They won't bother anyone anymore. They won't hurt my family. Or my son."

"You left town after that, didn't you?" I asked.

Westing nodded.

"But you kept in touch. With your son, with your wife. You wrote them letters."

Westing nodded. "I wrote Evelyn a letter every day until she passed. I wrote Bartholomew a letter when I thought he needed one. Maybe, he'd read one and wake up."

"Your son is dead."

Westing didn't smile. But he didn't appear sad, either. "You said that earlier. Why don't you tell me what happened?"

The doctor came first. He needed help getting Bartholomew down, and Harriet needed to be pried from my arms so I could help. He was shorter than me, but as we pulled him down, he seemed the size of a child.

We cut the noose and laid Bartholomew on his bed. His face was blue, his eyes bulged in their sockets. His mouth was twisted in what could only be described as horror. I tried shutting my eyes to block out the image, but it wasn't possible. I could already sense Bartholomew Westing's face creeping into the recesses of my brain, planning to haunt my dreams.

As the doctor looked over the body, I let Harriet weep against my shoulder. After a while I told the doctor I was going to walk her home. He agreed and said he and the police would be here when I got back. Before I left, I took the wooden box from my desk and the open letter that rested on Bartholomew's desk.

Harriet and I walked across the city, our silhouettes cast in gaslight. We didn't speak. The drinks we'd had earlier had worn off, as had the mood. Around us people laughed and enjoyed the evening.

After I dropped her off, I found the closest streetlamp and leaned against it. I unfolded the letter.

Dear Bartholomew,

I am writing you again to plead for you to realize what you've done to your family. You have broken us apart.

Your mother is dead. She died shamed. You cannot defend your family name. And now you've done what? You pay too close attention to girls you cannot expect to know intimately. You say you go to school to learn, to be a man.

You are not a man. This is the last correspondence you will receive from me. As of today, you are no longer my son.

Signed,
John Westing

The letter also contained a return address on it. I folded the letter and placed it in my jacket pocket. I took my father's gun from the box and secured it in my belt.

I thought about what my mother said a day earlier. That I couldn't always be there. I should have been. If I had stayed home that night, I would have stopped him.

I couldn't always look out for him. But there I could make it up to him.

I set off for Westing's town the next morning.

We left the saloon, Westing stumbling ahead of me. After I told him the story, he showed no remorse, no sadness. His anger scared me, but I had traveled a long way. I would not be deterred.

A few horses tied to posts muttered at us as we passed. I noted the stars glittering in the sky, stars I'd gotten to know well during my journey to this forsaken town. Being in the open, things that were familiar to me on my trip were familiar now. The sky, the smell of the air, the heft of the gun returned to my hip. The image of Bartholomew Westing's twisted face.

I stopped walking in the middle of the road. I stood next to a closed hardware store. The sign in the window advertised to prospectors. All their gold-digging needs could be found in that store.

It wasn't like this back home. Even at night restaurants bustled, people were in the streets, living. The gaslights glittered off expensive buildings. Candles flickered in the windows of houses where families enjoyed their time together.

For six weeks, I'd abandoned that comfort. I rode a horse in darkness. Now I stood among rickety buildings on weak foundations. Nothing moved, no one laughed. This town was dark and silent.

Dead.

Westing must have noticed his feet were the only ones crunching gravel. He stopped and slowly turned toward me.

I took out my gun.

John Westing eyed me, his hands at his sides. He stood a good twenty feet from me.

"I don't know what you've read about how things occur out here, but you're wrong. There are no draws, no duels. I'm not going to do that. And even if I were, you know I'd win. I should shoot you right now." He laughed and spat on the ground. "But I won't."

"Why not?"

"I've killed people, but everyone deserved it. You don't. You're trying to avenge a friend. I can understand that."

"You really think I'd come out all this way and not kill you?" I didn't want to say those words. There was too much of a chance they were true.

"Do you even know how to fire a gun? You're a college boy, probably like your father before you. You're following your path. My son didn't follow mine. He deserved what he got. He deserved it for what he did to my name. Where did you get that gun?"

I pulled the hammer back.

"It was my father's," I said. "From the war."

Westing paused, and his eyes widened. He knew then I would pull the trigger.

So did I.

"Don't," he muttered, but there was no conviction behind it.

I imagined my father, the smile on his face as he lifted me out of my cradle. I pictured my father returning from the war, his hair gray, his eyes sad. I wondered what he did in those years, what he'd seen.

I wondered what lay ahead for me. And what path I

was setting for my children. Then I remembered Bartholomew Westing would have no children. And would never set a path for them.

I squeezed the trigger.

Coda
by Laura Lippman

•

So, what do you think? C'mon, admit it, that was a pretty
fun ride, a roller-coaster journey in some very fine company. Aren't you curious to see what this bumper crop
of writers does next?

The bottom line is that one could argue *every* year
in crime fiction is a killer year, and this has been the
case for quite some time. After slumping slightly sales-
wise, in the 1970s, the genre of Chandler and Christie
came roaring back in the 1980s and now holds a significant amount of real estate on the *New York Times* bestseller list in any given week. Lee Child and I made our
debuts in 1997 (as did Joseph Kanon), while Ken Bruen
has been publishing since 1990. Other writers who came
on the scene in the nineties include: John Grisham,
Patricia Cornwell, Michael Connelly, Dennis Lehane,
George Pelecanos, Lisa Scottoline, Laurie King, and
Harlan Coben.

The striking thing to me about the writers gathered
here is not their camaraderie, but just how young some
of them are. I was thirty-eight when I published my novel
and felt positively precocious. Lehane, not quite thirty
when he published *A Drink Before the War* in 1996, was
crime fiction's official young'un. If thirty-somethings

were a minority wherever crime writers gathered, then twenty-somethings were simply unheard of in our ranks. Why, then, are more and more young writers heading straight for a life of crime?

I have a theory about this, one that no one necessarily supports, but no one has invested any energy in disputing it, either. In the 1980s, Vintage Books began reprinting James Crumley's novels in trade paperback editions that made them more widely available than before. These seminal works were discovered by various young writers—many in their twenties and trying to write mainstream literary fiction. I was one of them and I won't presume to speak for anyone else, but reading Crumley was a sock-in-the-gut epiphany for me. There was no *guilty* pleasure in Crumley's work, just pure pleasure. Here was a guy who had the chops to write whatever he wanted, and he had chosen the crime genre. In doing so, he blazed a path and a lot of us plunged down it, conscious of the fact that we might not be able to do what Crumley did, but there was no shame in trying. The result was some pretty exciting work, genre-bending work, most notably by Lehane and Pelecanos. Now those two writers are the most-cited influences among young would-be crime writers. But it really began with Crumley and, before Crumley, a youngster named Elmore Leonard, who started writing Westerns in the 1950s, then switched to crime with the so-called Detroit novels of the 1970s. But it wasn't until the 1980s that Leonard's critical and commercial reputation really soared, winning him the approval and awe of the literary establishment.

Also in the 1980s, a trio of female writers—Marcia

Muller, Sara Paretsky, and Sue Grafton—began breathing life into what had been presumed to be the moribund body of the private detective novel. All three women are significant, but I'm going to single out Paretsky because she was present, in 1986, at the creation of Sisters in Crime, which is a clear precursor to cooperative efforts such as Killer Year. A decade before the widespread use of the Internet, women—and men—were joining this new organization, which offered advice and mentoring programs to new writers.

In the 1990s, crime writers often toured together—in formal groups, assembled by publishers, but also in ad hoc arrangements hatched by the writers themselves. Walter Mosley was a member of one of those traveling caravans. So was Coben, touring with Jeff Abbott and Sparkle Hayter. In 1999, Lauren Henderson and Stella Duffy, two versatile UK writers, started the Tart City Web site, a precursor to the group blogs now thick on the web—First Offenders, Murderati, Naked Authors, The Lipstick Chronicles. In short, mystery writers have always been a collegial bunch, committed as much to the genre as they are to their own careers.

Killer Year, however, is the largest such enterprise to date and the first to be featured in its own anthology. Let's hope it works. You see, all too often, publishing plays out like a clichéd World War II movie: A diverse set of troops go out there every year, but not all of them make it back. Does it have to be that way? I don't know. But I'm for anything that increases writers' odds of enjoying long and successful careers. Let's hope *Killer Year* does just that, for these writers and generations of writers to come.

Author Biographies

Brett Battles is a Barry Award–winning author of over twenty novels, including the Jonathan Quinn series, the Project Eden series, and the time-bending thriller *Rewinder*. He's also the coauthor, with Robert Gregory Browne, of the Alexandra Poe series. You can learn more at his website: brettbattles.com.

Allison Brennan is the *New York Times* bestselling author of two dozen thrillers and numerous short stories. Reviewers have called her books "terrifying," "fast-paced," "wonderfully complex," and *RT Book Reviews* calls Allison "a master of suspense—tops in the genre." Lisa Gardner says, "Brennan knows how to deliver." She was a 2014 finalist for the Thriller Award; a one-time winner and six-time finalist of the Daphne du Maurier award; and nominated multiple times for best romantic suspense by Romance Writers of America.

Writing three books a year is more than a full-time job, and so is raising five kids, but Allison believes life is too short to be bored. When she's not writing, she's reading, playing video games, watching old movies or new television shows, and driving her kids to their sporting events. She also loves hands-on research, including SWAT role-playing, visiting the morgue, police ride-alongs, and touring the FBI Academy at Quantico.

Allison writes two series—the Lucy Kincaid thriller series (*Best Laid Plans*, available August 2015) and the Max Revere investigative reporter series (*Compulsion*). Her most recent books include *Notorious, Dead Heat,* and *Cold Snap*. Allison makes her home near Sacramento, California. For more information, visit www. allisonbrennan.com.

Ken Bruen was a finalist for the Edgar, Barry, and Macavity Awards, and the Private Eye Writers of America presented him with the Shamus Award for the Best Novel of 2003 for *The Guards,* the book that introduced Jack Taylor. He lives in Galway, Ireland.

An AMPAS Nicholl Award–winning, ITW Thriller Award–nominated novelist, **Robert Gregory Browne** is the author of the bestselling *Trial Junkies* series, as well as the Fourth Dimension Thrillers, *Kiss Her Goodbye*, *Whisper in the Dark*, and *Kill Her Again*.

Rob's book, *Kiss Her Goodbye*, was produced for TV by CBS Television and Sony Pictures, and his book, *The Paradise Prophecy*, is in development with Temple Hill Productions.

Rob lives in California with his wife and cat, and, in addition to writing, composes music, plays guitar and keyboards, and has even been known to sing now and then.

And you thought his BOOKS were scary. Find out more at robertgregorybrowne.com.

Bill Cameron is the author of dark, gritty mysteries featuring Skin Kadash: *County Line*, *Day One*, *Chasing Smoke*, and *Lost Dog*. His short stories have appeared in *Portland Noir*, *First Thrills*, *Deadly Treats*, and *West Coast Crime Wave*. His work has been nominated for multiple awards, including the Spotted Owl Award and the 2011 CWA Short Story Dagger Award. In 2012, *County Line* was awarded the Spotted Owl for Best Northwest Mystery.

Toni McGee Causey is the author of the critically acclaimed and nationally bestselling "Bobbie Faye" novels—an action/caper series set in south Louisiana; the series was released in back-to-back publications, beginning with *Charmed and Dangerous, Girls Just Wanna Have Guns*, and *When a Man Loves a Weapon*. She is also a contributor to the *USA Today* bestselling anthology *Love Is Murder*, as well as the *Killer Year* and the *Do You Know What It Means to Miss New Orleans?* anthologies. She has a soon-to-be-released dark southern/gothic thriller, *The Saints of the Lost and Found*, and is working on a lighter collaboration with Jenny Crusie, which has been more fun than she thought possible.

While pursuing an MFA in Screenwriting, Toni had scripts optioned by prominent studios and recently produced an indie film, *LA-308*, which now has offers of distribution pending. Toni began her career by writing nonfiction for local newspapers, edited *Baton Rouge*

Magazine, and sold articles to places like *Redbook* and *Mademoiselle*. In her copious spare time, she practiced her ninja skills, though she can't prove it because no one ever saw her.

She and her husband, Carl, thrive in the French Quarter where they're not the craziest ones on the block. Sometimes they're not even second craziest. She and Carl have owned and operated a civil construction company for over thirty years (hence the crazy), with projects all over Louisiana, Mississippi, and southeastern Texas. They are also working on a home/remodeling project in the Quarter. Her grown sons survived her (they might say "barely" but they don't get to write the bio, ha!), with one becoming a SWAT police officer and one becoming a firefighter. (In other words, Toni rarely sleeps.) Meanwhile, she and Carl are absolutely frothing-at-the-mouth proud of the two g-kids and three step-ish-g-kids (it's complicated, but it's all good).

One day, when she's grown up enough, she's going to get another puppy. This may take a while.

After graduating from Columbia College Chicago and the American Security Training Institute, **Sean Chercover** worked as a private investigator in Chicago and New Orleans. He has since written for film, television, and print. He's also worked as a film and video editor, scuba diver, nightclub magician, truck driver, waiter, car jockey, encyclopedia salesman, and in other, less glamorous positions. These days, he splits his time between

Chicago and Toronto and generally stays out of trouble. *Big City, Bad Blood* is his first novel.

Lee Child was born in 1954 in Coventry, England, but spent his formative years in the nearby city of Birmingham. By coincidence he won a scholarship to the same high school that J. R. R. Tolkien had attended. He went to law school in Sheffield, England, and after part-time work in the theater he joined Granada Television in Manchester for what turned out to be an eighteen-year career as a presentation director during British TV's "golden age." During his tenure his company made *Brideshead Revisited, The Jewel in the Crown, Prime Suspect,* and *Cracker.* But he was fired in 1995 at the age of forty as a result of corporate restructuring. Always a voracious reader, he decided to see an opportunity where others might have seen a crisis and bought six dollars' worth of paper and pencils and sat down to write a book, *Killing Floor,* the first in the Jack Reacher series. His twentieth Jack Reacher novel, *Make Me*, is available in September 2015.

J.T. Ellison is the *New York Times* bestselling author of thirteen critically acclaimed novels, including *What Lies Behind, When Shadows Fall, Edge of Black,* and *A Deeper Darkness,* and is the coauthor of the Nicholas Drummond series with #1 *New York Times* bestselling author Catherine Coulter. Her work has been published in over twenty countries. Her novel, *The Cold Room*, won the ITW Thriller Award for Best Paperback Original, and *Where All the Dead Lie* was a RITA Nominee for Best Romantic Suspense. She lives in Nashville with her husband. Visit JTEllison.com for more insight into her wicked imagination, or follow her on Twitter @ Thrillerchick or Facebook.com/JTEllison14.

Patry Francis is the author of two novels, *The Liar's Diary* (Dutton, 2007), which has been translated into seven languages and was recently optioned for film, and *The Orphans of Race Point* (Harper Perennial, 2014). Her poetry and short stories have been widely published. A mother of four, she lives with her family on Cape Cod.

Marc Lecard has published a couple of crime novels (*Vinnie's Head* and *Tiny Little Troubles,* both from St. Martin's), and his crime and supernatural short stories have appeared in anthologies, magazines, and on websites. After a stint teaching creative writing to middle-school students, he has begun writing stories with younger readers in mind. He recently relocated from sunny California to the dark heart of the Midwest, and now lives in southeast Michigan.

Laura Lippman was a reporter for twenty years, including twelve years at *The* (Baltimore) *Sun*. She began writing novels while working full-time and published seven books about "accidental PI" Tess Monaghan before leaving daily journalism in 2001. Her work has earned the Edgar, the Anthony, the Agatha, the Shamus, the Nero Wolfe, Gumshoe, and Barry Awards. She also has been nominated for other prizes in the crime fiction field, including the Hammett and the Macavity. She was the first ever recipient of the Mayor's Prize for Literary Excellence and the first genre writer recognized as Author of the

Year by the Maryland Library Association. Her twelfth Tess Monaghan novel, *Hush Hush*, came out in 2015.

Derek Nikitas is the author of two thriller novels with Minotaur: *Pyres*, nominated for an Edgar Award for Best First Novel by an American author, and *The Long Division*, a *Washington Post* Best Books of 2009 selection. The French translations of both novels were also *Elle Magazine* Readers' Choice Award finalists, and *Pyres* was nominated for a *Grand Prix de la Littérature Policière*. His next novel, *The Pastime Project*, a time-travel science fiction thriller for young adults, will be released by Polis Books in the fall of 2015. His Pushcart Prize–nominated short fiction has appeared in *Ellery Queen Mystery Magazine, The Ontario Review, Chelsea, Thuglit, Plots with Guns, New South, Washington Square,* and other venues, including the zombie anthology *The New Dead*, edited by Christopher Golden. With an MFA in fiction from the University of North Carolina at Wilmington and a PhD in English from Georgia State University, he is a professor of creative writing and the director of the MFA in Creative Writing at the Bluegrass Writers Studio at Eastern Kentucky University.

A #1 *New York Times* bestselling author, eight of **Gregg Olsen**'s books have appeared on the bestsellers' lists of the *Wall Street Journal, USA Today,* and the *New York Times* in both fiction and nonfiction categories.

Olsen has been a guest on numerous television shows, including *Dateline NBC, William Shatner's Aftermath,*

Deadly Women on Investigation Discovery, *Good Morning America, The CBS Early Show, The Today Show, FOX News*, CNN, *Anderson Cooper 360, Entertainment Tonight, CBS 48 Hours*, Oxygen's *Snapped, Inside Edition, Extra, Access Hollywood*, and A&E's *Biography*.

Deep Dark was named Idaho Book of the Year by the Idaho Libraries Association for its depiction of a mining tragedy in that state. *Starvation Heights* was honored by Washington's Secretary of State for the book's contribution to state history and culture, and Olsen's young adult novel, *Envy*, was the official selection of Washington State for the National Book Festival in Washington, D.C. His books have been translated into nine languages.

Olsen, a Seattle native, lives in Olalla, Washington.

Jason Pinter is the founder and publisher of Polis Books, an independent publishing company launched in the fall of 2013. He is the bestselling author of five novels in his Henry Parker series, which have been nominated for numerous awards and have nearly 1.5 million copies in print in over a dozen languages worldwide. His *Killer Year* story, "The Point Guard," was nominated for the Thriller Award. Visit him at www.jasonpinter.com or follow him on Twitter at @jasonpinter.

M. J. Rose is an internationally bestselling writer, the editor of *Buzz, Balls, & Hype,* founder of AuthorBuzz

.com, and on the board of International Thriller Writers. Please visit her Web site, mjrose.com, for more information.

Marcus Sakey's thrillers have been nominated for more than fifteen awards, named *New York Times'* Editor's Picks, and selected among *Esquire*'s Top 5 Books of the Year. His novel *Good People* was made into a movie starring James Franco and Kate Hudson, and *Brilliance* is currently in development with Legendary Pictures (*Inception, The Dark Knight*).

Marcus was also the host of the acclaimed television show *Hidden City* on Travel Channel, for which he was routinely pepper-sprayed and attacked by dogs.

Prior to writing, he worked as a landscaper, a theatrical carpenter, a 3D animator, a movie reviewer, a tutor, and a graphic designer who couldn't draw. He lives in Chicago with his wife and daughter. His website is MarcusSakey.com, or follow him on Facebook (Facebook.com/MarcusSakey) or Twitter, where he posts under the clever handle @MarcusSakey.

Duane Swierczynski is the Edgar-nominated author of nine novels including *Canary, Severance Package,* and the Shamus Award–winning Charlie Hardie series (*Fun & Games, Hell & Gone, Point & Shoot*). He's written over 200 comics for Marvel, DC, Dark Horse, Valiant, and IDW about characters such the Punisher, The X-Men, Birds of Prey, Judge Dredd, and that lovable scallywag, Godzilla. Duane has also collaborated with

CSI creator Anthony E. Zuiker on the bestselling *Level 26* series. He lives in Philadelphia with his wife and children.

Dave White is a Derringer Award–winning mystery author and educator. White, an eighth-grade teacher for the Clifton, New Jersey public school district, attended Rutgers University and received his MAT from Montclair State University. His 2002 short story "Closure," won the Derringer Award for Best Short Mystery Story the following year. *Publishers Weekly* gave the first two novels in his Jackson Donne series, *When One Man Dies* and *The Evil That Men Do*, starred reviews, calling *When One Man Dies* an "engrossing, evocative debut novel" and writing that his second novel "fulfills the promise of his debut." He received praise from crime fiction luminaries such as bestselling, Edgar Award–winning Laura Lippman and the legendary James Crumley.

Both *When One Man Dies* and *The Evil That Men Do* were nominated for the prestigious Shamus Award, and *When One Man Dies* was nominated for the Strand Critics Award for "Best First Novel." His standalone thriller, *Witness to Death*, was an ebook bestseller upon release and named one of the Best Books of the Year by the *Milwaukee Journal-Sentinel*. All three books have been reissued by Polis Books and are available wherever ebooks are sold. Follow him on Twitter @Dave_White.

Steven

আকাশ

৬২১

৬৮৩৫৩৫৩২
মানিক

উৎসব গ্রহণ